I0693108

1: Dining

1923, New York City, New York.

Mister's.
The name on the restaurant's sign swung in the light wind as the rain puddled on the cobblestones and muck in the gutters. Inside light spilled through cracks in the shutters onto the dark night streets.

Most were home, tired from a hard day's work at the factories or construction sites. However, those inside, well dressed and dining on exotic cuisines from Europe, were out for a night of decadence and flaunting their wealth.

Mister's restaurant had a wait list and you didn't just stop by for a greasy burger and fries or a bowl of pasta. No, it was an experience all on its own.

A lone man leaned against the doorframe. His bulky frame and keen eyes glancing about the street gave off the sense that he was not an easy prey.

Table of Contents:

The click of boots on cobblestones drew his dark eyes. His bald head swiveled to take in the newcomers as they closed the distance. He sighed as he recognized the pair of policemen. Fred O'Malley and George Johnson. No doubt here for another bribe. They twirled their batons as they strode along under the streetlamps. Their strides were purposeful and direct. *Yep*, he thought, *must be Thursday*. They were headed his way.

"Evenin', Duncan," the thinner, red-haired man said. He was a wiry man with a pocked face and long weasel nose. His red hair stuck straight out in all directions from under his duty cap. Duncan could see the look peering back at him from Fred's beady, hateful eyes.

"Evening, Officer O'Malley, Officer Johnson," he addressed each man.

The squat pug-nosed man canted his chin forward jerkily towards Duncan. The sour breath billowed out when he croaked out, "Your boss in?" It came out surly and menacing, as though he was offended by something. What it could be this time was anyone's guess.

"He certainly is, Officer. Do you need to speak with him?"

"No, wise-ass, I just asked 'cause I likes hearing's my momma's favorite son talk. Yeah, I wanna speak wid 'im."

"Ah. My apologies, Officer," He internalized another sigh, as he stepped backwards into the doorway pushing the door ajar and sweeping it out of the way, following it with his large frame, ducking his head easily to keep from banging it on the frame.

Piano music cascaded out the opening, a soft melody of tinkling ivory. As they moved inside the scrape of silverware against porcelain hissed under the music and quiet conversations.

His suit jacket dripped rain water as he slid it off and draped it over the nearby rack. Looking to the right, he spotted Ted. "Mr. Dremond, will you take these two to see Mr. Wells?"

"Of course, Mr. Caan." Nodding to Duncan, the younger man gestured to the two officers as they dribbled onto the floor. He turned towards the back of the restaurant and began striding along the wall. His black suit whispered as he walked. The two officers glanced at each other and followed.

Low lit table lamps and the bright lights of the stage illuminated the way to a narrow hallway to the side. The wooden walls gave way to stone as they neared the doorway at the end. The doorway framed a sturdy, white washed, wooden door set with a steel door knob. Ted stopped beside it and wrapped two knuckles against the frame.

"Mr. Wells, Sir, there are two gentlemen here to see you from the constabulary," he called.

"Thank you, Mr. Dremond. Show them in."

Duncan slipped his suit coat back on and slunk back outside, happy to just not have to be a part of the ordeal anymore.

Helena caught movement to her left and slid her eyes over to Duncan as he moved inside followed by two rain drenched policemen. She managed to keep playing, her moment's pause flowing in tempo with the piece she was playing.

She worried her lower lip with her teeth, keeping her eyes on the men shuffling in the hallway that led to Allen's office. She split her attention as they moved apart. Ted was leading the police down the hallway and a nonplussed Duncan was heading back out to guard the door. She wondered what that was all about. Only another hour until the restaurant closed and she could go out on top and spread her wings. Maybe she could convince Allen to come out with her. She smiled to herself as she tapped away at the ivory.

Allen Wells sat behind his desk, sipping three fingers of a new batch of Irish whiskey the boys were working on. The smooth liquid poured down his throat, burning a bit. The hickory and blackberries were a nice touch.

The knock came. Glancing at his calendar he didn't have anything scheduled until the restaurant closed. He frowned, as Ted talked to him through the door.

"Thank you, Mr. Dremond. Show them in."

The door opened smoothly. Ted stepped to the side and the two men lumbered in behind him.

"That will be all, Mr. Dremond."

"Yes, sir," Ted replied and stepped back out and closed the door behind him.
As soon as the door closed, the heavy man sat bodily down in the chair across from Allen, leaning forward, "So, I have it on good authority you got a bit more than a place where folks can spend way too many greenbacks on some booze." His angry glare no doubt melted most thugs. It was just that though, an angry glare.

"What do you mean, Officer Johnson?" Allen's voice came back calm, which seemed to infuriate the man further.

"I mean, Mr. Wells, that I got ya takin' people's wives downstairs, puttin' ya hands on dem, and forcin' them tah have sex wich ya."

Allen's eyebrows crawled up his forehead bumping up against his combed-back hair, "And why do you think that is the case?" He leaned back in his chair keeping an eye on both men. The tension in the room was palatable across his tongue. Now that he was paying attention, Johnson was fuming and O'Malley was itching for a fight. Both men gave off pre-fight pheromones. Anger and greed floated thick and putrid in the air.

" 'Cause my wife was here yesterday, ya dirty little shit!" Johnson slammed his fist on the desk, rattling the neat arrangement of pens and seals on the side and the ice in the whiskey.

"Hmm," Allen murmured to the outburst. He knew it had been a risk at the time. However, an angry husband so quickly was new. She must have really been neglected to have shown such a change so quickly. At least to have been noticed. Though, Johnson had been a bit sharper than most. "Well, I am sure there is a reason for such accusations, founded or not. But I have no idea what you are speaking of."

"She told me, you hinkty pill! That dumb dora can't hide nuttin from me. Ya think you're a sockdollager, doncha? But you ain't nuttin butta wurp. Maybe them otha boys don't give two shits what their dolls are doin', but I'm gonna lay you out and take ya down to the slammer," with this the wide man lumbered to his feet and began reaching over to pluck at Allen's collar.

This would not do. Allen slapped the offending hand away and pushed the desk toward the oaf, bracing his feet against the stone floor. The heavy oak desk caught Johnson against his knees and made him stumble back into his chair.

"I tell you what I will do, Mr. Johnson. I will double the weekly bonus. I know how hard it is during this trying time to relax, especially for a man of your caliber and esteem. I will send you home with a fine bottle of gin," the tone was dry and without emotion. It appeared Johnson had outlived his usefulness. Accidents happened though. Or maybe a tip to Internal Affairs that the fat bastard was working for the mob would give him something else to worry about.

"Dats Officer Johnson, nitwit," the red faced man spat, phlegm dripping down from his lip. He seemed to ponder the idea of doubling a payday and began to calm. "Alright, ya double the lettuce, and I'll let it go."

"Aw, Georgey, we aren't gonna drag 'im down to the station?" the whining voice came from the stringy man. Disappointment and greed washed off of him in waves. It seemed to stick to the top of Allen's mouth with the taste and texture of tar.

"I will extend the extra pay to you as well, Officer O'Malley," ground out Allen. *Looks like two instead of just the one.* He pulled four rolls of banknotes from a drawer and set it down in front of the two men. They greedily scooped them up, fitfully looking over their shoulders at the closed door.

They hurried over to it and Johnson called over his shoulder, "See ya next week, boy-o." With this last parting jab, they blundered out into the darkened room beyond, the jaunty tune Helena was playing washing over him.

The door opened behind Duncan and he quickly stepped to the side as the two police officers strode out and slapped each other on the back. "See you later, doorman. You keep that nose clean. I'd hate ta come back and drag ya downtown, after ya bossman paid us so much green," O'Malley called out spitefully. The two men had a good laugh at that as they pushed out into the rain.

Duncan watched them go silently. In his head, he imagined smashing them into the ground and ripping them with teeth and claws. He let out a deep breath and pushed his beast back down to that place it dwelled. He would not dishonor his alpha and these

men were not worth the effort. He resumed his vigil
as he let his anger flow away.

Allen stepped out of his office, swirling his drink in
his glass. He sipped from it as he locked the door
behind him. *Fuckers.* He walked slowly down the
hallway to the opening of the restaurant. A few
people still ate at a few of the tables. A few others
sat sipping coffee and just enjoying the atmosphere
provided by Helena's playing and the low light.

He spied Grace moving between the tables closing
checks and smiling prettily at each patron. Her blond
hair seemed to catch the light and her dazzling smile
brightened each person's face as she moved along.
Finishing her rounds, she turned to retreat and
locked eyes with him. He felt her power wash over
him once more and watched her smile reach her
eyes. She glided over to where he stood, her feet
barely making a sound. Her green dress swayed with
her hips, the frills and jewels at her neckline
accenting her allure.

"Evening, Sir," she purred as she slid up next to him.

"Evening, Ms. Grace. I do hope you are in the mood for something rough tonight. I am in foul spirits, though the sight of you has raised them."

"Mmm, yes, please," her arousal and pheromones were hot and needy as she spoke. "You do so know how to charm a gal with what she wants to hear, Sir," her sultry charm spiking with her heart. She winked coyly at him as she stepped off towards the back. As she walked her hips swayed more than necessary, her head turned to watch him watch her.

He could tell she was teasing him, but that would only lead to more fun later. She seemed to sass him more when she knew there was punishment to be had. He raised an eyebrow and he heard her giggle softly as she pushed through into the kitchen.

Helena stifled a frown as the two men hurried from the Owner's office. She could feel his anger through her mind. He would have a task for her soon, it appeared. She caressed the keys and the tinkling of her performance echoed through the dining hall.

As he stepped out into the restaurant proper she willed a trickle of power through the music, calming him and his bloodlust. She doubted he failed to notice, as his gaze found her and his beasts folded back in their cages. The sparkle of happiness at this was immediately turned into annoyance as his gaze moved to another. Of course, since it was closing time, Grace would be moving about. She felt his beasts sniff the air as he watched Grace. She swallowed the sigh. Maybe he would let her watch instead.

Closing time came and Allen Wells shook a few hands as customers recognized him. He gave each a firm handshake and thanks for attending this evening. The couple lagged behind the rest, Joseph and Meagan Lawson. Joseph asked if he had a moment. Allen schooled his expression and inquired what they had in mind.

Joseph leaned close and said softly, "Not to be a nuisance, but my wife heard you had... entertainment available for those willing to pay." His voice a whisper, he asked, "I don't suppose we can know in finer details what that means?"

Allen looked blankly at the two of them then gestured to his office. He spied Duncan coming in the doorway, shedding his suit coat. The muscled man looked weather worn and happy to be out of the rain. Allen raised an eyebrow at the man who gave him a brief wave. Satisfied that all was well, he followed the couple to his office, let them in, and settled once more behind the slab of oak.

"I would first like to know how you came by such information as any entertainment available at this establishment is confidential and in no way supposed to be bandied about," Allen stated curtly.

"Oh, sorry about that, pal. I didn't mean to put the screws on you. Just was hoping to get in on the new hotsy-totsy joint. I didn't know it was something that would be close to being under glass. We can take the bounce, if you feel we were putting you behind the eight ball," the unease coming off the young man and wife felt true enough.

These two were just kids with money looking for the next big thrill. A flaming youth and his flapper squeeze. He inhaled and let it back out slow. "All right. No harm done. Tell me who the canary is, and we'll see how it goes."

The young couple looked at each other and she shrugged. He sighed and motored out, "It was that doll, you got here working the tables, Gracie."

Allen felt his eyebrows raise at that. "Gracie? You mean Grace?"

"Yeah, that's her. She said that you might think we would be interested but didn't go into much more detail than that. We were hoping to hear from the high pillow on what the swanky game was," he cringed as he said the last sentence, almost coming out a question.

"Hmm," Allen let his face relax into a thoughtful expression. *I might as well let their pulse calm down.*

"Alright, I will let Mr. Caan know to expect you two for a private party on Thursday night. It will be one hundred dollars on the night of said party. Or now, if you are definitely interested. Though I am afraid I will have to refrain from adding any of the details until then." He placed his elbows on the desk and leaned forward on them, "This is invitation only. No more than the two of you. I will be sure to have everything ready when you get here. I will say this, you have the option to stop whenever you want. But, no refunds. My staff's time and loyalty is valuable to me. The fact that Grace has suggested this speaks highly of you two. You likely have been here before and caught her eye. So. With that in mind, I do have an appointment." He stood, staring not unkindly at the two of them.

He could tell this dismissal caught them off guard from the shocked expressions and awkward shuffle to the door. Joseph managed to squeak out, "Thanks, Mr. Wells. See you on Thursday night." His wife made a brief curtsey and the man closed the door behind them.

Grace, Grace, Grace, you naughty little girl.

She waited patiently in position for him. Kneeling on the pillow, with her palms on her knees, rump sitting on her heels, knees spread shoulder width, she waited. She squirmed a bit thinking about how rough he just might be. She couldn't help herself. She was pleased to have wrangled that young couple into a meeting with him. *He was probably fuming. She couldn't wait to see what kind of fun he would employ in her yearning flesh.* She shuddered with the thought of it. He had long rough fingers and calloused palms. *Yep, she was going to have to perform a ritual or two to recover from this night.* "Worth it," she purred.

Allen walked about the restaurant checking to make sure everything was moving on schedule. Tom and Jim were in the speakeasy clearing out the last of the men and women who had come in that night. That was fine with him. Shame most people couldn't handle their liquor otherwise being in there would not be such a hassle. Sometimes, on the nights when the high class patrons came in they were better. But he would almost prefer the factory worker that was just looking to spend his greenbacks than a self entitled sap from the upper part of town. Then there were always the little hangers ons. Sometimes, mugs or cons but usually just rich gone poor and trying to hold on to the coattails of one still in the game.

Whatever. He finished out front. Duncan and Ted had left with the crowds, hopping a cab together to head down to the apartment building they were staying in. He paid his people good money, so they could afford a bit of luxury. He had been in both apartments for New Years parties they had thrown, neither was gaudy or overdone. Both men were dependable, so if they needed the rest of the night off, so be it.

He walked back through the kitchen to the hidden door that led into the noisy room. Cigarette and pipe smoke billowed around the rafters. The clink of glass on glass and bedraggled conversations drifted from the corners as people got their coats or purses together. He could smell quite a few things beside the booze and smoke, too. Someone was in desperate need of a shower. That or the night had been the continued party of a night or two before.

He caught a look from Tom. *Trouble*. He clenched his jaw as he walked over to see what was happening.

A well-dressed man was arguing with Jim about the night coming to a close. Several men had stood up around the two of them. By the cut of their suits and cock to their shoulders, they had bean-shooters and were gearing up to burn powder. Probably mob. By the look at the big cheese and the brunos behind him, he was sure that was the lay of things.

"Good evening, gentlemen. Is there some confusion about where the door is?" Allen walked up to the group of men, pivoting to face the men across from Tom. "As you can see, we are closing down for the evening. I would ask you to leave and come see us another night."

"As I was telling your man here, we ain't ready to go yet. Bring us some broads and another bottle of that sweet giggle juice you boobs got here. Cause

Giovanni Russo don't take no line from no grifter in a dive like dis," the surly black haired man stated, with authority.

The man was average in every way possible. Average build, average face, average greasy hair. The only thing not average was his clothes. The suit alone was worth a fat penny. The goons leering over his shoulder at him were a bit cheaper dressed, but then they were muscle. It was highly likely these were mean men following a rich, mean man.

"Sorry, gents, no clappers here. I don't run a can house, though I do know of a few that I can recommend at this time. A bottle, I can do, but as it is after hours there is a markup."

This earned him a sneer from the average man and frown from the men behind him, "I ain't paying no mark up for booze. Tell you what I'm gonna do. I'm gonna drift on out of here and I ain't coming back. Neither will none of my boys. And I'll let the family know yous playing hardball."

Allen stared dull eyes back at the gangster, "Alright. Do you need help catching a cab?"

This seemed to frustrate the puffed up little man all the more, "Nah, we got boilers outside. I'll be seeing you later on, chum." He waved at the group. They pushed out into the night and rain, giving Allen a hard look each in turn.

Allen looked about the room. It was empty save for Tom and Jim. "Lock it up and go home," he waved and strode from the room.

Going back into the kitchen and pulling on the well hidden door near the freezer, Allen walked down the now exposed staircase. It spiraled under the building fifty feet, hewn from solid rock and lit by hissing torches every four steps.

As he reached the bottom he found Helena sitting on a bench, her hands in her lap. Cocking an eyebrow at her, he asked, "Not going for a lap around town? It is dark enough, and you did well tonight. Your melody was pleasing as always." He walked over and cupped her cheek as she raised it to him.

"No, Master, I felt your emotions tonight, and I was hoping you would want my company. But I felt you were going to see Grace this evening and was hoping to get a chance to watch. Or help," the curly brown hair bounced against her shoulders as she shrugged in acceptance of his decision.

"Grace normally is a bit shy, but she deserves proper punishment for tonight. Did I mention how well that blue goes with your skin, my little fallen angel?" he kissed her forehead as she grinned up at him.

"No, Master, you hadn't mentioned it yet. But I bought it on Saturday. I was hoping you would like it." She stood and performed a slow spin.

He watched the material flow about her and hug her curves. He noticed the back dropped low to just above her shapely bottom and was held at the top with a small clasp. He traced a finger up her spine and she froze at his touch. *She wants to show me.* Tracing the finger back down the pale almost translucent skin, he murmured, "I imagine it looks better with your wings out, as dazzling as you are without."

She spun to face him, "Oh. Can I show you?" Her glee and hope shone out her eyes.

"Yes, please. Just let me sit, so you have more room," he slipped onto the bench she had vacated.

"Yay!" This was all the warning he had before her black and blue wings shot out and took the entire hallway. The downy fluff of her wings beat once, and her countenance shifted. A light blue and black swirl lit under her skin. The light cascaded from her, not an overpowering brightness but warm and heady. He could smell her arousal and happiness as it came off her in thick waves. Her hair floated of its own accord, drifting about as though she was underwater. "Do you like it, Master?" Her voice was different too, dark and beckoning.

"It is a beautiful dress. And it suits you well, Angel. Silk?"

"Of course, Master."

"Very nice. Alright. Let's fold up those pretty wings of yours and go see my naughty little Grace."

2: Punishment

Grace shivered as she waited. *How long have I been waiting?* She did some mental math. *He should have been here by now.* She wondered what was keeping him.

Allen walked up to the door, Helena close on his heels. He turned, pressed down on the door latch, and pushed the heavy oak that was bound in iron straps into the room.

He continued into the room, seeing Grace kneeling on the carpeted area. Her bob-cut blond hair was fashionably styled and held in place by the jeweled clip he had given her last Christmas. Her petite form was clad in a new green lingerie piece. She readily seemed to find new items or have them made. This particular piece was lace and silk and pearls. Lines of silk traced the peak and either side of her breasts. Lace cupped under her breasts and concealed the nipples. A drape of lace was attached by two hooks and clasps along the front and, as he walked about her, two more along the back.

She quivered under his gaze, her eyes locked to the front. Her two small feet were clad in green hose, clipped to a green garter belt, small emeralds hanging from lace. Her panties were a sheer green and had pearls draped suggestively down the front and back from rings around the upper hem. She had fingerless lace gloves of the same green sheer material with emeralds and pearls sewn into each.

As he walked back to the front of her, he leaned down and cupped her cheek as she leaned into it. Her heart raced as she looked up at him, a question in her eyes.

"You look lovely, my little dollface. I love this look on you. Well done," he leaned down and tasted her lips.

"Thank you, Sir," she purred against his mouth.

She tasted of sage, molasses, charcoal, ginger, life, and need. Such a heady blend flowed into him as they explored each other's mouths, tongues dancing along each other, teeth and lips.

He pulled back and she breathed out a contented sigh. Her eyes were hooded and her breath was coming in short gasps. "Mmmm. Thank you, Sir."

"You're welcome, pretty lady," he held out his hand to her, which she took. He pulled her to her feet and slipped a hand around her waist. She pressed herself against him. She stood an inch or two shorter than him. Her light blue eyes looked up at him, her inner power gleaming behind them.

He kissed her lips softly then pulled away. She pouted at him. He raised an eyebrow as he walked over to a table, looking over the numerous collars displayed along its length.

The collars were made of various types, widths and materials. Clasps, snaps, and buckles. Thin, thick, and various in between. Leather, silk, cotton, and satin.

Knitting his eyebrows, he chose a medium thick, leather collar that had large steel rings at each of the compass points and was lightly padded on the inside. It had a duo of buckles that would hold it in place. He also picked a bell from the accessories that were at the side in a tray. He attached it to a hidden ring at the bottom of the collar. He then turned from the collar table to Grace. She smiled brightly and shuddered with anticipation.

He lifted the eyebrow again and one of his hands, twirling a finger. She gleefully spun on her hose covered toes and lifted her hair with both hands. He slid the collar around her neck and fastened the buckles in place.

He swatted her bottom as she quivered in delight, "The horse, lovely creature."

"Yes, Sir," she skipped over to the leather covered sawhorse bolted to the stone floor in the east end of the large room.

There were many implements arranged carefully about the room. Many brought in from long forgotten places and others made by Allen and others still made piecemeal throughout town.

The sawhorse was a sturdy piece made of redwood and covered in padding, followed by red leather. Rings, set in hinges to allow movement, were fastened on the corners and in increments along each length of the piece.

Quivering with delight, Grace stood in a standing display position near the sawhorse. Allen walked up slowly behind her, knowing that each moment not acting only heightened his playmate's anticipation. He watched the quiver of her body and smiled. He ran a hand up her inner thigh. Her scent blasted outward as her skin trembled with delight.

He slid the other hand up the other inner thigh then traced his hands under her butt cheeks, enjoying the feel of her skin, soft and trembling under his fingers. He continued up her form to the upper hem of panties, slowly traced her waist to her front, and began peeling the soft fabric down her body. As he reached the bottom of her thighs, he released the garment, letting it spill from his hands to puddle at her feet. He lightly caressed her butt. "Up," he said, smacking her on the rump once more.

Grace hurried to obey, clambering onto the piece. Her lingerie slid up to expose her sex and butt. He leaned down until he was eye level with her. "Good girl," he murmured and watched her pant out her thanks, "Now, we have some punishment to work through for you talking to people outside of this room about our personal lives. Which is against the rules agreed upon. Which you knowingly broke. However, they did seem to be a good bunch of kids. I did not sense evil in their aura or lies in their words. So, we will be doing a show on Thursday for them. But you will be in an assistant role, not participating. I have decided that Helena will be the exhibition submissive in this instance." A chirp of glee from the corner where Helena stood in the ready position. "Any questions?"

Grace worried her lips, "And tonight, Sir?"

"Tonight is going to be standard punishment. However, you, naughty girl, will be forgiven when we have completed the punishment. Which in this case is ten lashes with the strap. After which, will be post care followed by some fun." He arched an eyebrow, "Anything else, Submissive?"

Her eyes hooded at the last word, "No, Sir. I trust your judgment and will do my best to make you happy."

"I trust you will tell me if anything is more than you can bear, at which point, as your protector, I will shield you from all dangers. I will not fail to keep your trust in my heart and your safety in my mind. And so, we shall begin."

Allen stepped to the side and motioned to Helena, tapping his wrist and holding up four fingers, making a fist, followed by two fingers. She nodded as she moved to a table that had various restraints laid out in similar fashion to the collars. As she collected four two-inch-wide leather bands, Allen moved over to a rack and selected a wide leather strap. The strap was folded over and sewn together to form an easy to control leather implement. He tested the weight and feel against his hand. He tested the impact once against his hand as he walked back to the horse where Grace and Helena waited. Both women had lust in their eyes.

Allen stopped in front of the horse and kissed each of them, before taking the restraints from Helena, laying the strap across Grace's hips and securing her in place. Once he had each limb bound in place, he asked, "Comfortable?"

Grace twisted each arm, testing, then replied, "Yes, Sir."

"Count them. Failure will earn you an additional punishment."

"Yes, Sir," this reply was quick and precise.

He grinned. *She was halfway there.* He stood to the rear left of the horse and could see quite the dazzling view. Schooling his desire, he checked the lay of the strap. It would hit where he intended.

Then he began. The strap came down across her butt, the length of it going across both cheeks, but not past to slap against her hip.

"One, Sir!" came the count.

He could see the lash had pinked her flesh already. The strap came down beside the last strike.

"Two, Sir!" came the call, slightly less calm.

This last strike pinked as the last. He brought it down once more against her bottom beside the second.

"Three, Sir!" she called.

Again a little lower.

"Four, Sir!" her voice was a little more quavering.

This blow went across the top of her thighs.

"Five, Sir!" her voice suddenly husky as she called the count.

He moved to the right side and rechecked the lay. He brought the strap down across the pink of the first strike.

"Six, Sir!" her husky voice called.

He brought the strap down against his second strike.

"Seven, Sir!" she called.

He could see her arousal dripping onto the leather now. Again across the third blow.

"Eight, Sir!"

The next strike played across the fourth. Her sex was flowing with honey.

"Nine, Sir!"

He brought the strap against the top of her thighs again. Her body thrust backwards after the blow.

"Ten, Sir!"

"Good girl, my little Hellcat," He stroked her bright red ass. He looked to Helena. She moved to a nearby dresser, opened a drawer, and removed a jar of salve from within.

She stepped back over and handed Allen the jar. "Thank you, Angel," He opened it and scooped out half of a handful and began rubbing it into the red bottom. It was cool in temperature and the blissful moans were telling that it was helping.

When he finished he turned to find Helena standing nearby with a towel ready for him. He smiled at her, which she readily returned.

He took the towel and began wiping off his hands. Helena snuck in a kiss, as he cleaned off. He chuckled then turned and wiped off the excess from Grace's bottom. She moaned and hitched up her butt as he did. He swatted her softly, "Still, Kitten. Just lay still." As she laid back down shuddering with anticipation he murmured, "Good girl." He quickly finished wiping her off and handed the towel back to Helena. She strode off to place it in the laundry.

Allen moved about the sawhorse, quickly unlatched the locks holding the restraints closed, removed them from the rings,and closed the locks once more. He scooped up the bleary eyed woman, cradled her to his chest, and carried her to the nearby couch. She hummed into his shirt and vest, as he sat down and held her there. Helena came over a moment later and cuddled in beside, snuggling in as he wrapped the other arm around her.

3: Play

A few minutes passed as they held each other. Grace's fingers reached up to stroke Allen's face. Then she pulled it back and touched Helena's, who kissed her palm.

Grace pulled her head back from where it was buried in Allen's chest and turned it to the other woman, "You are such a dear, Hel. Come over here and kiss me."

"Yes, please," the brunette leaned over Allen to softly touch her lips to the blond's. The soft tangle of tongues and lips in front of him made his hardness flex in his pants. A soft content purr came from Grace as a soft moan slipped free of Helena.

Grace and Helena cupped the other's face. The kiss broke off and they pressed their foreheads together. "Mmmhmmm, thank you, Hel," purred Grace.

"Mmmm, my pleasure, Mistress," Helena intoned.

"Hmmm..." Grace seemed to contemplate that word. "No, I don't think that fits me. Only one in charge here is our Mister. Thank you, however."

Allen could smell the wetness of each woman. Helena's cinnamon, creme, and cherries mixing with Grace's heady flavor made his head swim and his lust spike. Helena tilted her eyes to him, likely feeling his emotions as they leaked through the magic.

"Oh, Master, we left you out of the kiss. Grace, we should fix that, no?"

"Hmmm," Grace tapped her lips on mock consideration, "No, I have a better idea." She wiggled free of his grasp and pulled one of the throw cushions out from the nearby shelf. She tossed it to a puzzled Helena and snagged another. As she dropped it on the floor next to Allen's feet, Helena quickly slipped free to join her. The two women unbuckled his belt, unfastened his pants, unbuttoned his fly, and looked up at him.

He shifted his weight to his shoulders as the twosome pulled his pants and underwear to his knees. He dropped back onto the couch. They slipped off his shoes and slid his pants down to his feet. Helena set the shoes and belt to her side, while Grace folded the pants and set them to the other side, setting his underwear atop them. Then the two women shared a look and leaned forward, kissing each other around the length of his manhood.

"Well, that is not a sight one sees every day," Allen groaned, grabbing a handful of their hair in each hand.

"Mmm," they murmured out around him. The vibrations strummed through him as their tongues battled each other. Grace cupped his balls with one hand, kneading them slowly, and cupping Helena's breast through her dress with the other. Helena responded by slipping a hand between Grace's legs, eliciting a gasp. Helena reached up with her free hand and took Allen into her mouth, eyes rolling back into her head as she sank down the length of him.

"You ritzy little sheba! Unn," Grace shouted and finished with a moan as Helena moved her hand.

Helena smiled and licked the other woman's hand cradling his balls.

"You two are killing me. I.." Allen flexed his hips, driving himself deeper still into Helena's mouth. She hummed her happiness as he pumped his seed down her throat. "Gods damned, Valkyrie, are you choosing me? You have me drunk on that mouth." He collapsed back into the couch. She kept pulling on him until he stopped shooting into her mouth. "Gods."

"Mmm, thank you, Master," she said after swallowing, a pleased look on her face.

Grace pouted next to her, "You distracted me." Her full bottom lip pushed out like that was so cute. And her attention to his balls never relented. He felt himself pulse and swell up again.

Grace squinted at Helena, who was feigning innocence, and pulled his rapidly rising member to her mouth. It amazed him how this sultry, gentile, knowledgeable, and powerful woman could act so miffed. Her tongue lashed out at the tip of him. The head pushed out from the foreskin as she worked the tip around the purple helmet, pushing the skin back farther and farther. She latched onto him then. Her hooded eyes looked up at his, as her head bobbed up and down on the head of his shaft. He could feel the purr of her happiness along his shaft where her tongue lapped and swirled, her lips tight and pulling at him.

She slid more of him in and out, the wetness of her saliva mixing with his own fluids and Helena's saliva. He felt her force him into the back of her throat and swallow around his length, the contracting muscles around him bringing him to the edge so swiftly. Then she licked and swirled her tongue about him as she lifted her head free. His member came free of her mouth with a pop and she licked her lips. "Sir, I want you inside me, please," she batted her eyelashes at him, sliding her barely covered breasts against his thighs and rod.

"Ah, yes, you've kissed him enough, I suppose," he mock-pondered, teasing her, drawing the squint and pout from her again, "Why don't you show me how sorry you are by sitting down here," he patted his thighs. "Make me come inside that sweet honeypot, Hellcat," he continued.

"Mmm-mm, yes, please," she let out a sultry giggle as she climbed up into his lap, her thighs straddling his. She leaned in, taking his vest in both hands, and they locked lips as she ground her sex against his. Her fingers worked the buttons of his vest then shirt, baring his hair covered chest to her fingers. She threaded them through the coarse and soft curls, as she played her tongue against his.

As she rocked her hips back and forth against him, he felt her lower lips play along the length of him, slick with her nectar. He drove his hips up and he slammed up into her to the hilt, her gasp muffled by his lips, as she shuddered against his chest.

"Good girl," he kissed her as he pulled back, "Now show me."

"Mm, yes, Sir," she purred as she rocked up and down on him, him in and out of her, her walls tightly around him. Her breaths ragged as she slowly drew more and more of him out of her and then slid back inside her. She let out a moan as she pulled him out to just the tip of his member splitting her wet lips. Her hooded eyes rolled back behind the lids as she drove him up into her mound.

Her breasts heaved as she shuddered and worked her hips back and forth, his engorged flesh deep within her. "Oh, oh, Sir, may I come, please?" she gasped out.

"Hmmm," he murmured, "I couldn't hear that. What did you say? You may have to speak louder."

"Please, Sir, may this submissive come on your dick, please, please, please?" she frantically gasped.

"Yes, my little Hellcat, come on my dick."

"Thank you, Sir!" she screamed out as her orgasm ripped through her as she wiggled on his lap, "thank you, thank you, thank you, thank you, thank you, thankyouthankyouthankyou..." she gasped out as she collapsed against his chest, fingers scrambled about his chest, tangling her fingers into the hair there.

The smell of sage and charcoal washed over him as she shivered. The smell of cherries and cream mixed into his nostrils as Helena rose behind Grace, a playful smile on her face. She leaned over the smaller woman, her dress falling to the floor as she stood. Her full breasts heaved with labored breathing, her inner thighs slick with her juices.

"Master, may I clean you two?" the lust flamed behind her eyes as she leaned over Grace until she was close to his face. He leaned forward and kissed her.

"Not yet, Angel. Let's go over to the bed and get started," he murmured into her lips. He leaned forward, watching Helena turn herself to the bed, a shimmer of black and blue tracing along her shoulders. Her bare bottom and swinging hips carried her over to it. *You lucky man*. He scooped up the half awake woman into his arms and followed the tall brunette.

By the time he reached the bed, Helena was in the ready position on the left side of the bed. He laid

Grace down on the right side, her eyes fluttering as she slowly came down from her bliss. He climbed up into the middle of the bed, settling between the two lovely ladies. He leaned over to Helena and they kissed briefly. She seemed to vibrate with energy as she waited.

"Show me your juicy, sweet slit. Bottoms up," he said. She complied quickly, moving to point her butt at him, her face turned back on the mattress to peer over her shoulder as she grabbed her thighs and pulled them apart to show him her dripping sex. "Good girl," he said as he moved up behind her, positioning himself between her feet. He teased her outer lips with the tips of two fingers, causing more of her juices to spill out of her as she whimpered.

"Fill my needy, wet slit, please, Master!" she begged, as she pushed back against his fingers.

He pulled his fingers free of the warmth of her sex. "Are you sure, my little fallen angel? You want me to put my dick inside you?" he asked.

"Yes, please, Master! Drive it deep into your naughty, little, spoiled Pet!"

He smiled, teased her opening, and pressed it slowly into her. Her moans were immediate as the lips seemed to suck him in. He began to move his hips forward, driving it into her mound slowly. As he slowly got close to halfway, she slammed her hips back against his. He watched her eyes roll as he pushed in and out of her. Her mouth opened wide. Her hips slammed back, meeting his slow strokes as he pumped her sex with his.

"Yes, yes, yes, yes, oh, yes, Master, plow your dirty Pet's wet hole!" she screamed, "Oh, yes, please, please, may I come on your sweet dick, Master? I need to come on your dick, Master! Please, please?"

"Yes, come on my dick, Pet," Allen replied, huskily.

"Oh!" she screamed, as she shook around his member, "Thank you, Master!"

Looking over to Grace, he saw that she had slipped out of her lingerie and was palm deep into her sex, her eyes locked on her bedmates. Her eyes moved to his as she slid fingers in and out of herself. A shy and sly grin spread across her face as she watched him watch her, "I'm sorry, Sir. I was enjoying watching, but my hand found its way to myself. The two of you were quite the show."

"Mmm, yes, Kitten, I understand. You are quite the sight yourself. I think it is time for some roughness," Allen slid his shaft free of the soaked Helena, who moaned the loss. He patted the bed in front of him and Grace hurried to obey. He reached over, taking both arms in his hands. Putting her wrists together, he locked them together over her head, pulled her right leg up to rest on his left shoulder, set his rod against her opening, and drove himself deep into her wetness. She gasped in delight as he thrust into her. He reached around her leg to play with her swollen bud at the top of her channel. She gasped out her pleasure as he teased it with a fingertip. He pinched it between finger and thumb, eliciting a moan. He slammed his hips into hers and tugged on the trapped clit. Driving her forcefully into the mattress, he pulled on his beasts as he thrust into her. Her gasps turned into cries of pleasure. He continued pummeling her wet sex and moved his hand from her clit to one of her bouncing breasts, squeezing it and teasing the nipple with the flick of fingers.

She bucked up to meet his thrusts as he slid his fingers up to twist the nipple. Mid thrust, he released her nipple and grabbed her leg, moving it across his body and pressing it into the mattress beside him. She pushed against his arms as he drove into her and withdrew and repeatedly drove into her. "Please, please, please," she began whispering. Even as he slammed his dick deep into her, he heard her pleas.

"Not yet, sweetling, I am almost there. Come when I fill you with my seed."

"Yes, Sir. Come inside me, pleeeease? Come for your little Kitty?"

With that plea, his reserves bled away as the beasts answered the swirl of her power building inside her. They became one in body as they came in unison. His seed shot deep within her as her body clamped down on his member, pulling at it as she came around him even as he filled her to the brim.

Falling atop her as his orgasm drained his strength, he heard Helena whisper in his ear, "Oh, Master, that was beautiful. Thank you, Master."

4: Rise

Allen woke the next morning with Grace nestled against his side while he laid on his back. Helena was nestled between his legs, her head against one leg, one hand holding his member against her face. Having someone that close to his most dear part was a bit unsettling, but as he watched she moved it to her mouth and sucked it into her mouth for a moment, before opening her mouth and letting out a contented sigh in her sleep. That's new. He watched her stir and pop it back into her mouth coming fully awake suddenly and staring back up at him with those light green eyes. "Good morning, Master," she said around him, sounding more like "Goo' moorin', Mawwa."

Wiping the last of the sleep from his eyes, he replied quietly, "Good morning to you too, Pet. Did you sleep well?"

She popped his lengthening erection from her mouth and whispered back, "Yes, Master." She paused and looked at Grace, biting her lip, "Will you come in my mouth, Master? I would like to start your day serving your dick as a good pet should."

"Uh, yes. That would be nice. Thank you, Pet."

She smiled and gorged herself on his member, which was twitching already from her talk. Her head bobbed up and down, her tongue swirling around the head, lapping at the very tip. She moaned softly as her eyes watched him watch her work. He felt himself begin to go not long after the sight and feel of her so early ticking off all the right boxes. "I am going to come in your mouth now, Pet," he growled softly. She nodded and he let go. He felt her slam his member to the back and swallow hard, sucking with her lips as the muscles of her throat worked the head. He grunted with the overload on his senses as he smelt rich cinnamon and creme hit his nostrils, pouring into his mouth.

Grace sat up with a jerk, arcane runes floating in the air as she looked about, bleary eyes watering. Taking in the scene, she dropped her arms and said, "Already? It is too early." She dove back into the crevice of warmth she had just exited under his arm. "Morning," she grumbled.

"Good morning, Hellcat," Allen smiled into her hair, kissing the top of her head.

She grumbled, "For a creature of the night, you sure are chipper this morning, Sir."

"You might be too, if Helena woke and immediately begged you to come in her mouth," he smirked.

"Will you come on my face, Ms. Grace?" piped up Helena from where she was licking his still half erect member.

"Gods, what?" Grace peeked out at the other woman. "You want to service me as well? I would almost rather get a few hundred more hours of sleep. But I can't say it doesn't mean I am not intrigued. You are a treasure. I am glad you are here. Sorry, about that," she trailed off at the end.

Helena smiled, "Don't be sorry. I would not have Master and you, if you had not done what you did. I feel redeemed by my service to Master. And the Master is not unkind. And I would service you if it gave you pleasure because it would give Master pleasure. My soul is the Master's to do with as he wishes." She ended this with a serious look on her face, then promptly put his rod back in her mouth and closed her eyes in obvious bliss.

"Gods, I imagine she is every man's ideal woman. She works you hard the night before, only to wake you the next morning to suck you dry," Grace snarled, eyeing Helena as the brunette licked and sucked his stiffening member.

"Ughn, maybe so. Good chance of that actually. Ah, mayhaps a demigod as well. She doesn't ever seem to want to stop. And, uhn, I am not complaining." He turned his attention to the woman licking his jewels while he was stuffed down her throat, "Ok, on your back, Pet. I am going to push your round bottom through this mattress."

Popping him free of her mouth and flopping backwards without a care onto the ginormous bed, Helena reached up and spread her lower lips, "Yes,

Master. Please, Master, show me how well I have done. Yes, please, Master."

He groaned his desire as both women's scents began to wash over him. He could feel his ties to both, thrumming through his body as he slid into her, her wet channel overflowing with her juices.

Grace laid alongside the two as Allen drove himself deep into Helena's petaled opening, much to the squirming, panting brunette's delight. Grace watched his shaft spread her lips, pulling more and more nectar with it. "As much as I love the sight of you, Sir, I need to get some tea and start getting ready for the day. May I have your leave to do so? It looks like you are going to be busy for a moment..."

Allen's eyes swung up from his partner to meet hers, still thrusting into her, "Ah, the shy Kitten emerges. Yes, Grace, you have my permission. Give me a kiss and we will catch up as quickly as we can. Make enough for all of us, please. I will miss you until then."

Sliding up and giving him a moment's lingering kiss, her eyes drifting half closed again, Grace then slid from the bed, "Thank you, darling Sir. I will miss you, too. See you soon." She swayed her hips as she walked out of the room.

He watched her hips and hair bounce with each step, "Pet, I am close already, come with me. I would like to get started on our day."

"Yes, Master! Please, fill my pussy with your seed! Please, come in me, please, please!" Helena gasped out as she thrust up to meet his strokes.

The two lovers cried out. Master and Pet's eyes locked together. Their hearts beating in time, echoing each other.

5: Tea

1908, Munich, Bavaria, Germany.

Wagner House.
The cafe and diner was a quaint shop and eatery, on the east end of Munich. Grace reveled in watching the people and savored the rich smells of earth and freshly cooked food. She loved the tea here. The small family that ran the shop were friendly enough and left her alone, which was a nice change from the usual, as she was a lone woman in the city.

The single men off to work the factory stopped in the mornings for sandwiches and thermoses with hot tea or coffee. They were doing so just now when the stranger walked in this morning. He waited in line, as the men jostled and joked with each other. Familiar ribbing and taunts bandied about as coin and goods traded hands.

She would be happy when it quieted back down and she could get back to her book. This fantasy world the author was taking her through was much different than any she had read. She liked the heroine and the hero was a darker and delicious bit. It wasn't often she found a book that had such fun aspects in it. Oh, and dragons and magic. Always quite fun. The build up was interesting. She sighed with relief as the last factory worker trundled out the door.

Now that things were settling down, she could relax, before going back to her research. She crossed one leg over the other at the knee. She propped her book on her leg, sipped her tea, and began losing herself to the world of Eastland. Something tickled the back of her mind, however, and she found herself looking back to the counter. The stranger was talking with the older daughter of the shopkeeper. She was seemingly entranced by him. Listening a bit closer, letting a trickle of her reserves into her eyes and ears, she caught his odd accent. It wasn't often that foreigners would be seen here.

His aura was a surprising swirl of contrasting dark and brightened red tendrils radiating out from him, teasing along the dull, pale green of the girl's. As the tendrils touched against hers it pulled back, like a hand on a hot surface. The girl's aura clung to her, barely draped over her form.

The girl behind the counter was speaking clearly, her voice breathy and almost giddy. They seemed to be talking about rooms for rent and the young woman seemed interested in knowing where he was going to lay his head.

She had come across to Grace as a bored young lady ready to leave the nest. She flirted with any man who caught her fancy, so long as her parents were not about. Likely, this was one more in a group of men denying her an escape from a bland life not to her liking.

The man spoke again, a rich baritone in broken German, as he asked the girl about some house. She giddily replied, giving clear directions to a place nearby.

Bored with their conversation she glanced over his clothes, they seemed a little worn and dirty from the road but of good repair. He wasn't a large man, nothing the size of one of the factory workers, but he wasn't small like a desk clerk. She went back to her book and the story within.

A day or two later, she was sitting comfortably on her usual chair, chapters deeper into her book. The hero and heroine had finally had sex, much to her relief. She was enjoying seeing the aftershocks of such a pivotal moment playing out between them.

A cough pulled her back to the present. Her face dropping into annoyance, she noticed the strange man from the other day was stamping off snow in the doorway. He coughed again, a faint shimmer rolling about him. She watched as he knocked the last of the snow from his shoulders and long beard. Patches of red and a single line of silver swam through the hair on his rugged face.

His jaw was cocked strangely with his mouth open as he breathed in. She had seen this gesture somewhere else, but she could not place it. His head turned to her, a question in his eyes. She was shocked by the intensity of his gaze. He looked to be a man that was unaccustomed to orders not being followed. His left eyebrow inched upward and he nodded to her.

She blinked once, blushed, and quickly looked back down at her book that had laid there in her lap forgotten until she averted her eyes to it. She took in deep breaths trying to calm her now racing heart. *He was something... more.* She could feel it now. Even now with her gaze averted, pretending to read the bouncing words, she felt his eyes on her.

As her heart and breath calmed, under her control once more, her eyes focused on the words in front of her. *Blushing, she continued stroking the hardening organ. She gulped and looked away from his eyes. The darkness there was deep enough to drown in. "I would like more, please, lord husband?"*

Gods save her, she was reading smut with this man looking at her. She gulped and peeked up, trying to not move her head and draw his eyes once more. He was at the counter, talking to the owner of the shop in his broken German. Was that an English accent?

He seemed to be ordering a full tea set. *Why...?* Suddenly, her heart was hammering in her chest again. He was alone with her in the shop. Breakfast crowds were long gone and lunch was some hours away. There was only one person he could be thinking of sharing tea with. Her.

She hurriedly gathered her bag, shoved her book down into it, and went to stand. He was three feet away and watching her with his eyebrow raised again, "I sorry. Offend you me is?"

His broken German was halting. As if he knew he was saying it incorrectly, but he didn't know the correct words. She stared at him for a moment with panic beating her heart against her sternum. "Um," she bit her lip, considering him, "I just have to go. I have research to continue and notes to verify..." She was shaking as she gave her excuses. They sounded lame to her. He likely didn't even know what she was saying.

"Sorry. I speak broke. Understand you word. Speak broke. I no good, offend, big presumption tea. Had questions," he turned to leave.

Her power was flowing through her eyes as he turned. She gasped as his red energy radiated about him, stroking against her flesh. *That would explain her shakes.* She could feel his ... source leaping off him. He was a bright red ball, tendrils of power lashing about the air. A star with a nexus of red energy swirling agitatedly about.

She bit hard on her lip. *Who was this man? Why was his aura lashing about like that? Well, not going to learn anything if you let him leave. And the shopkeeper is right there.* She opened her mouth to tell him to join her when another thought struck her. *What if they sent him? Have I been found?* The goose flesh along her arms made her shiver. *Gods help me.* "No, please, um, sit down. I have a question or several for you."

He turned his head back to her, "Is good? No trouble?"

"Yes, please, sit down at least. I am curious why you wanted to buy me tea. And also who you are," she watched him as he set the tea tray down and slid into the seat across from her. Willing some of her reserves into her eyes to see him, she saw the nova of red was somewhat subdued today. Though its focus was mostly edging about her, she could tell he was holding back the red tendrils. However, one almost appeared to be a large cat, its mouth open as his had been a few days back. Another appeared canine in nature with a watchful eye behind him. Then she blinked and she was not sure if she had seen them at all. *Odd.*

She wasn't sure what he was, but not from the coven. Maybe an agent? This didn't fit either though. He didn't give off a grainy feel or reek of a familiar or bound spirit. What was he?

"English speak?" the stranger asked.

"Ah, yes, that is fine," Grace answered.

Switching to English, he continued, "Thank you, madam. I was getting embarrassed by my struggle with my German. I was wondering, pardon me if I am too forward here, if you are a practicing magician?"

Stunned, she just stared at him for a moment. *Alright, not a coven agent, most likely. But how...?* "Why do you ask?" she asked in German, forgetting his switch, but remembering he understood her.

He began to pour tea as he replied, "Ah, well, you smell of sage, charcoal and molasses. If I judge correctly, they are spell components..." His words trailed off as if he gave away something he hadn't meant to.

She felt his power flex against his control. His eyes on hers as the dark brown within changed to a lighter brown. *Did his pupils change to a slit for a moment or was that her imagination?* Her eyes flicked to where she had seen the cat. *Nothing was there, but there was something unseen watching her.*

"Yes, I practice magic. Perhaps, you can tell me who you are?" *Or what you are?*

He replied in English, "Allen Wells, fraulein. May I ask for yours?"

"Grace, though I will keep my surname, Mr. Wells." The myriad of questions bubbled and swam in her head. *Considering he was blunt with his question, she wanted to know why he wanted to know that. Does he need something? Why is his energy changing so much?* She ran through anyway to ask them politely but came up short.

Sighing, she just let them loose from behind her teeth, "Seeing as you set a precedent for bluntness, I am just going to ask. Why did you want to know that? Do you need something? Why is your energy changing so much?"

He chuckled, "Being direct is in my nature, so please do not hold back. I wanted to know because I am looking to remove a curse. And as such I need a practitioner for the spell. If there is one.

"Why is my energy changing so much? I assume you are seeing my curse urging me to do... things. It is something I have dealt with for ... sometime now and have finally 'mastered' it, but it has kept me from lasting relationships with anyone," he said, his eyes fixed on her, appearing to gauge her reaction to his revelations.

"How does your curse keep you from a lasting relationship? If you weren't cursed, would you be in a normal relationship?" Grace was curious now.

"How does...?" he replied, "I thought you saw it?"

His eyes slanted forward as he knit his eyebrows. His mouth moved soundlessly as he worked through her words. "Perhaps you did not see my curse so much as the beasts trapped beneath the skin. You saw my energy though, yes?"

"Yes, I see that you are distinctive and unique. But I see a great deal of things. Things that others miss or overlook..." Grace haltingly said.

"Ah, well," he leans closer, glancing back over his shoulder to mark the shopkeeper. "I am one that changes under the moonlight. I have been for a long time. Recently, I managed to tame the beasts I become, but there are nights when it is still not safe to be around me. Hence, no lasting relationships. Or even to say ones that are close. To say, how often would you let go of the fact that your gentleman caller would be unavailable for four days out of each month? Would you not wonder what devilish things this cad would be about?"

"Yes, I can see what you mean."

Leaning back, he continued, "And again, I would be rid of it. That I may know peace and mayhaps know love. If you are unable to cure me, perhaps I should leave you be, and look for another," he stood. "I bid you good morrow, Fraulein Grace."

"No, no, sit. This is not a bother. And you haven't even asked properly," she sniffed, waving her hand at the couch that he had been sitting upon. "This sounds like quite the task and we haven't discussed payment or my busy schedule, Herr Wells."

He raised an eyebrow and sat bodily back down, "Payment. I don't care for money. I would happily pay any sum you think reasonable for services rendered." His voice had gotten icey and prickled along her skin.

"Ah..." her face flushed as her mind raced back to the book, the elf pressing the princess against the wall. She lost her train of thought as her heart began to race.

His eyebrows knit together as he watched her face, "Maybe I am missing something in translation. I know you are powerful. I can feel it rolling off you. So, is it a matter of not wanting to help me?"

She squirmed in her seat, his gaze fixed on her. *Is it even possible to do such a request? Remove a moonbeast's curse? Lycanthropes, could they be cured?* "I feel your frustration, I do want to help. But I don't even know if what you're asking of me is even possible. And I have my own mess of research I'm working on," she replied slowly.

"Very well. Let us help one another. I will help with your research however I can and you try to help me remove the curse?" he asked. "You intrigue me. And if something can hold your attention, it will probably be something that holds mine."

She blushed as she gasped out, "I intrigue you? You don't even know me."

"Your face is as lovely as the day. And I would like to," the look in his eyes showed no lie to the words. And, when she checked, neither did his aura.

"I can see you're persistent." *Or maybe insistent.* "I have to get back to work soon. Can we maybe talk again soon to discuss this further?" Grace asked.

"If that is your wish, then yes. Enjoy the tea," he stood once more, "Until next time, fraulein." He bowed slightly to her and left, donning his coat and waving to the shopkeeper.

"Hmmm... until next time, Herr Wells," she whispered, smiling to herself.

6: Dues

1923, New York City, New York.

After breakfast of tea, biscuits, bacon, eggs, and diced potatoes, Allen went up to his office to get his day going. Ted knocked on his door promptly at eight o'clock. "Enter," Allen called, scratching down notes to himself.

The young man opened the door, stepped in, and closed the door behind him. He walked over to the chairs across from his boss and sat in them, notepad in hand, "Good morning, Mr. Wells. Do you have a task for me today?"

"I do. I need you to take the file we have been compiling on the two gentlemen you brought to my office last night. Talk to our contact in Internal Affairs. I would like the full account to be in their hands by six tonight. Any questions?"

"No, Sir. I will get right on it, Mr. Wells," the young man stood, "Do I need an alibi for anything that I may or may not know about?"

Allen grinned maliciously, "I would go see your mother tonight. You had been saying you needed to check on her?"

"Too right, Mr. Wells. I will see you tomorrow then, Sir," he calmly replied, and strode from the room, closing the door softly.

Helena double-checked her equipment. Two pistols, a long knife, lock picks, and a billy club. She slipped it all into her small pack and moved up to the roof, her dark brown slacks swishing with each step. Her hair was tied back, a dark brown shirt covered her torso, and around her neck was a dark scarf. As she walked out onto the roof, she was ready. *Now came the wait for nightfall.*

Grace moved about the tables, setting silverware, napkins, glasses, and table settings. She smiled and hummed a song she had heard Helena play a night or two ago. *She was so giddy. The night hadn't been nearly as rough as she had expected. She figured the attention of the two women had distracted their delicious man and possibly even abated his frustration.* She sighed a happy sigh and kept working.

Duncan sat on a stool near the front door, waving to passing people. The day was a pretty one and not overly hot. He settled back against the wall, ready for a long day.

That, as these things happen, was when things got complicated. Mrs. Darlene Johnson was walking quickly down the street towards him. She was a short woman. She was a bit stouter than fashion favored, but her curves more than made up for it. Her flaming hair swung at her hips, loose and swinging with her strides. Her upturned nose was cute. Her green eyes sparkled with mischief. *Too bad she's married*, Duncan thought to himself. *I'd make her growl back at me as I...*

A knock interrupted Allen as he worked through the finances for the month. He finished the line he was working on then called, "Enter."

Duncan pushed into the room, a familiar short woman behind him. *Of course, she's here*, Allen leaned back in his chair. Its soft leather creaked with his weight. He looked at her for a moment, Duncan standing off to her right. Allen stood, walked about the room, and leaned back on the desk, "Good day, Mrs. Darlene. What brings you here today?"

She flipped up her fan, her blushing cheeks visible over the top. She snapped it closed and looked over at Duncan, "Perhaps, we could have some privacy, Sir." She turned back to him, batting her eyelashes coyly.

Allen stared at her for some time before he nodded, "Very well." Duncan gave a slight bow and stepped out, closing the heavy door behind him.

As the door closed, Allen nodded to her, "You may speak first, Mrs. Darlene."

The pretty lady slipped into one of the chairs, crossing her legs, "Is it too forward of me wanting to have another session so soon? My husband came home last night deep in the sauce. He has been asleep all night. He reeked of something awful. I thought I would see if I could coax you into using me as you saw fit."

Again, he looked long at her silently. Her smile fizzled as he continued watching her placidly. Finally, he leaned forward, a predatory look in his eyes. He spoke quietly and darkly, "You broke the fourth rule of the Dungeon. You are not to speak of anything that happens in the Dungeon or discussions in this office. You then come here expecting a cheerful smile on my face at your flirtatious attitude? You need to pay your dues. You have two choices. Neither of which you will like. One, you receive fifteen lashes across your rump and thighs. This option does not include orgasm. Two, you receive ten lashes in an exhibition for others to watch. I will then let Mr. Caan take his pleasure in each of your needy holes. This may include an orgasm but is not guaranteed.

"Either way, you will be forgiven after you receive your punishment."

She stared at him in amazement. Her mouth was agape as he could see her mind whirl behind those bright green eyes.

Ted walked into the police station, heading down the hallways towards Damien's office, a folder three inches thick under his arm.

Grace hummed as she prepped bottles for the night's festivities.

Duncan sat on his stool. He thought over the swish of Mrs. Johnson's skirts and the fullness of her blouse. He frowned as he cleared his mind.

Helena sat cross-legged on the roof, enjoying the fresh air.

Darlene stared at this delicious man. Anger thundered in his eyes, making her thighs slick with her juices. *He was such a prize.* She controlled herself enough to not lick her lips. *She hadn't meant to let on that she was in such high spirits, but Georgie never paid attention to her. Then last night, suddenly, he was in her face with that pistol. She had had no choice. But the thought of debasing herself in front of a crowd for their pleasure, especially without guaranteed release after, sounded like a bill too high.* "The first choice then, Sir," she said meekly.

Hours later, the restaurant and the speakeasy opened up for business. The lunch crowd came and went, fine cuisine and delicious desserts were eaten with gusto. Patrons tipped their servers well.

As night fell, the dinner crowds began creeping in, well-dressed men and glamorous women began arriving.

The piano on stage was played by a substitute artist as a winged woman flew from the roof and moved with the clouds across town.

Ted knocked on his mother's door. She answered soon after.

Allen sat in a chair. Sitting, naked on the carpet was Darlene. She was in the submissive waiting position. He stared down at her for another moment. He tilted his head up and sniffed the air. "Mmm, your fear tantalizes my palate," he began, turning his yellow and brown eyes on her, "I will begin by reminding you of the rules for the Dungeon.

"One. You will submit to the rules and follow them to the best of your abilities.

"Two. You will serve willingly while in the Dungeon and follow each command given as though it was your own thought.

"Three. You will remember the safe words. You will speak them, when you feel the need to do so, without hesitation. Safety is as important as the secrecy we practice here.

"Four. The secrecy that rule three alludes to is paramount to maintaining our personal safety, as some people will be quick to judge or impose their will upon us.

"Five. Pre-session. If there is anything you need to speak to me about, you will do so. We will come to an agreement before the session begins.

"Six. Post-session. If anything happens that does not require Red but still is a point of interest, we will discuss it during this time. This will occur after post-care. If for some reason Red occurs, we will stop all play immediately and begin post-care. Again, we will discuss the session and the reason for declaring Red.

"Seven. Respect. We will use respect with each other at all times," he finished the recitation, "Any questions at this time?"

"No, Sir. They are quite clear. I am sorry for failing to follow rule number four and understand why you must punish me to correct my thinking. I will strive to be a better submissive moving forward, Sir," her eyes were downcast, but she spoke clearly. Her fingers traced circles around her knees, lost in thought for a moment. She looked up at him as she asked meekly, "May we start the punishment? I would like to pay and move forward, Sir." A slight blush crept over her cheeks as she spoke.

He looked her over once more before replying, "I do not see why not. Take yourself over to the stocks and we will begin." He moved over to the can that held an assortment of stiff impact tools. Selecting a bamboo cane he had gotten on a trip to Asia, he pulled it free and tested its give. Satisfied, he strode over to where Darlene waited in front of the stocks in a standing ready position.

At least, she is a quick study. She had taken to learning the positions he had instructed her on quickly enough, only needing minor adjustments with the end of a crop and a quick smack on her generous bottom to correct her mistake. All and all, she would be quite the submissive for whom she wanted to pledge to when the time arose.

He lifted the stock on its hinges, letting it rest in an upright position. Gingerly, she placed her hands and neck on the rests for them. After making sure her hair was swept to the side, he slowly closed the stocks, careful not to pinch her skin in it, and locked them in place with the ready padlock.

He stepped to the front of the stocks and bent down, so that he was eye level with her, his eyes blazing with heat. He crooked his eyebrow, "Good girl. Now. You are receiving punishment for telling your husband about my attention to your willing flesh. If at any point you would like to stop the lashes, you may cry 'Red', and all punishment will stop. The lashes with this cane will hurt. Quite a bit. You are welcome to scream and cry. It may even help. But, so long as you count and do not use 'Red' we will continue. If you call 'Red,' the punishment will stop, I will see to your abused bottom and you may leave. However, you will no longer be welcome here in my Dungeon. Do we understand each other?"

She gulped visibly and squeaked out, "Yes, Sir."

"Good girl," he walked around and patted her butt. "Let us begin."

He twirled the cane between his fingers for a moment, watching her shake in the stocks, then, making certain to have a good grip on it, he brought it down against her bottom. She cried out then hurriedly cried, "One, Sir!"

He counted to three then swung again, bringing it down in a slightly different angle, laying this lash slightly to the side of the first.

She cried out again then hurriedly whimpered out, "Two, Sir!" The next blow pulled a strangled noise from her, followed by a sobbing, "Three, Sir!"

The next blow was received much as the last, her crying out, "Four, Sir!" She whimpered, the four red marks across her left buttock beginning to redden quickly.

Allen swung again, leaving the next stripe to redden on her cheek. She started crying, "Five, Sir."
"Good girl," he patted her bottom, eliciting a sharp 'eek' from her as he touched the tender flesh. "The next five will be quick, so numbers only." He swung quickly five more times, the blows landing along her thighs, alternating sides.
"Six, ugh, seven, Ayy-eight, No-iiiine, Te-hen," she screamed.

"Very good, submissive. We are almost done. Only five more. You have almost bought off all your poor manners," he stepped to the other side of her.

"Eleven! Sir!" she screamed, at the blow that slashed across her right cheek. She screamed out, "Twelve! Sir!" followed quickly by, "Thirteen! Sir!" then, "Fourteen! Sir!"

He waited a moment to see if she would break before he landed the last blow. She did not call out

'Red,' so he ended her torment by giving her the last lash.

She screamed, "FifTeeheen! Sir!"

He walked around to where she could see him. Her face was red and swollen with tears. Her hair was matted down to her forehead with sweat. He stroked her cheek softly, "Good girl. You did very well. I'm going to release you from the stock now and we are going to see to those lashes. Then I'm going to hold you." He unlocked the stocks and moved behind her, cradling her hips against him as he lifted the top up freeing her from its embrace. She leaned her weight against him as he moved her head and hands free of the device. He closed it and supported her to a nearby lowest table. It was padded for comfort and he laid her out down the length of it.

He walked over to the cupboard that held the healing salves that Grace had concocted for just such an occasion. Her whimpered cries reached him as he moved back, "There, there, now. Just some cream to take out most of the sting. Then we will sit on the couch and you can cry on my chest." He finished up and scooped her up, cradling her against him easily with one arm. He grabbed a cashmere blanket off a pile stacked on a shelf and wrapped it about them, sitting on the couch. She let it out then, racking sobs and unintelligible murmurs. He caressed her hair as she vented her pain into his shirt, soaking it through. He hummed softly as he cradled her.

Thirty minutes later, she was fast asleep.

Helena looked down at the second corpse she had made this evening. The skinny pile of refuse hadn't had a family so it had been more fun to kill him slowly. She had sewn his mouth shut, after knocking him out. It had made his screams of pain much quieter. *Delightful.* She chewed slowly on the heart in her hand. This one was delicious with sin. He had not been one with a bit of purity left in him. *All the better*, she moaned.

The first one was quick. Master had desired it so. A quick bullet to the brain. The fact that he was surrounded by all that white powder and half drank bottles of booze all the better.

Master will be pleased, she moaned again, as she finished her snack.

7: Echoes

1923, New York City, New York.

Allen laid the sleeping woman on the bed, taking a moment to pull the covers over her. She snuggled into his pillow, cooing something softly into the fabric of the pillowcase. He watched her a moment before leaving his place of peace.

As he walked through the restaurant, he stopped and talked with each table. Smiles and handshakes were exchanged. After talking with each table, while the young lady at the piano played Gene Austin's My Blue Heaven, Allen excused himself and made his way to the speakeasy in the back.

Heavy cigar smoke already hung over felt-covered card tables. Men and women sipped fine liquor or wines from glasses as the jazz band strummed guitars. Their soft melody drifted over the easy murmuring of hushed conversations.

After greeting the card players and a few solitary people, Allen walked up to the bar and tapped two fingers on the polished surface, "Some of the Irish."

Tom pulled a bottle out, dropped a few cubes of ice in a glass, and poured in some of the amber liquid.

Sergeant Dan Moses stared down at the mess on the floor. *This splatter of blood and spray of bits used to be a man. A man with a badge.* He looked at the slumped body next, the back facing towards the puddle of brain and blood behind him. Walking around the corpse and the table it sat at, he could see a pile of contraband and bottles of booze. The head of the now-dead Johnson was mainly empty. *Or at least emptier than in life*, Moses mused. The back of its head was a hole. The barrel of his gun, which was clutched in his hand, was stuck in his mouth. Looking along the revolver, into the chamber, he could see a round was spent. *Case closed. Suicide*, he thought. *Stinks in here*. "Pack it up, boys. We're done here," Moses called.

Disgusting in life, and now in death. Embarrassing. Fat waste.

Moses held his handkerchief over his nose. *What devil tore through here?* he thought as he forced his lunch to stay put. He heard gagging behind him and he turned to see a rookie pale green. He called over, "Wilson, go get some air."

"Yessir, thanks." The young man sprinted out the doorway and along the hall. They had been working on the second site for an hour.

Fred O'Malley was a grease ball and a sleaze but this...

Moses stood back in and took in the scene about him. The man was spread out like that Michaelangelo drawing. The man's mouth and eyes were sewn shut. A circle was spread on the floor as if painted. He leaned closer. The smell of copper was prevalent. *Blood?* Looking closer, he could see fingertips smeared in the "paint."

The torso was pulled apart from the neckline to the asshole. The skin was pulled out and spread out along the floor and resembled a pair of wings. Organs were torn free of the body and set neatly around the body. Ribs were broken and spread open and gaped wide like teeth from the mouth of some hellish fiend.

'Rat' was written on the wall in more of the macabre "paint." Shaking his head, Moses started writing down on his notepad. *Two more years, Dan, two more years.*

Fingers missing, nope, in the pockets. Heart missing. Liver missing... fuck me. Whoever did this is a sick sonuvabitch.

Helena finished showering, her hunger abated. She turned lazily in the heat of the water. She was so glad that Grace had managed to acquire the water and fire elementals. Hot water was a joy beyond measure. She thought about the upcoming show

Master was going to use her in. She moaned with lust. *Soon, soon, soon...*

8: Oath

1908, Munich, Bavaria, Germany.

'Quills, Mortar, Papyrus and Pestle'
bookshop.
Digging through her books, Grace set her
latest book on a stack. The stack was
listing back and forth due to its height.
Frustration had set in a day ago. Even with
all the books, she had at her disposal,
including the ones her teacher had given
her she couldn't find it. Plenty of spells on
removing hexes, rituals on expelling
possessions, destroying cursed artifacts.
However, lycanthropy itself was eluding
her.

She slumped back on her chair, she looked
over the swaying stacks. She had checked
them all three times. *Nothing*, she fumed
silently.

One book remained for her to read again,
though she had read it numerous times.

She had been fascinated with the rituals within. Service and devotion, binding one to another, and the summoning of powerful entities. Her teacher had stressed the difficulty of the spells within, but she felt she was close to being ready.

She remembered the one that had fixed in her mind the most. *'Service for protection, I submit to you, my life binding to your care, your life protecting mine, two become one, one by blood and gift.'* It had a response but it seemed to be one meant to be spoken of the heart. If they were not meant, the speaker would not know them. Perhaps that's why it always slipped from her mind. She tapped a lip, dismissing the train of thought.

There was a creak on the stairs. That was the only warning before the day was destroyed.

A brick by her head blew apart, peppering her face and the side of her neck with biting shards. She choked off the scream that was building up in her chest. Terror, an hour of it as she had run, clutching the only book she had been able to grab. It was by far her most treasured possession.

Her teacher wouldn't be gifting her any more books from his collection, since Elana had inspired rebellion and burnt his tower to the ground, with him inside. That shrivel hearted sorceress was of course the one who sent Grace's attackers.

Another black ball slammed down into the cobblestones behind her. More knife-shaped rocks cut into her calves and lower thighs. The many cuts along her body oozed blood. Her clothes were torn and coated in grime, brick dust, her blood, and muck from the gutters. It was only a matter of time until her pursuers caught her in one of those blasts and she was the shards raining down. Tears streaked her face. *I was so careful this time. Why, why, why?*

She had been running for hours. She had managed to evade the blasts and slip through a shadow to pull herself through to another. She had broken their line of sight.
That, of course, was when the hellhound had been summoned. She now just ran.

She had stopped crying after an hour and a half. She was drained of all moisture. Her lips were cracked and covered in soot. Her hair in disarray whipped back and forth against the many wounds on her neck.

She stumbled once, twice, then fell. Her palms scraped against the cobblestones of the alley she was traveling along. Her knees slammed into another group of stones, jarring her with pain.

She let out a dry sob and began scrambling back to her feet. A long shadow fell over her and she went rigid with horror. Have they summoned a larger fiend to finish me? She looked up to find a strange sight. It was a large man that was partly a cat and partly dog. It was very odd to see and her heart thundered in her chest as she crouched its gaze.

A gravelly voice rumbled from the long dog snout that had a cat's eyes above them. The ears that twitched above were short but a blend from both genus. "Frrrraulein Grrrrace, what is going on herrrrre?" He looked over her until unnatural growls and barks came from the street at the end of the alley and drew his eyes.

Allen? Then her brain skipped to the noises, *They found me!* "What... what are you?"

"Rrrun, I will deal with..." the creature that loomed over as it moved past her. She watched him move, lithe, and sure.

Her heart slammed in her chest as she finished getting to her feet. She watched him as he stood in the alley. Then the first of the hounds rounded the corner.

Black chitinous scales flexed down the creatures as their muscles moved along their torsos. Large mitts slammed into the cobblestones breaking the ground up in chunks. Black flaming drool dripped and burnt the ground. Eyes of insanity stared at her as the hell creatures fought with each other to be the first to rip her apart.

She had just gotten to her feet when the first cruel abomination tried to pass the monster that was Allen. A large claw shot out from the end of the arm before he punched down into its back and ripped its spine free. Lava and flames shot out of its back as it flopped onto the ground, twitching but still dragging itself towards her.

She screamed then. Next, she knew she was running again. Her legs burned and her lungs ached as she gasped breaths.

She fell again. She could go no further. Damn them but she just couldn't. She was unable to move from the puddle she had fallen in. *The thing behind her would kill her soon enough. Maybe it will be hungry and it will be quick. She knew this was an unlikely event, but maybe, just maybe.*

She stirred to a gentle hand tugging at her. *Gods, I fell asleep?! How in the...* she looked slowly at the hand tugging at her. Her brain slowly dragged its way out of the exhaustion. Fearfully, she took in the mess clutching to her hem. *Allen?*

His skin was torn everywhere and burnt by hellfire. His eyes were half-closed with exhaustion. He mumbled in his English, "Grace, found... you." He coughed up a handful of blood and fell to lay near her feet.

Goodness, gods help us. She struggled to sit up, her mind swirling in a chaotic mental mess of pure exhaustion and complete gratitude for him saving her. He lay there, his breath ragged and labored. She screamed in panic and shook him so he wouldn't fall asleep. *Please, please, please, don't die. You don't even know me and you saved me. I need you not to die, not like this, not for me.* She shifted her position and looked down at her right hand. There, dirty and bloody was the book. Her teacher's gift. "You're not dying on me, Herr Wells!" she rasped out loudly. Her fingers flipped through the worn pages. She found the one she was looking for. She began to work. She drew her knife cutting into her raw hands, drawing the required sigils. She cut fast but precisely. Double-checking the runes she had carved, she pressed her hands to his wounds.

The words poured out of her. She felt the words fill with her power. Her vision swam as their auras came alive to her eyes. "Service for protection, I submit to you, my life binding to your care, your life protecting mine, two become one, one by blood and gift."

His eyes cracked open as his mouth moved, his eyes locked on her. The words of response reverberated with her own. As she watched and he talked, his previously fading aura bloomed like the sun. His bright red aura meshed with her violet waves. She couldn't tell where one stopped and the other began. "I give my protection (cough) to you, I accept the gift of your service, two be- (cough) come one."

Violently his wounds began to close, power screamed between them. He screamed as the last of the wounds closed. Then he slumped back to the ground, unconscious. She tucked her book into her bodice and heaved him up to a sitting position. "Sure, now is a grand time for a nap." She dragged him down the street.

9: Exhibition

1923, New York City, New York.

Joseph Lawson marveled at the door that he had been led through. His wife and he had been led down a spiral stone staircase. It seemed to be carved straight out of the bedrock below the building. Along the stairs, on both sides, was an ornate, black handrail. It seemed to be fused into the rock at the bottom and a second support extended at regular intervals into the wall.

A minute or two later they reached the bottom of the stair that led into a dark cellar from a castle or something. The long hall was easily twenty feet wide and a good hundred feet long. Seven doors stood out in sharp contrast against the stone, their dark wood and iron seeming to shine in the torchlight.

Mr. Caan led them down to the third door and opened it, gesturing for them to proceed him inside. Stepping past the large man, they stepped into a large room with curtained areas. Looking to the right they saw five couches arranged in a semicircle around a long table. There were several bottles sticking up out of ice with several champagne flutes arranged in precise order. A tray of various types of cheese, crackers, and bite-size fruits was next to that.

Joseph glanced over to their escort, unsure. Mr. Caan motioned for them to sit, "You're welcome to begin before your host arrives, but I would suggest you wait on opening any bottles. There is a bit of theatre to it all I'm afraid."

The young couple sat down on the comfortable couches. "Mmm, is this velvet?" Meagan asked the big man.

"Yes, Mrs. Lawson. Mr. Wells likes the material and had these imported from Germany. Speaking of, I believe he is on his way. If you have any more questions, the Owner will answer them. Good evening," Mr. Caan said and stepped from the room. The two left in the room helped themselves to small morsels for a few moments, savoring the contrasting flavors of cheese and fruits.

The sounds of steps came from the hallway, announcing the arrival of two hooded and cloak covered individuals. The lead person, draped in the gray cloak, held a long, thin, silver chain in his hand. The chain pulled on a ring protruding from under a blue cloak on the second person's collar.

The cloaked figure dropped the chain. The second figure immediately knelt on the floor, her cloak billowing to show a glimpse of blue lingerie underneath. The figure in the gray cloak swirled the cloak off his shoulders and head, revealing Mr. Wells in a three-piece suit. A fitted black coat hugged the man's form over a red vest with black brocade swirling along the length. The man eased into a couch next to the couple.

"How does this evening find you two?" Mr. Wells asked as he leaned over to the bottles and pulled a bottle of champagne free of ice, water dripping down the length. Popping the top, he plucked a towel from a shelf under the table and wrapped it around the bottle. Balancing three glasses between his fingers he filled them and passed two over to the young couple.

"This is the cat's meow, Mr. Wells!" Joseph gushed then sipped his drink. "Thank you for having us. I... sorry, just spilling from my yap."

"Not a problem, Mr. Lawson. I do say, you both look quite keen in your glad rags," Mr. Wells replied, tasting his own drink.

"Thank you, Mr. Wells. You look dapper yourself."

"Thank you, Mrs. Lawson. Now. I have a few rules, covered in the documents you signed before coming down. I am going to expand on them, as well. And I will answer any questions you two may have.

"One. Once the scene has begun you must remain silent for the purpose of letting us stay in our headspace.

"Two. If the scene brings out the desire to begin intercourse with each other, please use the bed to the right. It has fresh linen and has a good view of the stage. And these couches were a touch costly to have made and shipped here.

"Three. And this is the most important one, do not speak of anything you see here or we talk about.

"Any questions at this time?" Mr. Wells finished.

"Use the bed?" Meagan squeaked, "Where you can see us?"

"I can assure you, seeing you two having sex while she is on stage will only make the experience that much better for Helena," Mr. Wells replied, a smile tugging one corner of his mouth up into a smile, something dark passing behind his eyes. "You are both adults. You'll understand more when we start. Anything else?" The two young people just gaped at him. "Very well," he chuckled.

He walked over to the kneeling Helena, "Stand." The order was firm yet calm. She immediately responded, popping up to her feet. He took the blue cloak, as it shimmered lightly under the torchlight.

The cloak came away as though it was water, flowing off of her form. The torchlight fell across lace and leather, both blue and covered in various brocades much like the ones on Mr. Wells' vest. He played his free hand over her stomach's straps and frills. "You look very pretty tonight, Angel," he said, voice thick. "Thank you, Master."

He stepped over to the couches, draped her cloak over it, and walked back over to her. A blue leather collar with four rings was secured around her neck. Her bra was sleek and wrapped about her breasts, blue lace, and leather alternating along her pale skin. A harness of blue leather was buckled to her collar and made triangles under her bra. It connected to additional straps that flowed down her torso to her waist to attach to another harness on each leg. These wrapped around each leg perpendicularly five times from a strap that moved down her leg to mid-thigh. Her underwear was a frilled blue piece that left some to the imagination though it was smaller than either Lawson had seen. She had on a pair of long blue hose with the brocade stitched on it clipped into place on a garter belt of the same material.

Allen walked to where he could see her standing. He watched as her eyes followed him, her head facing forward, her body perfectly still. He raised a solitary finger. Her hands moved to be clasped against the back of her head and she stood straight and tall for him.

"I love your eyes on me, Angel," Allen began circling her, admiring her curves and the lay of the leather and lace trimming them.

He ran a hand around her hip as he walked, pinching and rubbing here and there. He cupped her bottom with his hands. "Delicious, Angel. I'm looking forward to spanking this."

"Thank you, Master."

"Turn left." She did as he commanded. "Stop." She was facing the curtains, her mostly bare bottom facing their audience. "You like the attention of your Master and being watched while your Master touches you?"

"Yes, Master," she said as she shivered.

"Good girl," he said, before patting her bottom, "Bend."

She bent over at the waist, grabbing her ankles. He reached up and pulled her panties down over her hips. They slid over her garters and hose and puddled at her feet. He patted her bottom again and moved her left side. He teased her slit, her juices quickly coating his finger.

"You are very wet, Angel. Are you always this wet?"

"Only for you, Master," she shuddered as she spoke.

"Hmm. Such lovely petals on your flower. And your clit is quite swollen. You are quite needy, aren't you?"

"Yes, Master," she gasped out.

"I'm sorry, what was it you were agreeing to? I would like you to say it for our guests." His finger traced over her mound and wound in between each fold of her. It never entered her and made a small circle on her love button each time it reached the swollen spot.

"I am soaking wet, Master. I need you to touch me. To fill me. To own me, Master."

"Good girl, Angel," he smiled at the beautiful words. He slid a finger into her and felt the warm and wet tightness as she trembled to his touch.

Sliding it in and out of her, he teased in a second finger. She whimpered at the assault as he explored her inner flower. Finding her clit with his pinky, he rubbed back and forth against it. His exploration found her sensitive spot inside her and he alternated fingers pressing into it. She twitched against his hand as he felt her get closer to her orgasm, the pressure around his fingers building.

"May I come for you, Master?" she pleaded, desperation in her voice.

"No, not so soon. We have just begun," he clicked his tongue, slowly pulling his fingers away, wiggling them furiously inside her as he did.

She shuddered as she gasped out, "Y-y-yes, Master."

"Stand up." She obeyed. "Turn about." She turned to face the young couple. "Open your mouth and stick out your tongue." She complied, holding her mouth open as wide as she could. "Good girl. Let's see that tongue." He pinched it between two fingers pulling it straight out. "Very soft, Angel. Almost as soft as your petals. Clean my fingers for me. You got them very messy." He released her tongue and held his fingers he had used on her up.

She took them into her mouth and began sucking on them. Her desire radiated out from her eyes as she watched him watch her suck on them. She ran her tongue up and down each finger and her lips pulled at both.

"Good girl," he said as he pulled his fingers from her.

He circled her again, tracing the lines of her body and occasionally unlatching buckles until all was loose on her. "We won't be needing that anymore, Angel. Show them my beautiful body that you gave to me."

She smiled as she began, "Yes, Master." The rest of her outfit began to clatter and fall to rest along with her panties. He began circling again. He cupped each breast. He ran his hand across her belly. He cupped each butt cheek. He pinched her sides, eliciting a squeak from her. He clicked his tongue. "Bend." She did and he immediately popped her bottom. "You need to be quiet, Angel, unless I direct you to. You know that, yes?"

"Unhn, yes, Master." Her eyes seemed to have locked on something out in the audience. He turned to see what had broken her attention. The young couple was doing a bit of fondling of their own. The woman's dress was hiked up to her hips and the man's member was out. They were transfixed on the stage as they touched each other.

Allen raised an eyebrow. "Unless you want to buy that very expensive couch I would suggest moving to the bed post haste."

Startled, the couple realized they had been caught and scurried to the bed and began disrobing. It was cute and endearing. Such young love. He rested a hand against Helena's sex, sliding a finger in and out of her as the audience finished getting undressed and comfortable on the bed. She whimpered again, as she tightened around him.

"Well, now that our guests are being honest with themselves and my body of yours has been inspected, we can begin. Stand in the ready position, Angel."

He moved away from her as she stood, interlocking her fingers behind her back, shaking from her near release. He moved to the curtains and pulled a cord. The clasp above detached. Two weights, one on either side, began to descend. They were affixed to steel cables that ran through pulleys and were fastened to the heavy felt curtains. As they fell, the cables pulled the curtains to the sides, revealing an assortment of large fixtures. Some of them were mounted on casters while others were bolted to the ground.

"The St. Andrew's Cross, Angel." He watched as she turned fluidly and began walking to the indicated piece. Ebony wood padded and covered in black dyed leather. Several rings were bolted in place on each leg of the sideways cross.

Helena stepped up to the cross and returned to the ready position. He smiled as he walked up behind her. He selected restraints from a nearby table and began to strap them on to her arms and legs, tracing each limb after buckling them into place.

He selected four locks and said, "Up." She stepped on to the cross' steps and faced it. She spread her legs wide and set her hands up along the fastening rings on the upper arms of the cross. Allen opened the locks and, pulling each leg and arm into place, locked them on the restraints and nearby rings.

The young couple was being a bit noisier now, but nothing he couldn't manage. "They are enjoying the show, Angel. How does that make you feel?"

"Happy, Master."

"You would really like to come for me in front of them, wouldn't you?"

She inhaled sharply before replying in a soft, husky voice, "Yes, Master."

"Too quiet. You are going to have to say it loud now. What is it you want, Angel?" he commanded.

She tugged at the locks and restraints as she whimpered, "Please, Master."

"No. You want something. But you need to ask me for it. Convincingly."

"Please, let me come for you, Master. Please let your Slave come for you, Master. I am aching to come for you."

"Hmmm. Not good enough. We will just have to see," he stepped over to a rack of various hanging crops, paddles, straps, and canes. Selecting a crop with a long leather strap and long handle, he walked back to her. He traced the leather strap across her butt cheeks. She quivered, her excitement dripping down her inner thighs.

He flicked the tip of the crop softly against her bottom, thighs, and calves. She whimpered at each flick. He stuck the crop through his belt. He traced his fingers along her cheeks. She shook visibly under his touch.

"Now for some spanks on that delicious bottom of yours. I do so much love spanking my ass of yours," he stated. He began lightly slapping her cheeks from the bottom to the top.

She whimpered and her back arched, pushing her bottom back towards him. He increased his speed and force gradually as he moved his hand around her bottom. She shuddered as he spanked her, gasping and dripping down her legs.

Her butt began to pink and redden as he worked on her. She whimpered and began to beg him, "Please, oh, Master, please! Oh, gods, uhn..."

"Not yet, naughty Angel, our guests haven't come yet. Do you think you should come before them?"

"Umhn, no, Master, oh, gods, unn."

He could hear the passion building behind him, a quick glance over his shoulder showed the two coupling. They were both facing the stage. He was behind her as they thrust against each other. They were watching as he reached back and popped Helena once more. Both of them cried out and collapsed against the footboard in an embrace.

"Ah, the guests have finished. I want you to come on my fingers while I spank your ass now."

As he slid his hand down her stomach and slipped two fingers into her sex, he heard her reply, "Yes, Master! Please, Master!"

"Good girl, Angel," he began spanking each cheek in succession, firm and quick. She shook as the orgasm ripped through her. The constant stream of juices jumped to a spray as she bucked and jerked in her restraints.

She screamed, "Oh, gods, thank you, Master! Thank you for letting your Slave come for you! Thank you! Oh, my gods! Thank you, Master!" Her ass cheeks flexed and her legs shook as she continued to thank him and come on his fingers.

The young couple had thanked him repeatedly for the show as he had held Helena on the couch. After a quick shower, they had redressed and been led out by Duncan.

Now, he just held her. She mumbled something in her sleep. Her head rested on his shoulder, her hair draped down her bare back.

A short while later, he noticed Grace standing in the doorway, leaning on the frame, a smile on her luscious lips.

10: Summons

1910, dilapidated ruins on the outskirts of Kristiansand, Norway.

Grace checked against the book for the hundredth time. This rune was a pain in her butt. Why couldn't runes be easier to draw? She wiped out the binding rune. She went slower and drew the chalk piece along the stone floor. Slowly and carefully, she completed the process then checked it against her teacher's book. Her book.

She scooted back in her skirts, giving herself room for the next rune. She heard Allen sip his coffee. She sighed as he said it again, "Are you sure this is a good idea? You don't know what you are going to pull through this ... spell."

She knew he didn't doubt her abilities, but he seemed leery about new forms of magic. Untested, untried. Everything in the book was new to her but ancient. "No, maybe, yes? I don't know what we are going to get from this spell. That's true. But it... just feels right. And we need more strength. More power. We don't know when she is going to try to kill us again and I want to be ready this time. I will not be a weak, scuttling, cringing, whimpering fool waiting to die. And I won't sacrifice you to her ambitions either. I know what you were going to say. You'll keep me safe. But... But we need to get stronger. And this is how." She finished the last rune. "There. All done." She looked up to his skeptical smile. She squinted at him and stuck out her tongue.

He chuckled, "Oh, alright. Let's see. Can't be worse than the time you summoned the greed demon."

She frowned, "I didn't know what that rune meant. That wasn't my fault." She waved a hand over her last several days of work, "I've double-checked all the runes. Life. Power. Binding. Time. Power. And that one is Lust. So no greed demon this time." She pointed to the runes as she named them and looked back at him again.

"Very well. Close it and we will see," his beard was long now, almost to his belt. He ran a hand down the length of it as he readied himself.

She skipped over to her big strong man, pecked him on the cheek, and pulled out her little dagger. Its silver blade glinted in the moonlight dancing about the room. She pricked her thumb and squeezed out a drop onto the chalk.
The second the drop hit the chalk, she felt it.

Power. Anger. It washed over her. It was not her own or Allen. It radiated out from the blue fire that licked along the circle, scarce inches from her face. The flames roiled along the cylindrical wall and recoiled to strike again and again.

The scent of sulfur and cinnamon hit her nose as she began to catch sight of the being within. A taller woman wearing armor with a long sword stood in the fire. Grace realized she wasn't standing in the fire, she was the fire. The noise of roaring flame changed to that of a thunderclap and the flame was replaced by feathers. They pressed against the wall of the circle. Blue and black lightning danced about slamming into the barrier.

The woman was staring at her hatred and rage crackling in her eyes. Blue and black lightning coursed under her ivory skin, long hair rippling in an unfelt torrent. The sword in her hand came up and she lunged for Grace.

Grace screamed as she toppled backward. The sword had stopped at the barrier and Allen was suddenly in between her and the winged woman. This couldn't be right. Why would an angel answer her summon? The barrier suddenly fell, a spider-webbed reflection of magic washing over them as the woman drove herself forward with a flap of her outrageously large wings.

Allen at once was in between them. Grace hadn't seen him move. He slapped the sword aside to his left. The woman spun around with a flap of her wings and brought a rising cut to his left side with both hands.

He leaped back as he snapped his right hand out to slap the sword again this time skyward, knocking one of her hands loose.

The woman jerked her sword to her hips and then let loose a barrage of jabs. Each time Allen would step or lean away from the blade.

Then she whirled and a spray of blood flew. He bent over holding his slashed arm and abdominal muscles. She took advantage of him staggering back to rush past him and lunged at Grace.

Again Allen was there, one hand on her neck driving her back, jolting her movement to a stop before slamming her into the ground.

"No, you will not hurt what is Mine!" he roared as he took his cat form. White fur with black spots shot out along his arms and legs, which had blossomed in size. His head snapped forward as he had a feral gleam in his slanted eyes. A tail poked out of one of his pant legs as he slammed his clawed palm down against the attacking woman's face.

A shriek of pain came from her as her sword drove itself into the wall to the left. Allen continued to pummel her. His fist jerking back and slamming back down. "MINE!"

11: Service

1923, New York City, New York.

Grace smiled at the sight of Mister being gentle with her third. He was gentle as he was firm during the time after a scene. She loved the softness as much as his domineering side. He glanced over at her. She smiled broadly and said, "Aren't you a sight for sore eyes. May I join you, Sir?"

"Of course, my little Witch. I have another knee..." he smiled tiredly at her. He balanced the sleeping Helena, holding her firmly against him.

She smiled back, undressed out of her work uniform to kneel down before him, and rested her head against his knee.

He smiled wider, ran his fingers through her hair, and pulled her chin up towards him, "Come give me a kiss then tell me about your evening."

She beamed up at him. She loved it when he ran his calloused hands through her hair and plucked at her chin. *This man. Mmm.* She pulled herself up onto her knees and extended herself up to meet his forward lean and kissed him. His tongue lashed out to push through her lips and claim her own. Her heart thrummed with joy. She playfully bit his bottom lip. "You look tired, Sir. Come to bed and I'll tell you about my evening."

"Very well. Help me get Helena to bed and I will happily climb into bed." He stood slowly so as not to jostle the sleeping woman. Grace jumped up to her feet quickly and stabilized him. He moved the sleeping woman to a cradling carry and nodded. The two of them walked the hall together. Grace rubbed his back and butt, earning her a knowing grin from her Mister.

She smiled back and skipped ahead knowing he was looking at her butt as she did. She pulled the door open and he slipped through into Helena's room.

If Grace didn't know better she would think this was a young girl's room. But the large rack of bladed weapons and full plate armor on the mannequin spoke to one of Helena's two sides.

The other was in the little things that sat around the room. On the left was the pink and blue tea set. Mister had gotten that five years ago for Helena and she had squealed with delight. The huge collection of stuffed cats, bears, wolves, and China dolls lined the walls on shelves. The pink bedding and blue drapery on the four-poster bed. All spoke of such an innocence that made her smile.

Mister took Helena to the bed and Grace pulled back the blankets. He slid Helena from his arms and kissed her forehead. She snuggled into the pillows and Grace tucked her in. He put her two favorite stuffed animals into bed with Helena, a fierce wolf, and an adorable white leopard. As if sensing they were there, Helena pulled them down into the covers with her. She mumbled something in her sleep.

They watched her for a moment before leaving and closing the door softly behind them. They walked to his room and she again skipped ahead to open the door for him. He didn't slip by this time. Instead, he stopped and claimed her mouth once more. It started soft and gentle. But soon his arms were around her, crushing her to him and claiming every inch of her mouth. They gasped out their breaths as they came apart.

"Please, Sir, let's get you undressed and ready for bed," she said, as she sucked in air. He nodded and stepped into the room. He grabbed a chair and sat heavily into it.

Grace walked up to him and began unbuttoning his vest and shirt. She untied his necktie and slid it slowly along his shoulders. She pushed his clothes free of his chest and ran her fingers through his chest hair. She helped him out of the vest. The garment and tie fell to the floor as she took a sleeve and pulled it free of his arm. She moved to the other side of him and tugged the other arm free. Peeling the shirt from him she began running her hands over him. She worked the chest pushing hard and trailing fingertips over his pectoral muscles.

She stepped behind him and began running her fingers through his scalp. He let loose a soft moan. *Mmm. I like the sound of that.* She rubbed his temples and jaw. His head rolled back against her bosom and his eyes closed. She smiled as she worked his neck and shoulders. Another groan escaped as she found a knot and worked to break it up under her fingers. "The evening was great, but I did miss Helena's music. Her energy has a way of speaking to my soul."

She pressed her breasts against him as she leaned forward to run her fingers back through his chest hair. Her fingers trailed along his stomach until she could reach no further. She pouted. *Shame*. She laid a finger on his chin and ran it up to his lips. Then she kissed him softly as she moved around in front of him. "I spoke to the Lawsons after your exhibition. They were quite impressed. I'm sorry I didn't get to see it myself."

She knelt in front of him, sitting on her heels and resting her cheek on his knee. "They would like to come back for more..." His eyes fluttered open and fixed on hers. Need rose in her to mirror what she saw in his eyes.

"Hmm. I'm glad the evening went well. I didn't have an issue with the Lawsons. They seem like good people. But more importantly, I am glad you brought me in here. I want to see those pretty lips wrapped around me, little Witch," he said as he ran his fingers through her hair.

Grace sat up on her knees a bit, running her hands up his thighs to reach his waist and unbuckled his belt. She unfastened his buttons, revealing him pressing against the fabric of his undergarments. She got a grin on her face as she caught sight of what she wanted. She took him in her hand as her lips softly kissed the tip of him. Then she carefully pulled his foreskin back and rolled her tongue around him, getting him drenched in her saliva. She looked up at him, so she could see his pleasure radiating out from his eyes as he watched her. Still looking in his eyes, she opened and slid her mouth over his head and down his length. He groaned and she could feel him rumble with need through her lips and hands. Her eyes rolled back in her head as her lips met her hand to work him together. Up and down she went as he swelled in her mouth. *Mmm. Mmmm. Mmmmm.*

He ran his fingers through her hair, the tips curling her hair behind her ears as her head bobbed up and down on him, "Oh, that is good. Such a good girl." She moaned around him as his member pulsed in her mouth.

The soft words were met with a twinkle of an unspoken "*thank you, Sir*" in her eyes. She rolled her tongue around his head and then licked the underside all the way down. Then she came back up and began bobbing faster up and down his shaft.

His fingers curled into her hair at the nape of her neck, not pushing just pulling on her downward stroke. "Gods, that is ... ugh, delicious, Kitten."

She, still holding all of him in her mouth, grabbed the hem of his pants and tugged at them. He hopped up partly out of his seat, allowing her to yank his pants and undergarments out from under him. She pushed them to the ground as his stiffness pressed into the back of her throat. She felt her gag reflex try to push him out and she choked slightly as she grabbed his thighs and pushed herself farther down on him. "Mmmmm. Mmm mmmm," she moaned out as her saliva dripped out around him.

He ran his fingers across her cheek and one down her nose, "Is that what you want? You want me to make a mess of your mouth? Do you want to swallow me down and suck me dry, Hell Cat?"

"Mmmhmmm," she moaned into him, as she went back to furiously working his tasty meat with her lips and tongue. He groaned again as she stroked and sucked on him. His member flexed and twitched in her mouth. *Mmmm, not much longer now.* She curled a hand around his balls and rubbed them with one hand and he twitched again.

"I'm about to go, Kitten. If you want it, just keep doing that... ugn."
Her eyes rolled back in her head as he came on her tongue. His pleasure satisfied her to the core. She kept working him up and down as he shot out his cum, then she slowly came to a stop. Then she looked up at him, swallowed, and softly kissed the tip.

"Sweet little Grace. I'm going to take you out to eat and you're going to dress up pretty. I'm going to think about a good reward for that. And then I'm going to give it to you," he continued after a pause, "...tomorrow. Let's get in bed." He leaned down, kissed her firmly again, and pulled her to her feet. They padded to the bed and slid in together.

Soon, they were asleep, arms and legs intertwined, her head on his chest.

12: Binding

1910, dilapidated ruins on the outskirts of Kristiansand, Norway.

Grace pushed herself up on her elbows. Allen had pushed her out of the way of the last strike the crazed angel woman had swung at her. She badgered herself mentally. *Not again!* Followed quickly by, *This is worse than the demon.* Then she furiously flipped through her book to find something or somehow to fix this.

Then she realized nothing in the book could help fast enough, so she jumped up and ran towards Allen's side. The woman flapped her wings, punched, and kicked up at him. He snapped another strike down at her, rocking her head back against the stone floor.

"Allen!" Grace called as she neared him. He flicked a glance over his shoulder at her, his eyes awash with yellow and his iris a wide vertical line. Grace finished her run, closing all but the last three feet. "If you.. if you hold her down, maybe I can bind her. We need this and..."

He growled as he grabbed the woman's throat and bounced her head twice more on the stone floor. "Hurry then." His voice was gravelly and strained. She could see the blood he was losing. *Damn, damn, damn.* She hurried back to her supplies and grabbed a bowl and rushed back to the struggling pair.

She leaned in and caught the dribbling blood in the bowl. She dodged an attack from the woman as Allen grabbed the offending arm. "Uh, uh, hold it out and still for me," she pleaded. He complied, giving her a look. The woman struggled as Grace pulled her silver dagger free of her belt again and sliced a gash in the woman's arm.

Blood spilled free and Grace caught it in the bowl. The hot, red liquid sizzled as it mixed with Allen's. She took a second to dance away from a kick and settled a good meter from the fight. She knelt down, slashed her own hand over the bowl, and poured out magic with her blood into the mixture. She stuck three fingers into it and ran back to Allen.

"What are you doing?" he growled out. The woman was still pummeling him with kicks and punches on his side while he tried to grab her other arm.

"Uh, uh, just stay still. It will be fine," Grace hoped out loud. She drew the binding rune on his back as he struggled with the woman.

Grace finished the rune and began drawing the rune for power when she felt the woman break free from his grasp and kick her in the side. She sailed through the air, coming to rest on her back.

She looked back to the fight to see Allen slamming devastating blows down on the woman as she fought back and blocked. Grace hurriedly drew runes and symbols on the cold ground. She backed up again and called to him, "Bring her here! Put her on the mark and force her submission!" He didn't seem to hear, but she knew he did. He always heard her, even when she didn't want him to. "Please, Sir, you'll kill her! And ... and we will be the same as we were! We need her! Please!"

He looked over at that. He huffed and pulled the woman up off the ground by her neck. She continued her assault on him as he dragged her over to where Grace pointed. He slammed the woman down on the markings and a trio of colors jumped up and drove into each of them.

Oh, that hurts. It was the only thing she could see or feel. But there was something else. Her Mister's voice. "YOU WILL

SUBMIT! IF YOU DO, NO ONE SHALL EVER FORCE YOUR SERVICE AS YOU WILL BE MINE! I PROTECT THAT WHICH I OWN! YOU SHALL BE MY SLAVE, BUT I WILL OWN YOU! I WILL BE THE MASTER! ALL WILL KNOW MY WRATH IF THEY WANT TO HARM YOU! SUBMIT!"

"You, you will own me? And protect me? Yes, please! Please, be my Master! I submit to you and will serve no other!" The voice was new. A sing-song melody. And the pain was gone.

And darkness swam over her.

13: Dinner

1923, New York City, New York.

Jerry's Place.
Grace and Allen followed their waiter through the semi vacant tables. The chandeliers overhead splashed a soft light from the myriad of candles lit there onto the fine white and black tablecloths and the centerpieces on each table. The house band was playing a soft melody on the stage.

The waiter, a gaunt gentleman that was well-dressed with tails, led them to an area marked off with velvet ropes. After moving them through the barrier, he led them over to a table set with fine silverware. A tea service and coffee pot simmered on a trolley with a small wood stove atop it. Another waiter stood nearby watching the fire. This young man looked up at them as they approached and began moving to fill the tea kettle with boiling water.

As Allen pulled out her chair, the two began setting cups in front of their seats. The younger man set the tea service down on a fold-out tray, followed closely behind by the coffee pot. He moves away with the stove trolley.

The older man turned to them and his voice had a soft British accent, "Your orders of shrimp primavera with linguine and garlic butter sauce, salad with olive oil, and garlic and cheese bread will be out in ten minutes, Master Wells. Will you be needing anything else, sir?"

"Not at this time, Mister Sampson." Allen slipped into his chair, his eyes fixed on Grace.

"Very good, sir," the man said and stepped away, bobbing his head in a quick bow.

Allen leaned heavily onto his elbows toward her. His fingers touched together in a steeple. He set them against his lips. "You look fantastic in that dress, Fraulein Grace."

"Thank you, Sir," she beamed a happy smile at him as she ran her hands across the material. *It was that red he loved her in. She had worked hard with the tailor to get the cut just right. A level or two above scandalous, yet classy and form-fitting. Truth be told she had needed Helena to get the buttons in the back for her.* She was overjoyed by his enthusiasm for her in it.

"I would like to slide your dress up to the hip, and trace the hem of your stockings." There was almost a growl in his voice. One she recognized to be full of want. She gulped as her eyes shot up to his. They were backlit with a red flame and were locked onto her.

"Tie your wrists together and attach it to a winch, lift it up until you are on your stockinged toes."

Grace tried to hide the excitement yet the fear of hearing her fantasy spoken of from across the table. She whispered, "Sir, someone will hear you!"

He continued after he lifted his coffee cup to his lips and sipped, "Then just tease your flesh."

Grace looked down at her hands while biting her inner lip.

"Inner thighs. Calves. The back of your arms. Earlobes. Hips. Bottom of your spine. Neck. All along your bottom cheeks."

She blushed and looked up at him with a twinkle in her eye.

"Your tummy. The valley of your breasts. Your shoulders. The side of your breasts. Back of your thighs. Valley of your lap, just above your mound."

She let out a breathless "Sir..."

"Then I will begin on your nipples. Lick. Nibble. Pinch. Twist."

Her mouth dropped open in want while she sat up and subconsciously pushed her breasts towards him.

"The mound of your honeypot."

She squeezed her legs together at the mention.

"Kissing along the outside of the lips. Licking along the line of the lips. Teasing the tip of my tongue into it. Bumping your clit."

She squirmed in her seat, "Sir! I...."

He interrupted her, the growl of his voice rumbling, "Flicking it repeatedly with my tongue. Sucking it into my mouth. Working it with my tongue as I suck it. Nibble it then bite and suck hard."

She sucked in a breath, glanced around to see if anyone was listening, and let out a desperate whimper.

"You, of course, would be allowed to come here, if you remember your manners."

She looked back to him quickly and gave him a grin with a twinkling wink, "I always remember my manners, Sir." She giggled breathlessly and quietly.

"Then, of course, we could move on to something both of us need."

"Oh, I love the sound of that," she sighed out with a devilish tone.

"After touching every part of you, I would start light spanks across your buttocks."

She tried once again to contain her excitement and took a sip of tea.

"Then your thighs, calves. Fondle your breasts. Grope your bottom. Spank your butt, one cheek at a time. Alternating between them."

Grace bit her lip and writhed in her seat.

"Then tease your petals."

She sucked in a breath.

"And continued light spanking."

She let out her breath, "Mmmm, gods, you get me."

"Then I would clean my fingers off your juices where you could hear."

Her mouth dropped open in astonishment.

"Oh, yes. I forgot to mention the blindfold."

She came back to herself and teasingly said, "Oh? How could you forget that?"

He raised an eyebrow and continued, "Then I would take your mouth. Your juices and my saliva mixing with yours."

Her eyes widened in surprise.

"Then I would pink your bottom with my hand."

Again she bit her inner lip and her want poured out of her at him.

"Then your thighs. Calves. Bottom of your feet. Then slow slaps on your sexpot. Slowly increasing pace and intensity."

"Sir! I....need you..."

"Sh, sh," he hushed her, "Then when you're shuddering, I'll push two fingers into your sex, telling you to come on my hand."

She let out a whimper of longing, "Sir, please. Your words have me aching and so wet."

"Then I would take you to the horse and tie you down to it."

Her inner excitement escalated with the thought of scenery change.

"Then I would explore your mouth with my tongue. Then I would trace lines on your back. Kissing each place I touch."

She smiled and said, "You're so sweet to me."

"Then bite each place I kiss."

She squinted, "Yet not."

"Until I reach your backside again. Then I would lick and nibble your sex and ass cheeks. Then lick deep into your sex."

"Oh, gods!" she muffled her exclamation with her hands.

"Sucking and licking. Nibbling your lips. Flicking your clit with my tongue. Teasing your rosebud."

Her eyes widened in surprise and she looked him in the eyes to make sure she heard correctly.

"Licking and sucking at it. Alternating between the two as I pinch and slap and grope your ass, back, thighs. Until you are begging me to let you come. Then I would let you come as I slam two fingers into your sex and tease your rosebud with my tongue."

She shook as she struggled to keep composure. "Goddess, help me."

"And once you had come for a few minutes I would let you stop."

She let out a breath she didn't know she was holding.

"Kiss my way back up your back to your lips. Taking your mouth with mine as I hold your neck. Pressing deep and fucking your mouth with my tongue."

She smiled, her cheeks blushing red.

"Then I would fetch the floggers."

Her smile vanished as her jaw dropped again, eyes flaring wide once more.

"Starting light, I would work your back, bottom, thighs, calves, feet."

She sucked in a breath and fanned herself.

"Slow soft slaps. Slowly increasing the pace and intensity. Moving along your body. Once you were close I would dive into you, sucking and biting at your clit. Until you came on my face, with permission."

She squirmed again in her seat and looked for others watching or listening, but no one seemed to be paying them any heed.

"Then a paddle," his growling voice breaking through her worry.

Her eyes jolted back to him in surprise.

"Soft slow pops. Increasing slowly in pace only. Then stop until you wiggle at me."

"I don't wiggle!" her mock indignation seemed to fall on deaf ears as he continued.

"Then pop you good and square across both cheeks."

She closed her mouth tight.

"Then slam two fingers into your sex and tease your rosebud with my tongue as I use my hand across your bright red cheeks."

Her cheeks flamed with an amber blush.

"You, of course, would be allowed to come when you asked."

She managed to get out, "I always ask..."

"Then... hmmm." His voice stopped as he tapped his lips. "Then I would maintain the state of mind you were in there. You should be drifting in subspace by then or fucking my face... once you came down, I would hold you for cuddles."

She was lost in her excitement, "May we pleeeease go home for dessert now?"

"No, we still need to eat. But now, you will have an appetite," he winked at her.

Just at that moment, their food arrived. 'Goddess, help me.'

14: Development

Allen watched as the normally reserved Grace ate with gusto. He chuckled as he spun his fork through the last of his noodles.

She squinted at him as she chewed the last of her shrimp. She was squirming in her chair. *Gods, this woman is a doll. I can't wait to get her alone. I'm glad Sampson brought the check earlier. She might fling herself at me if we don't get out of here quickly.*

He slipped a few bills into the small leather folder. He rose and moved over to give the agitated woman a hand up out of her chair, as he slid it out for her.

She took his hand as she stood, "Thank you for dinner, Sir. It was delicious."

"Of course, Kitten. I'm glad you liked it. I had ordered it for this time while you were in the shower," he grinned as he led her from the restaurant holding her hand.

"You always pick the best meals," she pulled his arm back against him, pressing it against her and resting her head against his shoulder. He did not think it was by accident that his arm was pressed between her breasts.

"Ah, yes, well, I have to keep my pretty lady happy," he smirked as the door was opened for them. That was when he saw the men in suits. Quite a bit of men in suits. Glancing over them he saw every one of them had a firearm tucked behind designer jackets.

"Mr. Wells, Mr. Francisco Russo would like for you to speak with him. The lady too," the man nearest to the lead car said, opening the car.

Allen glanced at Grace. She had stilled beside him. He cleared his throat and replied, "Of course, mister?"

"My name isn't important. Get in the car. I won't say it again."
Raising an eyebrow at that, Allen sighed and moved to help Grace into the car. He climbed in behind her.

The man slammed the door and climbed in the front, joined by a driver. They drove away from the restaurant at a rapid pace.

Arriving at a large manor, Allen let out a low whistle from the back seat. A long walk led from the driveway, composed of white flagstones bereft of dirt or debris. On either side of the ten-foot-wide walk were ten-foot-tall, well-manicured hedges that followed along with it and tapered off to a large courtyard that held a massive fountain with a sculpture at the center. The sculpture seemed to be a woman talking with cherubs. An elaborate staircase led up to the house proper. Vines grew along the sides of the house and reached skyward along the top.

"The landscape is a dream. So well kept," Grace said in a dreamy and light tone, as she squeezed his arm. Something about the way she said that made him look at her. As happy as the words sounded he could see a bit of her lower lip sticking out just past her upper.

The plan of a fun afternoon and evening being derailed had been jarring for her. He patted her hand where it was squeezing his arm. "I will uphold the agreement we discussed, with the gusto you showed at the meal," he murmured to her. "I am sorry for the delay."

"What could this possibly be about? I hope whatever it is, it doesn't take long," she murmured back, softly running a hand down his arm to his hand.
During this, the two men up front got out and opened both doors to the back. In short order, they were hustled up to the big house and through to the back yard.
It was, of course, as opulent as the front. There was an overly large table, with an elaborate lunch. A roast chicken. Platters of sandwiches. A bottle of white wine. A bowl of potatoes au gratin.

Seated behind that was what they assumed was the man they were here to see. He was a medium-sized, older man, a bit of gray feathering through his hair at the temples. A cruel grimace, sunken brown eyes, and a crooked nose that spoke of breaks set well made up the jagged lines of his face. He stood and smoothed out the nonexistent wrinkles of his blatantly expensive suit. "Mr. Wells, I heard you had a conversation with my son. I would like to revisit things you said," he said as he walked toward them.

Allen kept himself from retorting with the first thing that popped in his head. *Your son was a jackass and I wanted to make him squeal as I pounded him into the ground.* "Yes, I remember the conversation, Mr. Russo. What would you like to revisit?" Allen said calmly.

"You disrespected him. In public. I don't appreciate your attitude and lack of hospitality for my family. I understand you didn't want us in your establishment after the evening. Do we have a problem, Mr. Wells?"

"If I remember correctly, Mr. Russo, I was letting him know that we were closing for the evening. It was late and we have no women of the night on the premises under my payroll. I asked them to leave and your son took offense. He also stated he would be telling of the event and that none of the family would come to my establishment. I did not require this condition. It was self-imposed, I'm afraid. If he thought I was disrespectful, I am sorry that he took that as such. However, I would be happy to have the Russo family in at any time, as my House is neutral ground and safe for anyone that would like to have meetings there."

"Hmmm. There is also an odd thing that has happened recently. Seems a few of my screws got themselves on the bad side of a mark or racket. Know anything about that?"

Allen gritted his teeth. Even in death, those two shits are going to cause me grief. "I am afraid they were being disrespectful. They seemed to have thought they deserved more than I did. I apologize if you needed them for an operation."

The mobster seemed to ponder this as he glared at Allen. Long seconds went by as he continued to stare unblinking at him. Allen returned the look with a placid face. "You seem to know your business. I would like you to host a meeting with the De Luca family. Their son is coming into town next week.

With your house as the meeting ground maybe talks can go better than they have in Italy," he waved his hand and walked away. "I will have a man come by to let you know when you should expect us. Good day, Mr. Wells."

"A good day to you as well, Mr. Russo." Allen pulled Grace's hand as the men who had escorted them to the patio returned wordlessly and showed them back out to the cars.

Allen sat in his chair pondering the day. Grace was draped over his lap and he spanked her as he thought.

Her wrists were bound together as were her ankles. She was no longer in her dress and hadn't been wearing underwear he had found out with delight.

He decided he might as well plan for the family to try to take his business and kill as many of them as needed. As they like to say, sometimes you have to crack an egg or two to make an omelet. He looked down at the pink cheeks under his palm. He appeared to have been lost in thought for some time. "Thank you for your sweet bum, Kitten. Let's begin your reward now."

The next several hours were just what they both needed. For him the feel and aroma of her skin and the way she called out her pleas and thanks sung a sweet melody. A calm stole over him as she came for him for the umpteenth time. For her, it was a welcomed mix of pleasure and pain. A much-needed release of tension that she didn't know she was holding on to until he took it from her. She felt light as a feather afterward.

15: Preparations

Duncan leaned against the hood of the army surplus truck. Night had fallen hours ago, but their contact still hadn't had the decency to show.

He grumbled something about lack of professionalism under his breath. Allen sighed as the large, bald man let out more half-heard obscenities.

Seconds ticked by as they sat waiting in the darkness. "Mr. Wells, I don't like it."

"I am aware, Mr. Caan," Allen replied. "Just be ready." Allen checked his own revolver. Still loaded like it was five minutes ago. He sighed again.

Allen looked about the courtyard they sat in. The factory buildings that surrounded them had the clatter of hammers on iron, no doubt working on the newest shipment of goods. The scrape of shovel on coal and grunts of men working sung through the moment between clang of the hammers.

A rumble of a truck engine cut through the relative stillness. "Finally," Allen heard Duncan mutter bitterly.

As the truck came to a stop several men clambered out of the back, weapons in hand. Squinting through the headlamps of the other truck, Allen could make out five men. All of them had heavy coats and fedoras. In their hands were guns.

The lead man tapped his brim up to let the light of the nearby lanterns play across his rugged features.

Allen had not needed it to see the red beard of John Mac Byrne. Irish Republican Army. He had seen the man on the docks. He had heard stories, whether or not they were true, of the cruelty this man was capable of. None of this mattered to Allen.

"I assume we can begin?" the Irishman called out. "I have what ye'd be asking for."

"Thank the gods," Duncan murmured, softly enough Allen was sure he was the only to have heard. That was until the entire group of men turned their heads toward him. And John 'Breaker' Mac Byrne squinted his eyes and sneered.

"Ye be having some'tin on yer wee mind d'be needing sharing?" the red mane shook as he spoke.

Duncan shook his head. Allen noticed his fists clenched into white balls of fury however. John seemed to have noticed it too, since he continued. "Then keep your Limey loving mouth shut!" The Irishman's head swiveled to Allen. "The price d'be going up. Be taking some work to be getting it here and ye be paying for me effort."

Allen hated dealing with things he could not control. He let his breath steam out his nose, "We had agreed on the ridiculous price of three thousand dollars. How much more are we talking about?" The words came out cold and flat.

"Five thousand be what ye be paying."

He felt Duncan's anger ripple off him. "For three crates? No. I do not think that is acceptable. I will pay that much for an additional crate and your trouble or find out if the Jewish gentleman can hold to their deals."

Tense moments dragged by as the two men stared at each other.

"That d'be smarting for the troubles. But ye be talking true that we did be saying a price. Deal struck and I d'be thank you so."

The two men reached out, clasped hands, and shook once. Duncan fetched the satchel with the money and the Irish loaded his truck with the crates. Not another word was said.

Transaction complete, the IRA drove off and disappeared into the fog and gloom.

Allen let out the tension in his shoulders. The two men loaded into the cab. Two minutes later, Tom and Jim clambered down off of the neighboring houses and into the back, rifles slung over their shoulders. Allen turned the key and away they drove.

16: Knotted Up

Allen stormed into the room, the last few members of Mister's steering clear of him as he thundered past them. Duncan came in behind, followed by Jim and Tom, a crate of weapons under each arm.

Allen watched as they stacked them in the back room. He felt the rage boiling under his skin. He needed a break from the stress of all this. Too many people depended on his preparation and planning.

"We are closing early. 'Ask' whoever is in the speakeasy to go home. Then lock up and go home yourselves. Good night." Allen strode from the room as he heard the 'Yes, sir' being said from those behind him.

He needed to get out of this foul mood and he knew just how to do so. He stomped his way down the steps to the lower rooms. As he neared the bottom of the spiral stairs, he could feel Helena's presence in his mind through their bond. He felt her happiness fade as her concern replaced it.

He smelled her down the length of the hallway. Her scent changed as he neared. He caught Grace's join Helena's, but it was slightly smothered by soap and lavender. Fresh from the shower? Delicious. His spirit rose at just the thought of seeing his two pretties.

The two of them stepped out of either side of the hall. Helena was in a short, blue, lacy sleep shirt. The garment hung off of one shoulder and barely covered mid-thigh.

Grace was wrapped in a red silk robe that caressed her ankles. It was bound closed, yet was open enough to give him a glimpse of her mounds. Her nipples pressed up against the thin fabric. Her hair was wrapped in a towel.

He felt Grace touch his aura with hers. Another level of tension bled off him. *Gods, he had lucked out snagging her.*

Both beauties blinked once, smiling concernedly. "Sir, what's the matter?"

"Sandblasted micks took a bit more money than I wanted to spend on hardware. It will be alright. But I am going to devour both of you tonight," he replied in a controlled growl.

Grace reached for the belt holding her robe and slid the loose knot free. As the robe fell open, revealing her lovely flesh beneath, she demurred, "It would be our pleasure to take your mind off all that stress, Sir."

"Mmm-hmm, Master, yes, please! Use us!" Helena chirped, pulling her shirt over her head and dropping it to the floor, her breasts bouncing with the motion.

Allen chuckled, "Very well, my pretties. Let's go to the Room So Black. I am in a mood. and it shall be grand to watch you squirm in there."

A huge smile bloomed over both women's faces, filling his soul with happiness and desire. He waved his hands at them and they almost skipped towards the door aforementioned. He chuckled again and followed behind them, enjoying the view of their swaying hips. Helena's right hand played across Grace's bottom through her robe. The shorter blond pulled her towel from her head, spilling her wet hair down her back, and smacked the brunette with a section of it across her back. The taller woman laughed as she lunged for the lead. Grace was squinting at her as he caught up to her.

He grabbed a handful of her backside, earning him a kiss. He leaned into her pouting lips. Their auras crashed together and licked at each other. He growled into her mouth, as he took all of her into him.

Grace sighed and melted into him, her naked form and silk robe wrapping around him. Her hand rubbed against his hardening member and his hands explored her in return.

His fingers pushed and pulled at her flesh. He squeezed, pinched, and scratched at her skin. She whimpered at his attentions. Minutes flashed by and she shuddered repeatedly as he teased her.

"Oh, Sir, please, please, please..." she murmured into his mouth as he kept probing hers and biting at her lips.

"Mmm... my little Witch, I am going to stick you on a spit and gobble you down," he rumbled into her mouth. He flipped his buckle and yanked his belt free. Her hand slid into his pants and tugged at him. He dropped the garment to the floor and seized one of her legs. He pulled her knee up and hooked it over his arm. He pressed his hips close to hers. She easily guided him to her entrance and he thrust into her to the hilt. She was gasping breathlessly and shuddered with his suddenness of entry. He grabbed both of her arms at the elbows.

He slid out to his tip and drove himself forward to the hilt. He repeated his assault in and out of her quickly. The sound of flesh on flesh slapping filled the hallway. A soft moan pulled his attention and he turned his head to see Helena working at her sex with two fingers and pinching her nipples.

His attention shifting from her brought her eyes to the audience. She gasped in embarrassment and blushed, but he felt her clench around him with excitement. All three groaned and moaned in unison. "Come for me, my Pretties." With that he began flexing and spasming inside Grace, filling her with hot sperm.

"Yessssssss, Master!" cried Helena, bucking against her own hand. A clear puddle began growing about her on the floor.

"Thank you, Sir!" Grace managed as he kept driving into her, pumping his softening member.

He held her against him for a moment as he calmed. "Gods, I do not deserve either of you," he sighed into Grace's hair. Helena padded over and wrapped them both into a firm embrace.

"Do you feel better, Sir?" Grace cooed to him, as she stroked his hair.

"Much, thank you," was his honest reply. He felt much lighter as the women slid hands over him.

Helena released the pair and took their hands in hers, "Please, use your Pet for your pleasure, Master?"

She seemed to be swinging her hips more than needed for her stride. *Jealous? Or just the need to be used that great?* The striking woman looked over her shoulders at him, her eyes a bright blue. Eagerness and need evident on her face. *Good, just the latter.*

A huge grin spread across her face and he couldn't help but smile back, "Of course, Pet. You were very patient. I must reward you." They entered the dark black room. Candles sprung to life as Grace waved her free hand at the room.

A soft glow played over the numerous implements and devices stored here.

A medieval rack, freshly polished, sat to one side. It was made of oak and black iron.

A St. Andrew's Cross sat next to it, shining with wax across its ebon wood frame and black leather padding.

A series of chain winches connected to large iron rings occupied another. Each ring twinkled with the flickering candlelight.

A set of four wooden whipping posts nestled into their stations near the floating winch rings. The iron rings and the redwood gleamed against the dark.

A cage sized for a humanoid being with not much room to sit in was in the corner. The steel bars hardly reflected the lights.

A table that could be raised to stand on end with numerous chains and straps sat in yet another corner. Its top showed signs of recent polish also.

Impact tools of all shapes and sizes hung from a circular rack in the center.

He took in the room and tapped his chin. He was unsure of where to begin.

He leaned over and kissed Grace on the cheek, "Thank you again, Kitten. I need to see to my Angel now." He nipped her ear as he walked towards the rings, pulling Helena behind him.

"My pleasure, Sir," she purred from behind him contentedly. He heard the whisper of silk on leather as she sat on one of the nearby blackened steel and leather chairs.

He stood Helena by the collection of rings. He turned her to him and kissed her deeply until her eyes closed and her hands danced along his body. He broke off the kiss and looked into her eyes. They fluttered open and she smiled broadly at him, "Mmm. Thank you, Master."

He chuckled, pecked her once more on the lips, and moved to the area with the numerous ropes. The collection of ropes was expansive. Each rope was hung neatly and was cut to a specific length. They were arranged by type, then again by length. Grabbing a half dozen of his forty-foot hemp ropes, he strode back to Helena. He began moving her about and fastening the ropes about her. A corset harness, followed by a ten wrap collar and thirty wrap single column ties to each limb.

He teased her nipples with pinches, her bottom with playful slaps, and opening with traces of knuckles and fingertips as he worked the ropes about her. By the time he completed preparation for suspension, she was panting and there was a drop of her excitement dripping from her needy sex. Her eyes were bright and her mouth was half open with anticipation.

He began feeding the ends through the bights on the corset. Now, with that done, he created a harness for her hips and connected it through her corset to the ring above her.

Double-checking circulation and tightness, with 'gentle' teasing, he moved to the hoist ropes. With a yank, she was pulled upwards, the corset and hip harnesses supporting her weight. He manipulated the ropes for her limbs. Her arms were pulled over her head towards her back. Her legs were pulled up towards her bottom. Hanging forward in the harnesses, her dark hair spilled over her face. He took a moment to admire his handiwork and her gorgeous form. Her breasts heaved over and under the tight coils. The midnight black of the ropes accented the pearlescent white of her skin. He had her flying just above standing height.

"Angel, nothing pinching?" he asked her softly.

"Mmmm, no, Master," her voice came to him heavy with arousal.

Smirking at that, he strode over to the impact tools and selected two long special made bullwhips. They were carefully woven to be smooth in braiding and ended with a single strand of leather strap an inch wide.

He looped them over his shoulders and walked back to her. He caught a glimpse of her eyes as he strode back. Her hips bucked and the droplet of her juices was now dripping easily five inches from her. He grinned at her and uncoiled the two whips. He heard her moan, as he took his time.

Then he began with his right hand, flicking it out to crack and flick across her exposed thigh. The left followed a moment later, tracing along her exposed belly. The rapid crack of the whips echoed across the room, as he continued bringing them back and forth, tracing lines across every inch of her flesh. Thighs, shoulders, stomach, hips, bottom, back, arms, feet, and breasts. Her cries of pain quickly changed to pleasure as the shock of the first few strikes turned to the lingering sting of red. Minutes passed with cracks of his whips and whimpers and moans from her lips.

"Master! May this Pet come for you, please!" she cried out after a strike across her bottom.

"Yes, Pet. Come for me and make a puddle on the floor," he replied as he caught her against her back.

She jerked and screamed as she did just that. A stream of her juices dripped down, puddling below her as he continued his assault against her flesh.

He slowed his strikes and finally stopped altogether. He lowered her back down to rest hips level with his own. Her body continued jerking and jumping in the restraints. Her body was covered in angry, amber lines, criss crossing over each other. He traced a few of them. She moaned at the gentle touch. He watched as she began to heal slowly and could feel the draw at the symbol carved into his back.

He tilted her chin up and devoured her from the mouth down. She worked her tongue against his as she spasmed in her bindings. Breaking the kiss, he tilted her forward downward in the sling of the harnesses. She eagerly took him into her mouth and suckled him. He swung her back and forth, sliding himself in and out of her as she continued working him with her lips and tongue eagerly.

He reveled in the feel of her for long moments. *Gods, he could let her do this all eve.* Breaking the trance she was putting him in with her attention, he pulled free of her lips. She let out a disappointed sound, which broke off as he spun her around. A surprised cry followed by a moan of pleasure as he drove himself into her as she swung around.

He swung her away from him and let her weight drive her back down onto him. She cried out in delight each time she slammed down his length. Soon, he could feel her clenching around him grow more urgent. Her cries turned once more to gasping moans.

"Master, please, let this Pet come for you! Please, let her soak your hard cock with her juices!"

"You may come again when you feel me come, Pet. Not before."

"Ugnn, yes, Master! Come in your Angel! Breed her needy hole! Fill her with your seed! She needs to be full of it!"

"Good gods. Then she shall have it," he grunted out and began spraying her velvet walls with his sperm. She really knew what to say to stroke his ego.

She screamed out her orgasm as she clenched around and her walls worked on him pulling more from him.

17: Tether

Catching his breath, Allen began lowering the quivering Helena back to the floor. He made certain she was stable on her feet then began to unravel the ropes, dropping them on the floor.

He carried her over to a chair next to a blushing Grace, cuddled her to his chest, and checked over her welts. That done, he looked over at his Witch. She was biting her lips.

"Need some more attention, Kitten?" he grinned, his eyes darkening with desire.

"Only if it would please you, Sir," Grace softly sang out.

"Oh, well, in that case, I do not want to tax you, lover," he said mercilessly, rolling his head away from her. He wondered what she would reply to such obvious baiting.

Grace squinted her eyes and her mouth dropped open. She seethed, he wasn't supposed to buy that, he was supposed to force his will on her. She thought, two could play at that game.

"That was an impressive scene, Sir. May I get you anything? Perhaps a cold drink?" she surprised him with her reply.

"Hmm. Yes, please. That would be lovely. Thank you," he said as he leaned over to snag a kiss.

"My pleasure...," she stood up to get the drink and dropped her robe to the floor as she walked away from him, she looked back and added, "...Sir," with a flirty wink.

He grinned openly in response to her playfulness, watching her hips swing as she stepped from the room. *Gods, he was going to make her come repeatedly when she returned.*

Minutes passed and Grace walked back down the stairs. She was quite proud of her little stunt. It had gotten just the result she had wanted. Maybe a bit of playful teasing would get her some of that delicious roughness he had just given Helena. She salivated at the thought of his big hands forcing her to...

And she turned the corner. And all thoughts left her.

Allen watched her turn the corner and nearly drop the drink she had 'been told' to go get. He did a jig in his head at the obvious success at her being so jarred. But it was the little things that counted.

She walked up to him, her eyes never leaving the contraption Helena was locked into. A rubber shirt that allowed one to be bound with their arms locked down at their sides. He heard that psychologists were going to use them to help those patients that were mentally unstable.

He had modified it greatly from its original design. Instead of it being a jacket that you tied in the back, it had buttons up the front. A peek-a-boo section had been built to allow access to the breasts. The arms now were strapped down hands over the shoulder. There was a strap each connected to the elbow and sleeve, with an adjustable length so it could be loosened or tightened.

That wasn't the only thing that Helena was wearing either. She had a hook with a ball on the tip of it instead of a point. The hook was at the end of a two-foot rod that came to a keyhole fastener that he had a rope attached to. The rope was run through a pulley and swung in front of her dazed looking eyes.

Once more this wasn't the end of the delicious torture he had concocted. She was astride a fine chain strung up between her legs to rest at her most sensitive areas. He reached over and spanked her lightly on the rump, which sent her forward an inch, which in turn pulled her along the chain, and moved the hook inside her.

Grace seemed to lurch her hips forward with the sound of the slap as well. *Good, she wants to partake.* Her eyes found his. He could see evidence of several emotions warring for the forefront. Jealousy. Lust. Curiosity. Rejection. Need.

He crooked a finger, and she sauntered over to him. "I have another jacket. Would you like to put it on?" He flicked a thumb at a nearby table that held the aforementioned article. Her eyes followed his movement. He watched as her face washed over with glee and excitement. She pranced over and began to pull on the garment. She pulled it tight and fastened it in place. It fit about her like a sheath to her slender form.

He felt his cat pace about under his skin at the sight of her as she skipped back over to him. He could smell her arousal thick in the air. He perceived their powers taste each other. Her spices tickled his nose and his member flexed towards her. Her eyes darted down and she grinned with pleasure. He reached up and adjusted her arm straps to mirror Helena's.

He led her over to the chain, helped her put a leg over, and walked over to a nearby table for her hook. He rubbed some of the lubricant Grace had concocted to allow for ease of entry and walked back over to the chipper duo. He checked on Helena, who appeared as delighted as Grace at the new scene. He stepped back to Grace and gently pressed the ball of the hook against her back entry. She visibly relaxed and the ball eased slowly into her. Reaching up he grabbed the rope and pulled it down to tie it to Grace's hook.

She shuddered with obvious delight as the rope tugged up a fraction as the pulley centered between the ladies. He stepped back to the table and collected the final piece of the scene. A steel collar that would fasten about each of their necks and keep them a minor distance from one another. Their eyes tracked him as he strode back to them and began to fasten the apparatus about them.

That completed he stepped back and regarded his two lovers. His cat leaped for them. Only able to keep it at bay by a margin, he closed his eyes and calmed the beast. He slid his eyes open and pulled a wooden spoon from a nearby hook. "Well, ladies, let us begin," he grinned as he popped Helena on the right cheek.

She was startled and reflexively moved slightly forward on the chain, pulling on the hook. This pushed Grace back along the chain and pulled on her hook. Both women let out a gasp and seemed to reassess the situation. He was grinning wickedly now. "Yes, just like that."

Soon the room was alight with their synchronized moans and whimpers, as he moved them back and forth along the chain. He alternated between Grace and Helena, and which cheek he was spanking. The two were panting and gasping out in near orgasm.

He felt a surge of happiness flow over him as he watched them twitch with his next blow. The two women were teetering at the edge. Their wanton eyes followed him as they moved from the latest blow across Grace's right cheek.

Helena suddenly called out, "Master! Oh, gods, please let this Slave come for you! Oh!"

Grace turned her lust filled eyes to Helena, "I win, Helena." Her eyes flitted back to Allen, "I get to sleep in his bed."

Helena let out a whimper, "Please! Master!"

"Yes, Angel, come for me," Allen replied as he contemplated Grace's statement. *Did his pretty ladies have an agreement or running bet?*

Helena bucked her hips forward, driving Grace back and yanking at the hook in their butts. Grace's eye flew wide open, "Stop moving! You are going to make me come!" Then both their eyes rolled back in their heads as both women came hard and pitifully. Allen dropped the spoon and held each one up by their armpits. Once they had both slowly come down from their ecstasy, he made sure they could hold their weight with their feet. He then dropped the chain from its fastenings and untied the hooks.

Allen then slid two fingers into each woman's sex, tapping the hooks with his thumb. Helena shuddered and Grace gasped. Sliding his fingers from their soaked slits, he licked his fingers, while they watched him in a rapt attention. Next, off came the collar. As each woman leaned into him, he eased out the hooks. Then he removed the straps holding their hands in place.

He kissed each of them and slid the hooks from them while he explored their mouths. They gasped into his mouth with delight and shuddered with their whole bodies. "Grace, stay here, I am going to tuck in our Angel," he commanded softly as he undressed Helena and scooped her into his arms. She snuggled into him and was softly snoring by the time he had walked into her room. He pulled back the covers as he held her with the other arm. He eased her into her bed and pulled the covers over her and the two stuffed animals she always slept with.

"Good night, my fierce warrior." He kissed her forehead and she smiled in her sleep.

Making his way back to the room, he found a kneeling Grace, her face still red and flushed from the forced orgasms. He smiled at her as her eyes found his. She returned it twice as brilliantly. He beckoned to her and she crawled across the floor to him. He leaned down, scooped her up into his arms, and whispered into her ear, "You were forced to come by Hel's climax, so you are not in trouble for that. That being said, I want to crush you against me tonight. So, yes, you won... We shall see if you truly won."

He left the room, with her curled into his arms.

18: Arrival

West Docks.

Giulia De Luca stepped off the gangplank to the pier and over to a waiting car. The driver popped the door open as she approached, and she slid into the back seat. She hated the ocean, but it had given her some time to think as she had made that long journey. Her favorite part of the trip was the peace of mind that they were safe. Yes, it had cost two would-be assassins their lives, but they had not been prepared to dispatch her fully. The fact that they had attempted to kill her had been enlightening, however. And being at sea, it had been just a matter of tossing the men overboard, followed shortly by their heads.

She looked over to where Matteo was still talking with the ship staff. She sighed. Her brother could be so particular, but since he oversaw logistics and security... She waved the thoughts away. She smoothed out her dress and pulled her hat off. Her long black hair fell into her face and was batted out of her eyes with the swipe of her hand. If it wasn't so unrefined, she would have it all lopped off. She tossed an envious look at Matteo's short black curls before looking over the notes of the interrogation with the second assassin. The first one, of course, had needed to die to set a precedent. He had been very helpful. Well, all the way up to when she had torn his head off his shoulders, she giggled.

The driver glanced at her. She met his eyes with her own and he quickly looked back at the road. She watched a cold sweat drop roll down his neck and could taste his fear in the air. *Good. Half-wit.*

Matteo lumbered into the cab, slapped the driver's shoulder, and barked out, "Roosevelt." The driver was flooding the small car with his fear now. No doubt recognized her brother. She leaned against the glass of the window and stared at the skyline. She was always treated as decoration or ..., she gritted her teeth. She was never going back to Italy. She would die first.

"This place smells of regret and fish," she said in Italian to her brother. He chuckled and shrugged. The cab lumbered down the cobblestone streets.

There were dockworkers moving crates, wives doing laundry in tubs or hanging them to dry on lines, dirt-smeared children running about to and fro. She envied their simple, pitiful struggle-soaked lives. Hers was one full of deals and death.

Most men saw her as the way to marry into the line of De Luca, not as a thinking being that had dreams of her own. Her brother though at least treated her well. Truth be known he had asked her for advice often enough as a child, they had come into adulthood knowing he would be the heir, but that she would be the decision-maker.

It was just the way things had been ever since that night. She shuddered and let out a sigh.

Giulia sipped the tea as she leaned on the stone railing of the balcony of the suite. The long, fluttering drapery snapped in the light breeze behind her. The hubbub of movement was visible far below but muffled in the storm that had rolled into the congested city. There was no rain as of yet, but she could smell it in the air and it was a matter of moments until the clouds opened up. A peal of thunder crashed, and she glanced up at the darkening sky. Sighing at being forced back inside, she turned from her view and slipped into the well-lit room. Several small lamps dotted the ostentatious atmosphere. Large, overstuffed chairs and couches offered seating. Ornate frames held works of modern art. A large mahogany desk, with entirely too many flourishes and trimming that held no purpose, sat at one end of the suite with a leather chair behind it. Her notes and a stack of papers sat waiting for her atop it.

She kicked off her slippers and swept into the desk. Thumbing through the pages, she found the outline for Father's requirements and stipulations for peace. So many petty little things. She dropped it back on top of the pile, dismissing it.

A knock sounded from the door, bringing her out of her sullen reverie. "Yes?"

Matteo called from the other side of the door, "Giulia, I grabbed dinner. Would you like a plate?"

Smirking, she called back, "Yes, thank you, Come in. I'm dressed." He pushed the door open and waved at a hidden person. The bellhop pushed in a trolley with various plates of pasta and a basket with bread. The steam was wafting up into the chilly room and she caught a hint of it as she smiled. "Worried I would forget to eat again, brother?"

He grinned over at her, "You get wrapped up in all the details and forget to take care of yourself." He handed the bellhop a handful of coins. The man's eyes bulged out and he bowed low before leaving, closing the door behind him. *Jenkins?* She shrugged, he wasn't overly important. But sometimes remembering a name would do more than a large tip.

She grabbed a plate of linguine and a stick of bread. She hastened to eat, her stomach having rumbled in agreement with Matteo's statement. She groaned in delight and spoke around her mouthful, "Where did you get this? It is divine! Would give Nonna a challenge. Not that I would say that to her, mind."

Matteo was also shoveling food into his mouth. He nodded. Too polite to talk with his mouth full. She snorted at him and he replied with a wink. The two ate in silence for long minutes. The food was heavenly and rich. A much-needed change from the week of poor fare on the ship. Even though it was a cruise liner and the cook staff had been gifted, there are only so many things you can keep fresh that long in such an environment.

Sighing out in unison as they finished together with the last plate, the twins leaned back in their chairs. She stood, walked over to the tea set, poured them both a cup of tea and brought it back over to where he lounged. He took it gratefully and they sipped in silence.

"I think I shall go look over this establishment we are to meet at, Matteo. I can slip in and out easily since I am not the heir..." she stated, catching his gaze.

He frowned back at her, "Are you going to take an escort?" The question was soft as he spoke it. He seemed worried.

"I shall take a pistol. Not that I need one."

"That is not what I'm worried about. At least take a car, I do not want to have to take a bunch of guys to go clean up whatever gang has the misfortune of trying to grab a pretty lone woman off the streets."

"I had not thought of that... Very well, I shall take a car," she replied and he visibly relaxed. He raised the teacup towards her and peered out the open window. She followed the gaze and saw the clouds had begun to open onto the street below. Rain pattered on the balcony. The sweet cleansing smell rolled into the apartments and tugged at her hair. She leaned back and enjoyed its scent.

19: Subterfuge

Giulia slid out of the town car in front of the black brick building. Before her were two elaborate sconces lighting a door, with a sign reading MISTER'S, and a well-built mountain of a man. The large bald man stepped to the side and opened the door for her, as she smoothed out the wrinkles of her white slim business suit dress. She nodded to the stranger and stepped through the open portal.

There was a slight murmur of hushed conversations overlaid with the tinkle of the ivory from the stage. Looking over she was surprised to see a dark-haired woman playing a grand piano. A half-smile graced her lips at the sight.

"Can I see you to a table, ma'am?" The cheerful sultry voice pulled her eyes from the stage to a slim, pretty blond and her dazzling smile.

"I would like that, yes."

"Anyone else in your party?" the lady asked.

"No, just myself."

"Very well. Follow me, please, Miss..?"

Giulia hesitated. *Should she tell them who she was?* She hadn't expected this so soon. *Blast. What would it hurt?* "Giulia De Luca."

The blond's head turned slowly back to hers, never missing a step as she led Giulia to a table. She seemed to reconsider and turned and strode over to a staircase. She smiled at Giulia again and proceeded to climb the stairs.

A tall, slender man sat near a velvet rope. He jumped to his feet at their approach. He unclipped the rope and stepped to the side. "Miss Grace," he said formally, bowing his head to her.

"Thank you, Mr. Dremond. Will you tell Mr. Wells he has a visitor and grab a bottle of that red wine from the reserve?" the blond now known as Grace said in a direct tone.

"Of course, Miss Grace," he bowed again and clipped the rope behind them. He hustled down the stairs straightaway.

Grace led her to one of the three tables arranged on the upper landing. The hushed conversations from below seemed to be muffled more so by some kind of acoustics. Giulia nodded with approval. *Very nice.*

"Miss De Luca, do any foods make you sick or anything of that nature?" Grace asked as she turned to face Giulia.

"Ah, no. I don't think so."

"Then if you will be seated, the Mister will be up to see you and we will have a meal brought up for the table," Grace said as she turned to leave.

"Pardon me, but does a guest not order a meal here?" Giulia asked, confused by the statement.

"Oh, no, not in this section. Most people on the lower level go along with the waitstaff's recommendation as well," the blond woman's tone was cheery but measured.

Interesting. That and the deference from the section manager. This one may be higher than most women of her station. She scrutinized the woman as she turned to leave.

Blond hair is precisely styled. Emerald earrings. Amethyst stone set in a silver bracelet, with some sort of inscription wrapping about it. Black three-quarter jacket with a vertical green pinstripe. Matching skirt. Green, almost emerald, shirt. Silk or Egyptian cotton, if she had to guess. Stylish black flat-soled shoes. Very business professional. She could easily be a Don's relative with that quality of attire.

Thinking hard, she slid into one of the chairs. It was an ornate piece, yet functionally sound. And comfortable. *Heaven.* A good chair was always welcome.

She smelled him before she heard him. A strong musk mixed with soap and grass. Then she heard the clip of his shoes on the stairs. Her heart began racing, for a reason of its own accord. *What the heavens?*

Then she saw him begin to rise over the top of the railing for the staircase and upper floor. Her curse pushed at her restraint. She pushed it down inside her as his eyes bore into hers.

A dark color. Brown? Black? They didn't seem to blink as he worked the clip, one-handed without looking or hesitancy. He turned and she sucked in air. *Who was this man?*

He turned back to her and she felt her curse throb once more through her whole being. Then a blanket of warmth fell over her and her curse settled low in her stomach. She was panting as he finished the last few steps to her table.

Without asking, he pulled a chair out and sat down across from her. "Still taming her I see," he said as he unbuttoned his coat and smoothed the black and red vest underneath.

"What?" she replied stupidly.

"The beast that ... nevermind. I have ordered a hearty meal. Grace will be joining us," he adjusted his tie and locked those dark windows onto her soul. She just stared back, unblinking.

Allen climbed the stairs as the scent of a Moontouched slammed into his nose. He grimaced and stepped wider, taking two stairs at a time. The woman at the table struggled with her animal as he crested the banister. Getting through the rope he felt her power leap for him again. A moment more and she would lose control. He reached out with his own, drove hers deep down, and wrestled her to her back. The woman just stared. He sighed inside. He knew what followed that display.

She could barely breathe. She felt her sex slicken as her chest heaved. *Who? What?* She couldn't think. She needed to think. Badly. About something besides tossing this table to the side and taking this man roughly on the floor.

She managed to shake her head and clear her thoughts. She wrangled the emotions blasting through her.

"Ah, a hearty meal. Yes. Food. I could eat," she choked out. *She sounded like a lunatic.* She tried again, "Giulia De Luca, and you are?"

"Mr. Allen Wells, a pleasure to meet you, Miss De Luca," he bowed his head to her.

"Right, of course, the owner of the establishment. That makes sense..." she trailed off dumbly. She looked down at her hands in her lap. *What the heavens am I doing?*

A clamber of footsteps on the stairs brought her head up and she slid her mask back into place. *Nothing to see here. All is well. Just two business people having a private luncheon.*

Grace appeared with a bottle in hand, followed by two men carrying trays. One man was broader than the other, though their build was hard to tell through their dapper suits and ties. Well-fit suits clung to them, obviously not off the rack. *What was this man paying his staff if they could dress in such a manner?*

She looked back to Mr. Wells, who watched the approaching group. *Was that a smile?* She glanced back at the group to see Grace smile back at him.

In a few moments, the group arrived and began to serve out familiar dishes. Matteo, you jerk. Three plates of linguine with a red meat sauce. Fresh breadsticks, gleaming with butter and garlic. Three glasses. A plate of breaded chicken with an alfredo and pepper sauce. Another three plates of salad topped with a creamy vinaigrette dressing and feta cheese.

Her eyes boggled and her stomach rumbled with its thoughts. She blushed red and she could feel the warmth of it creep down her neck. She squeaked out, "Ah, excuse me."

Mr. Wells chuckled, "Well, Miss De Luca, you are at a restaurant. I should hope you brought your appetite. Please, help yourself."

"Ah, yes, it all looks so good, I would have no idea where to start, perhaps you could decide for me?" *It was weak as far as flirts went, but she was uncertain of how brazen she should be. Usually, she would do as she liked, why did he unsettle her so?*

He blinked at her then glanced at Grace. The blond had an eyebrow cocked up as she slid into her chair in between him and her. The two men were walking down the stairs by this point. *Heaven, she hoped they hadn't heard her.*

"I... I apologize. That was not ... courteous. And you have been nothing but civil and kind," she stammered out. She looked down at her plate and began serving food onto it.

"No, it's alright, Miss De Luca. Just odd to have a person of the Family be polite. Even if it is soaked with flirting," he said, as he loaded up Grace's plate with a bit from each dish.

She stopped and watched him move. She glanced up at Grace's face. The woman was watching her placidly. A hint of a smile on her face. She tilted her head towards Mr. Wells and raised an eyebrow. Then she frowned and shook her head.

Giulia frowned herself then stared back at her plate. Her mind raced as she turned this over in her mind, mechanically moving the food to her mouth. Her mind stopped as she tasted the forkful. *Heaven, this was delicious.* Minutes passed as she worked through her plate and twice more as she refilled it from the table.

She sighed as she sipped her wine and leaned back into her chair. She could get used to America if this was how they ate here. She dabbed at her lips with her napkin.

"I have to ask, do you have an Italian nonna running your kitchen?" she asked with a smile.

"Mrs. Ricci is one of the esteemed chefs, yes. She is a fine cook. I believe she learned from her grandmother who in turn learned from hers. I was extremely lucky to have been able to hire her. Her uncle is still upset with me," Mr. Wells stated with a half shrug.

Her mouth dropped open. *The Ricci family? And the way he spoke with such disregard about the uncle being upset. Surely it wasn't the Ricci Don's niece working in the kitchen...* "You certainly don't mean..?"

"Yes," he interrupted with a heavy sigh, "that Ricci. But she was looking to get away from family politics. And she has proven herself time and again. And her aunt and parents love me for giving her the chance. She has taken some time off to spend with her grandmothers and family. She is well worth any trouble that may arise." He waved his hand and continued, "What brought you here this day, Miss De Luca?" His eyes were on her and pierced into her.

"I wanted to see your establishment and assure myself that it would be an equal footing for our meeting. To be fair, I do have someone do so every time. I had hoped to get in and get out as an unseen guest. But Miss Grace threw me for a loop when she asked my name. I wasn't sure what to say. So, I just told the truth."

"I see. Very well. Do you have any other questions for me?"

"Not at this time, Mr. Wells. I do not think I could have had a finer meal at another place in town," she said.

"If you would excuse me then, Miss De Luca," he stood, scooped up Grace's hand, and kissed her knuckles. He turned back to Giulia, gave her a slight bow, and walked from the upper dining room.

The thrum of her beast through her simmered and faded. *What is he?* She turned to Grace and started, "I..."

"No, I don't think you should ask that here. You do not have the same protections he has from prying eyes and ears. Should you want to know more it shall have to wait. Would you care to help me finish this bottle of wine? It is an old vintage and I would hate having to drink it all myself. Well, that's a lie. But Mister would be annoyed with me, and I can't have that. At least not too often," she had a conspiratorial glint to her eyes and tone as she poured them both another glass.

20: Tension

The speakeasy was closed that night. The restaurant had been closed hours before and non-essential staff were sent home. The thirteen of them waited in the gloom of the smoke-addled room. The musicians were off for the night. Their bandstand was empty save the chairs Allen lent them when they came to play.

The card tables were brushed clean and unopened card boxes sat in neat stacks next to the men that had volunteered for a few hours extra pay. All the chips sat in neat stacks next to the cards and the stools were freshly cleaned.

The bar was polished to a sheen of glass. Behind it, a wide variety of his stock of liquor was on display. Grace and Helena stood behind the bar, waiting to serve beverages. The two of them had their usual outfits on, with one minor change. A revolver under each arm and a speed loader for each in either pocket. Helena also had her shortswords sheathed under the bar surface. Allen hoped it never came to that. He had sparred against her with many weapons, but he found he had more wounds after a night when she used those two wicked obsidian blades.

The four compass points held James, Theodore, Thomas, and Duncan. Each man held a loaded Thompson submachine gun. Tommy guns, most ruffians called them. They also had two revolvers under their arms with speed loaders and another load for their long-guns.

Thomas had a look in his eye. Allen snapped his fingers at him. The man looked at him. "I would appreciate it if your patron remembers she lent you to me. I do not need you half-cocked this evening," he called to the blushing man.

"Guessed it in one, Mr. Wells," Thomas replied, sheepishly. His head cocked to the side as if listening to something whispered. He blushed, "She says that she misses you. She... she says she has been lonely in Ireland since the ceannasach left her alone. She's saying more, but I would beg her not to share such things with me, much less for me to speak aloud."

Allen sighed, "Tell her if she would be so kind as to stop, as it breaches the contract we have sealed with blood."

Thomas sagged in relief. "Thank you, Mr. Wells. She was getting fairly graphic," he said with a bright red face.

Allen shook his head. *Looks like a trip back to Ireland was to come in the future.* A movement to his right drew his attention. Grace was looking pointedly at him. Helena was smiling coyly as she watched him out of the corner of her eyes. He waved his hand at them. Grace scrunched her nose at him, drawing nervous chuckles from everyone else in attendance. He leaned closer to her and tapped the tip of her nose with a fingertip. "I will give you a surprise soon as an apology. I did not know she would keep pressing to alter the deal made. She has not yet broken it, so we should not either. Hmm, Kitten?"

She huffed at him, "No, Sir." She looked away.

Knowing there would be a later conversation about it, he pushed it to the side in his mind's eye. The roll of rubber on cobblestones outside brought the room back to a serious mood. All attention turned to the door as Allen stepped to it. He opened the peep window and saw that the Russos were first to arrive. He clenched his fist. Then worked through the thought again. *Perhaps Don Russo would be more agreeable with a couple of fingers of liquor in his gut. He knew that the Russo kid was not worth counting on, but hopefully, the father could be reasonable.*

A troop of the agreed-upon sixteen men trooped up behind Francisco Russo. Sixteen if you did not count Giovanni Russo that is. Which Allen did not. The De Lucas no doubt would, however.

He opened the door and ushered them in, the Don stopping to shake his hand briefly and moving to the bar. Allen eyed the last man as he walked in. Sighing inwardly, he realized he had been doing quite a bit of that lately. *Vacation in Ireland may be just what he needed. Close down ... scratch that. Leave the bar in Theodore, Duncan, and James' hands... No. That would not do either. He trusted them but he needed a woman to see to the table settings. And to flirt a little with the regulars. I need to see to that soon. Who to wrangle?*

He brushed the thoughts aside as the De Luca's three cars pulled up. He had been in the process of closing the door again as they did, so he swung it open once more. He felt Duncan ease up beside him. The big man was uncomfortable with the arrangement. Allen glanced over at the guests already inside and saw most of them were sitting down to card tables with glasses of dark liquor.

Allen waved to the De Luca woman. She returned the wave awkwardly, as she fought to keep her beast under control. He pushed her beast down and felt James and Duncan look at him quizzically. He shook his head softly and the De Luca troop marched forward. Again the expected sixteen men, but this time it included one of the De Luca siblings. Looking at them as they approached he got the feeling they were fairly close in age. *Possibly twins?* He ushered in the group, stepped to the front of the room by the bar, and began,
"Gentlemen and lady.

"I want to welcome you all to the Mister's. The drinks are on me this evening. I would like everyone to have a good time.

"I would like to say that the cards are fresh from the factory. The dealers are impartial. They are paid to work past their regular shift to be here, so please be respectful.

"If you have had too much to drink, you are welcome to sleep it off in the cars. However, if you are told to sleep it off, you should follow this advice. You will only be told once. Then you can take it up with Mr. Caan.

"The lovely ladies serving your drinks are taken. They will be polite and courteous. Do not take that as their need or desire to be shown what 'a real man is like.' Failure to treat them with respect will immediately have you begging them to stop hurting you and to let you walk out of your own accord. "Any questions?"

Allen stared out at the stupefied audience. No one said a word. There were some mutterings, but none were said where he should have been able to hear them.

Nodding to the crowd, he turned to look at Francisco. "You have an extra man," he stated with a touch of anger creeping into his words.

"The boy needs to learn how these things go. So, he will be joining us for the talks," the old Don replied, self-assuredness and contempt dripping from his words.

Allen turned to the De Luca siblings and raised an eyebrow at them.

The male sibling piped up with a rich tenor, "We can accommodate as my sister will be joining me."

"Women should not be a part of talks about important issues," the older Russo hissed.

"Seeing as you broke the agenda before we even started, I do not see that you have a leg to stand on, Mr. Russo," Allen said firmly.

The Russos fumed. Francisco was keeping it under control, but the boy was about to lose his mind.

Allen leaned closer to them and said quietly, "Do you really want to start this in public?"

That seemed to reel them both in and the Don shook his head. "Good. Finally, I will need you to take the weapons out of your holsters and set them on the bar. You will receive them back when the talks are completed. Or we finish for the evening."

All four were glaring at him now. Each of them had weapons on them. He could smell the gun oil and powder on them. Two on each of the men and three on Giulia. He just stared blankly back at them.

Grace could feel Allen hold Giulia De Luca's beast in check. The thrum of his power in the air had all of the other-worlders on the edge of violence. Guns and thirty-odd men were not going to save any of them if it boiled over. She eyed the oblivious normals as they took their drinks from her, grins on their carefree faces as the ice clinked against glass.

The four Misters in the corners tensed as her Sir stared back at the hostile glares fired back at him.

Giulia felt him pressing down inside her, her beast pushed back against the paw holding her in place. *Or was that a claw?* Her anger died away as she picked up a soft lilting song under the chatter of men. Her eyes flicked to the side and saw the arm of the dark-haired woman behind the bar flex as a hand curled around the hilt of a sword. *The piano player?*

Her mind clicked and whirled as she took in the scene around her. The family was not the threat here. She took in the men at the corners. Now that she was aware of them she could feel their pressure on the air. A bear. A wolf. A ... not man. The last was ... she couldn't feel him. And the two beautiful women behind the bar thrummed the air in concert.

Then she looked once more at Mr. Wells. The focal point of the maelstrom. He held life and death behind his tongue. The anger she had been clutching to was gone with this realization.

She moved then. She slid the two revolvers from her underarm holsters. She laid them on the bar. She popped open her handbag, pulled the small derringer pistol out, and laid it beside the others.

The other three heads of the family looked confused at her for a moment. Then Matteo shrugged and did the same, slipping his two pistols out of his jacket and setting them beside hers.

The Russos exchanged glances and did likewise. Each produced two pistols. The younger one, getting a sharp look from the older as he laid the first one down alone, had relented and slid one out of a calf holster.

Mr. Wells had a half-smile on his face, and she felt the tension bleed out of the room. The big bald wolf leaned back against the wall corner as the shorter, yet no less muscular, bear lit a cigarette.

She let out a breath she hadn't realized she had been holding. Mr. Wells made a slight nod to her and led the group from the speakeasy.

21: Meeting

Allen led the group to a well-disguised door that led up to a large office room. He would come here to do late-night work when the women were out and the restaurant was closed. He also did a fair amount of business up here when he needed a discreet meeting with 'well-to-do' businessmen.

Pulling out a chair and waiting for all to be seated, he sat down at the long oak table. The families had arranged themselves on either side.

He steepled his fingers and said, "Since the Russos are hosting, perhaps we should start with them."

Giulia marveled at the interior of the simple room. Nothing screamed decadence and money except from the quality and care each piece was given.

As they walked in the room from the chilly stairway, she felt the warmth of the room fall over her, though there was no fireplace or stove to be seen. As though the comfort of the room gave off the warmth in the essence of itself.

A long bookcase took up the entire north wall with few spaces for more books upon them. She wondered if he had read them all. *Who would have the time?*

A long oak table sat in the center of the room. Black leather rolling chairs sat around the outside of either side, with a red leather chair at the head of it.

A smaller oak desk sat in the corner. Atop it was notes and stacked papers, arranged pencils, and an old fashioned inkpot. There was a brown bound leather book sitting to the left. It had odd markings along the spine. She couldn't tell what they were but perhaps another language.

Matteo pulled a chair out for her and she swept her skirts as she sat down. She looked over to Mr. Wells as her brother pushed her in. He wasn't even looking at her but she could feel his continued controlled pressure on her inner beast, pinning that part of her in place. Her curse snarled at him. He seemed to press her further into herself and her curse went to a highly passive state. A moment more and that part of her seemed to fall asleep.

Her heart was racing. *Who? What? Could he be a wolf? His power was so that she couldn't feel the flavor as much as drown in it. Wait. Was that a cat claw drawing back from her? No. Now it seemed to be a wolf paw. Or bear. Or ...* her mind locked back on to the discussion as it continued.

Matteo and Russo argued over the points she had lined out for her brother. She had put them in an order for him. The order was important, building up to their goals. Giving away small menial things at the beginning unspooled Russo's leverage on the things her father had wanted to get as his portion. Just as she had known it would. Francisco was playing hardball, but she knew in the end it would resolve the way she had planned. She had done her research well. Goad for gold she called it. She smothered the smile that wanted to pull at her mouth, presenting only the mask she wore for others.

This meet was over in all the ways but time. She stole another glance at Mr. Wells. He was taking notes absentmindedly. His penmanship was astounding considering he wasn't paying the slightest bit of attention. And his notes were phenomenal. She could make out most of what it read upside down. She watched as he scratched a note down before Matteo and Russo could begin the argument about it. It was the final point of the outline she had laid out. And Matteo only referred to her outline for a moment between each discussion. *Had he seen?*

He rolled his eyes as they went back and forth over the previous point. *No. He had not seen. He had deduced it?* Her brain was a whirl.

The argument over something the De Luca siblings did not want was grating on his nerves. Why push so hard for something you did not want? The only reason had to be they wanted to make Fransisco think he had made a good deal when they stole what they truly wanted. She had almost smiled. There it is.

What is not on the table yet. The east shipyards. They were known for their ability to carry and outfit ocean-faring vessels. He jotted down, 'East Shipyards - De Luca' and covered it with his hand.

He caught her staring at him again. Inward sigh.

It was done. All the things they had wanted with all the things they didn't need. Now all she needed to know was how this man knew her true goal. And HOW IN THE SEVEN HELLS he was calming her curse. If... if he could cure her... she could ... she could have a life. Truly live again. Instead of being afraid all the time.

22: Cursed

1917, Ravenna, Italy.

Giulia was in heaven. Binidittu had taken her out for the first anniversary of their first date. The fact that he was a Lombardi was not lost on her. She didn't care about the family squabbling. *Why would she care about that?* She was in love. Her father had only been against their seeing each other until he had learned Benny was the heir to his family fortune and rank. She was not about to ruin that for her father and let him know that he was not interested in the Families. He loved cooking. He didn't care about politics.

He wanted to open a restaurant and make all his favorite dishes his nonna had taught him. Today he brought a picnic basket. They had watched the sunrise with freshly made orange juice, fluffy biscuits and peach marmalade. He, of course, had made the marmalade, squeezed the oranges, and baked the biscuits. It was divine.

They had walked the streets of Ravenna, admiring the mosaics and ancient architecture. She had loved seeing the Basilica di San Vitale, the Mausoleum of Galla Placida, the Tomb of Dante Alighieri, the Basilica di Sant'Apollinare Nuovo, and the Basilica di San Francesco. So many lovely murals and paintings and oh she could go on and on...

Then they had stopped to eat lunch at a local beach where he had pulled out another delicious meal. Piadina went so well with the atmosphere she had almost been ready for a nap. After packing back up, they had set off down the beach.

Finally, he had taken her to a small restaurant for some of the best mussels and risotto. She had come to find out he had come here the night before to cook all the meals himself. This was to be his restaurant. She had shouted out with amazement and joy for him. They hugged and she kissed him.

Then her final dream came true. He had taken a knee and asked her to be his forever. She had happily cried and accepted. What a day it had been.

Now, they were peacefully taking a stroll back to where they had parked the car.

The stars were lovely and the moon was so full! It was almost as full as her heart. She looked back up at his grinning face. She smiled up at him as he smiled down at her. She had waited twenty-two years to be here this day, with her other half of her soul.

Of course, that was when the monster had attacked them. Of course it attacked two people madly in love. Of course it had waited until that exact day to strike at them.

It had leaped from the nearby brush, lashing out at them. She screamed and Benny leaped in front of her. The swipe of the creature's claws slashed Benny across the stomach. He slammed back into her, knocking them both to the ground. The creature leaped forward, snagging her leg, its cruel claws digging deep into her calves. Benny had punched it in the large canine muzzle. It stopped trying to get her into its mouth and snarled at him.

Binidittu had thrown himself at the beast then, screaming for her to run. She was ashamed to have done just that. Barely able to see, she had run. The fight behind her had not lasted very long. The sounds of the creature followed her along the street, as it gave chase. But Benny had slowed it down just enough to let her make it to the car. She jumped inside the car with the creature just behind her, its claws scraping on the door and its blows smashing the windows. Its muzzle and claws were covered in red. All she could do was slam her foot down and drive away knowing that her love was no more.

She still cried on clear nights. Especially since she found the touch of its claws had been enough to turn her into a creature just like the one who killed her beautiful Binidittu.

She had turned to Matteo, forcing him to lock her in a steel cage on the nights of the full moon. Her father still did not know. And she would keep shunning all the suitors until the day she joined Benny in heaven.

23: Sidhe Said, She Said

1472, Unknown Forest, North of the Pale, Éire.

Allen had been trudging through the wet underbrush slowly for hours. He was sure he was closing on his quarries for some time now.

He had tracked them from the burnt-out village he had seen on the edges of the Earldom of Desmond. They had left only bits and pieces of their victims behind. Not a corpse to be found. He had found shuffled steps. They had followed behind the foul men he had been hired to find and end.

The fact that he would and could have ended them without being paid and without hesitation, he did not share with his client. The church had its own prejudices. He was glad none who would know him still lived. They would have a bounty on his head the same as his prey.

The copper tang of blood hit his snout. It broke up the mix of greens, rot, and decay he had been following since the revered fairy mounds.

Leaning forward he sniffled about with his snout for the scent. There. A wet leaf. The splash of vibrant red on a purple leaf. His man brain caught up with his senses. *Purple?* He craned his neck up and looked about him. The dew-soaked foliage about him was varied shades of violet and a dark purple. The trees about him had odd flowers he had never seen before. *Where was he? Had he stumbled through a gap in the planes? He had not been watching the change in scenery, so focused had he been on his hunt.*

He blinked and sat back on his haunches. He curled his tail about his rear left leg to keep it out of the wet soil. No doubt about it. That was what had happened. He cursed inwardly as he thought of being unable to return. There was no telling when he would return or if he could return at all. He grimaced and struck out along the trail again.

Minutes later he found a desiccated body with three green-fletched arrows in its torso and a removed head some feet away. He could smell the rot of the creature that had once been human. She had been a homely woman in life. The head was cleanly sheared at the collar and stabbed through the eye.

Another splash of red blood on a nearby bush. He wondered who those he followed had crossed paths with. They would not have slain one of their creations. Not given the high cost it took to create them. He pondered this as he smelled the stench of dead things grow in strength as he padded forward. He was gaining on them now and rapidly so.

He came upon a littering of dead things.
Their heads were all removed or sliced in
twain. There was also a grey-robed man,
freshly killed. A beam of ice jutted out of
his back. It was covered in gore and held
him half a meter off the ground. His limbs
were splayed about him in an awkward
way. Death throes. Sinister markings and
lines were scrawled over every exposed
inch of skin.

Allen felt his lips curl in a snarl. A
thunderclap rang out suddenly and he
hunched lower looking towards the sound.
A tree toppled in the distance. He blinked
his eyes in astonishment then loped
forward, doubling his pace from up to this
point. He could see the conflict. Perhaps
he would find the spell weaver ahead.

- - -

As he neared the ruckus, he felt the wind
shift and flow in an odd circular direction.

His fur twisted and moved with it. Something substantial was afoot and he needed to get closer to understand what was coming.

He found himself on the edge of an unnatural clearing. Remains of the resurrected villagers lay torn or crushed all about it. Exploded or rapidly decayed trees and wilted shrubbery were strewn about, littering the forest floor.

In the nexus of the area were the surviving members of the necromancer party he had been chasing. Their hands moved in rapid motion, flinging black or green balls at their opponent.

Arrayed against them was a silver-haired woman. She held a shortsword in one hand and an amethyst tipped rod in the other. She flipped and danced about the fray. She dodged spell after spell, but he could see her limits were upon her. Even as he watched her, she slowed as the spells grew closer with every leap. As he thought this, one of the mages switched to a different pattern and a red sliver raced forward and sliced into her leg.

He watched as she began to fall. Her numerous attackers readying large orbs of sickening shades of black and green. He rushed forward, making his decision.

His body elongated to more of a man. His rear legs tore into the remains of the turf and he lashed out at the closest man. A swipe of his lengthening claws and the ball the man had been feeding swept into his neighbor's head. The man let out a minute scream as the spell absorbed his flesh and decayed the bones beneath. That man's spell screamed off into the next man. It slammed into his legs and melted him as a candle held upside down. His piteous cries drew the other two men's attention and they halted in their castings. Their wicked spells swirled above them.

Allen leaped to the side as they flung them at him. He rebounded off a nearby shattered trunk and tore into both of their chests. He ripped their tainted hearts from their chests with a quick motion of his clawed hands. They both looked down at the dripping holes and gasped out their last breaths.

He rushed back to the first man he had attacked. The mage was frantically cutting a pattern into the soil. He wrenched the man's head about and received the crackle of snapping bones as payment. Satisfied, he checked the clearing once more.

The woman was laying there on the ground panting. He stared back at her and she lowered her arm holding the rod. Now that she was not aiming it at his face, he let himself relax.

He took stock of the carnage. The mages would have to be cut cleanly with a sword to remove the heads in a manner that did not look like a wild beast had attacked them. He needed to continue to guard his secret.

"Who are you? And why did you help me?" the soft voice carried to his ears and he flicked them back towards her. He glanced over to see her healing herself with a trickle of magic. It seemed he had caught up in the nick of time for her fortune.

He let his form drop to that of a man, the wolf falling away content to sleep within.

He took a long moment to inspect the woman before him. Her silver-white hair had an ethereal glow to its locks as it cascaded down her back. And as she turned her head it fell back to reveal long, pointed ears. *One of the sidhe?*

Her clothes were made from strange materials. It shimmered with her surroundings, but sturdy enough to possibly slow the slash or thrust of a blade.

Her leg had stopped bleeding by this time and she looked up at him with a frown. She seemed to be satisfied with the healing of the wound. "Well?" she snapped, her tone icy and sharp, "Do you not have a tongue? Or did you save me only to ogle me?"

He grinned at that. He liked the attitude. It was much different than that of the women of this age. A warrior and mage. Her haughty demeanor suggested she had a noble birth perhaps. "You may call me by the name Wanderer."

She pursed her lips to the side of her mouth, "Ah, not a true name, but something you answer to. Very well, in keeping, you may call me Nevvie. None has called me besides my brother." She clamored to her feet, wobbling ever so much as she stood. He watched her cautiously as she swung her arms about still clutching to the sword and jeweled rod. He glanced back at the cooling bodies momentarily then looked back to her. "Wanderer, pray why are you in my forest? You have wandered far to be here. Surely you did not presume to hunt in my woods without my blessing?"

He mulled her words over for a moment before replying, "I was hunting these men, as that is my occupation and happened into your forest by no choice of my own. I would not have entered your woods without your permission had I known they were yours, yet I followed after my prey and now here they lay."

"Aha! And yet you have..." she began a wry smile dancing up onto her lips, but he interrupted her.

"More the better, I should happen this way as you surely would have perished under such a barrage they had arrayed against you," he said. He was glad for the sparring he had in dealing with the church as of late. They had presented a fair amount of careful wordplay and bartering that would get him the money owed. Now, he could see she was trying to allude to owing and rather catch him at a point at which he owed her. More's the shame for her. He did so enjoy a job that paid twice.

"I see." Her playful happy expression had died with his words. She could see his point and was now frowning as she pondered her next words. She arched a dainty silver eyebrow at him. "And what price do you think to be fair in recompense for such bravery?"

She was baiting him. He could taste it on the flavor of her words. He would have to be especially careful here. "Hunting rights in your woods against those not under your sway and a favor from you at a later date would be my price, should you agree. The details of the favor to be subject to both parties' approval at the date upon which the favor is called due."

She smiled at that, "Such careful prose. I accept. I hereby do swear you Friend of these Woods, so long as you remain so. And grant a favor upon a later date of our choosing. Safe travel back to the world of men."

He had forgotten that he was not in his own world. Gritting his teeth, he said, "Yes, that shall be a bit of doing. Good morrow to you, Nevvie."

She laughed, "Do not you want to know how to leave? Too soon a favor?" She waved her hand as she turned and walked out of the clearing. "Good morrow, Wanderer."

24: Waking Want

1923, New York City, New York.

Grace faded back to consciousness, slowly taking in her surroundings as she faded from the dream's gifts. Groggily, she noted fingers playing over her breasts, hips, and bottom. Her nipples were erect and aching. The calloused fingers pulled at each of them softly and traced her areolas. She let out a gasp as her assailant flicked one sensitive tip and slid down her stomach towards her valley.

"Good morning, Kitten," Allen rumbled softly into her shoulder as he bit down on it.

She pressed herself back into him and sighed out a sleep choked, "Good mmmm-morning, Sir." She felt his hardness lay between her cheeks as she ground back against it.

Suddenly, he was moving.

He snatched her wrists up with his left hand as his right hand scooped up her knee and pressed it into the down of the mattress. Then he swung up above her and set himself against her opening.

She felt her heart begin to slam against her ribs as her excitement escalated as he eased into her channel.

She felt her lips spread as he pushed farther and farther into her, painfully slow. He halted before his hips were pressed against hers. She felt him there, filling her and stretching her walls.

"Gods, Kitten, I love how your body pulls at me. I could sit like this all day, just enjoying the softness and tightness of your wet flower," he growled into her shoulder as he bit her again.

She smiled over her shoulder, a light blush on her cheeks as she inadvertently angled her hips to allow for a better angle for his entry.

"Ah, mm, I, I will clear our schedule, but may I please have all of you?" she managed.

A soft moan slipped free of her throat as he pushed slowly into her, still moving at a pace much slower than she would like, "Mmmm."

"You want all of me, lover? Deep inside you?" Allen's voice vibrated along her skin as he bit his way across her shoulder towards her neck.

She heard the hunger in his voice as he bit her again, a shudder ran down her body as her fingers flailed uselessly in his grasp. She cried out, "Oh, Sir, yes, yes, please!"

He bit into the back of her neck and slammed the rest of his length into her. Their hips met with the resounding slap of flesh on flesh. Her back arched with the fullness and completeness she always felt when he took her for his pleasure. The way her heart sang at his need for her filled her to overflowing.

His hips moved backwards and crashed back into her, from tip to hilt. "Tell me again, Kitten," he murmured between his teeth as they pulled at her.

Her eyes rolled in her head as his teeth pulled her skin taut. She squeaked out, "Gods, you feel incredible! Don't stop!"

His teeth let go of her neck momentarily as he pressed his lips against the same place, "No. Kitten, tell me of your needs. I want to hear it. I want to hear you say it. Plead it. Want it." With that his mouth spread wide and he bit her once more.

Her head swam with the need pulling at her from her core. Her mind couldn't concentrate on what he was saying. It was singularly locked to the slow pace of his hips sliding away from hers, the length of him drawing out of her. His head and shaft stroked her innermost muscles. She managed to whisper, "Please, please, please, please..." Her words trailed off as the head of him halted once more pressed against her entrance.

He grunted into her flesh. "That will have to do for now. You will make it up for me later." He drove himself fully into her five times before holding himself inside her.

She shook with pleasure with each rough thrust, "I need more. Please, Sir!" Her voice was a wisp and faint, but she felt him flex inside her in response to her words. She shuddered again as he slid out at half speed and smashed his way into her slickness.

The sound of their earnest rhythm echoed in the chamber as he continued his assault. Her eyes half closed as she felt him beat against the drum of her soul. She heard the music play against their powers as he took her.

His right foot came up as he drove into her to take the place of his right hand on her knee, pressing it more firmly into the mattress. His hand, now free, pinched and pulled at her nipples, squeezed at her breasts, scratched at her waist, then slapped down hard against her bottom. Soon her body was singing her praises as she felt his power twine with hers. She smelled crushed pine and ferns. She could hear the growl of a wolf, the yowl of a panther, and the crackle of a fire. The heat washed over her as she felt his lips brush along her earlobe.

"Come for me, my little Hellcat. Come for your Sir." Immediately, her dam broke as if summoned and they became one in all things. The crash of him against her as the wave of his need drove into her. She felt him fill her with his seed as he drove into her sex.

"Mmm, good girl," he murmured as he rested the full weight of himself against her hips.

"Thank you, thank you, thank you, thank you..." she gasped out as they both drifted back off to sleep.

25: Snow and Steam

1908, Alba Wilds.

Snow hung from boughs of trees. Crisp air tasted of rebirth and refreshment. Clumps of snow fell and gathered in drifts.

Grace watched the swirl of the snow along the winter covered grass. She clutched the blanket about her naked frame a bit closer against the chill that pressed in through the slats.

They had been on the move since he had awakened from his battle with the hellhounds and the coven members. Winter had settled in full since.

The coven had followed them somehow across Germany. But crossing into France seemed to have slowed their pursuit. She pondered if the coven had put a tracking spell on them. Either way, leaving the country seemed to have broken whatever it was. A few days with no attacks gave her an idea for the salt baths. That had broken whatever traces had been left. She had to hope they hadn't gotten any of their blood. *Gods, they certainly had left enough behind.*

She watched a snowflake as it spun and danced with the breeze. This time of year had always seemed to be charged with magic. Even the mundane seemed to feel it. Yule, or Christmas, was a happy time. Gifts, hot chocolate, loved ones, carols, and decorations had always been a delight growing up. Even her old master had grown almost chipper during this time. The grumpy old goat had a bit of a child in him still it had seemed. A pang of loss speared through her center with the remembered loss.

She heard Allen move about behind her. And she glanced over her shoulder to watch him. He was crouched in front of the wood stove feeding small logs into the growing blaze. He had strung up a line across their small hostel and had draped their wet clothes over it near the fire. Her eyes drank in the sight of his naked form. Layers of muscles moved under his skin, moving a network of crisscrossing lines. Jagged swirls, white stars and squares traced areas around his sides. A long quartet of lines ran along his back from left shoulder to right hip. She was baffled at how a lycanthrope could have scars. *Did they not heal all their wounds?* Maybe soon he would tell her his tale.

He glanced back at her over his left shoulder, an eyebrow raised over his dark eye. Her heart raced as she felt his amusement through their bond.

The magic surged between them and she could feel his beasts sniffing along her skin.

She swallowed her fear down as he watched and she remembered the words they had said. They were bound deeply. Those had been old words in an ancient book.

He turned back to the fire but she could still feel his emotions play against her skin. Amusement, sorrow, and traces of something else. Something that tasted dark and warm. She walked over and, tucking the blanket under her, sat beside him.

The flames danced and sparks jumped as he slowly tended the fire, poking small dry branches in under the larger logs. A kettle resting atop the stove began to slowly whistle.

The blend of crisp air, crackle of the fire, and the shrill of the steam was soothing, deep to her core. She felt her eyes slide halfway closed with contentment. She pulled the blanket even closer around her body. She rested her chin on her knees and sighed. Her breath came out in a wisp and disappeared in the heat.

Allen moved next to her, bringing her out of her reverie. She always was startled at his fluid movements. He seemed to move from one position to another with effortless ease. He pulled a thick rag from a pile of torn blankets and lifted the protesting kettle from the stove.

She watched him glide to the nearby oak table, set it down, and begin to shift out leaves from one of her pouches. She smelled them clearly and knew it was from the black tea he had gotten for her in France before they had fled to the United Kingdom.

Her senses were sharper since the days they spoke the words. She heard much softer noises, smells were much more distinctive, and her eyesight was absurdly more acute. The crunch of their boots through the snow to the hostel had been deafeningly loud to her. She had cringed with each step, but the owner had been outside chopping firewood and had not noticed their approach until they had broken free of the trees.

Allen had said something in a beautiful tongue. Which the stout bearded man had chuckled at then replied in the strange melody of a language. Coins had been exchanged and the man had produced a key and waved towards the small shack they now occupied.

"Pardon me, sur. Dae ye hae a room whaur mah fair lassie 'n' ah kin be getting ourselves freuch 'n' taps aff?"

"Aye, ower thare. If ye hae th' coins tae be usin` it?"

"Aye, indeed. Howfur muckle ye be thinking?"

"A marc fur th' week, ah be thinking."

"Fair enough tae me. Ta."

"Na trauchle at a'."

Allen felt her eyes on him as he seeped the tea. Another wash of cold cascaded over his back as the wind picked up. He felt her earthy power resonate with his beasts as she watched him. He could smell her arousal as it built up between her legs.

He pretended not to notice. She had proved much more capable than he had imagined on their trip. He had guessed her to be a bookish woman and had not thought her an outdoorsy type. But that night in the woods she had used flint and steel as surely and swiftly as a practiced hunter.

But her desire at this moment was palpable. He wished he could act upon his desires. She was unbelievably fetching, her mind was sharp as a dagger, and did not hesitate to act when the need arrived. This much was evident from his continued existence.

And her laugh and smile. Gods. He breathed her scent in. It rolled over his tongue and he bit into it. Earth magic, sugar, and a myriad of what he had come to realize were the tools of her trade. He shivered and managed to not stiffen. He could not and would not give in to his darkness.

Grace took the wooden mug from his calloused fingers, with a smile and quiet thanks. He nodded to her as he collected his own and sat down on the dirt floor. They sipped the tea and watched the flame's dance.

Her eyes slid over to watch him out of their corners. She was intrigued by this man. They had crossed countries and spent months together. And as they were bound together, they could feel the emotions of the other. And yet they had not been intimate. She had teased him with glimpses of her. And yet. And yet.

A wicked thought crossed her mind and she set her mug down on the earthen floor. She let go of the blanket corners and stretched her arms out high over her head. She thrust her breasts out and moaned softly as her back shifted and popped. Letting out a sigh, she dropped her arms back into her lap. Her blanket pooled around her and she glanced over at him sidelong.

He had stiffened. His fingers white knuckled about his own mug. His eyes were on her, piercing deep into her, something dark behind his eyes. She felt his need wash over her and her own flame roil and grow fueled by his own.

He became a flurry of movement. His wooden mug clattered against the wall where he had thrown it. He was standing over her, one hand curled in her hair, wrenching her head back and eyes up at him. His eyes were slotted and yellow. The darkness had slid into full view and she could feel him tremble. She glanced down at his waist and saw that he was swollen and pulsing there, straining with his need. "You are not being fair, Frauline Grace. Would you like me to lose my restraint and tempt the fates and gods with infecting you with my curse? We are bound but would you risk that? To be an animal in the moonlight? You are precious to me. I would not take you without your knowledge of the risk. And if we do we will never not be apart, your magic be damned. You will be mine to do with as I wish, for your pleasure and mine."

"Can't you see that's all I want? To be yours?" she answered, her voice tight with her emotion and desire.

"The curse burns bright even now. And you would risk it. Say it thrice, and be it true."

"I want to be yours..." she whispered.

He grunted and waited. She could feel the press of his power rolling over her and into her.

"I want to be yours," she said more determinedly. "I need to be yours," she said with every part of her body and soul. Her magic swirled inside her and crashed into his beasts, becoming one and whirling the dust about them.

"Then you are," he said solemnly and pulled her crashing up into his mouth. She felt his tongue explore her mouth as her eyes fluttered and hooded themselves. She slid her arms around him as he curled an arm around her and pulled her roughly against his body. His member pressed against her stomach just above her sex.

She felt him pull her hair back as he broke off the deep kiss. Her eyelids fluttered as he pressed his hardness into her. Her eyes shot open as his teeth bit into her neck. She moaned as he sucked and licked at the trapped flesh. She ground her hips against his leg as he released her neck and bit her again an inch or two lower.

His rough hand grabbed her right breast and he released her neck to bite into it. She felt her nipple roll between his teeth and the flick of his tongue against the tip of it. She sucked in a breath in response. He opened his mouth wide and more of the breast was pushed inside. Her breath slipped from her as the warmth of his mouth filled her. His teeth bit into her flesh and his tongue flashed over it and swirled over the nipple. His hand moved to her left breast and pinched the nipple spinning it into a twist that pulled the skin taut and aching. The pain seemed only to make her wet. *Was it the joy of his touch or the pain that excited her?* He released the nipple and cupped the breast as he released his hold of her right and fed her left into his mouth. As he bit into her left breast she caught sight of the purple bruise already forming around her nipple. Four or five inches wide, it sang with pain and the kiss of cold on the damp flesh. As gooseflesh rippled over her, she realized she enjoyed, no, needed all of it, the pain and the pleasure of him touching her.

She felt his teeth dig into her breast as he pinched the right nipple and pulled hard. He laid her back on her pooled blankets, his teeth pulled at her left nipple. It came free of his teeth when he released it and she could see the bruise his mouth left there. The sight made her drip and salivate with desire.

She felt his fingers trace down her sides, his dark eyes were drinking her in. She shivered to the attention of his gaze and the feel of the cold wind on her flesh. His fingers drifted to the valley of her legs, sliding to the slickness there. They teased over the lips and she shuddered again with his touch. The dampness spread about her petals as he teased in the opening. "Oh, yes, please?"

Goose flesh spread over her skin as he slowly dipped in and out of her. She felt his fingers slide in and out deeper each time. None too soon he was resting his palm against the button on her channel. The palm pressed down in pulses against the swollen clit as his two fingers moved about in her. They rubbed on her walls and explored her deepest parts. She felt herself respond and clench tight about his fingers. *Gods, yes! Finally!*

The fingers rubbed slowly as she clenched around him. Her eyes fluttered open. *When had they closed?* His dark, intense eyes. Her heart fluttered in her chest as he drank in her heaving breasts, the way she ground her sex against his hand, and her whimpering and gasping breaths. She was close to release and his yellow eyes locked onto hers as the dam began to tip to overflowing.

"Not yet, Kitten. Hold onto your release until I allow it," the deep rumble of his breath stole away her will. It was his now. She was his. Not that his fingers slowed their pace. If anything they were moving faster now. *Oh my, yes, much faster.*

And now he moved in and out of her. The fingers slammed in and the palm slapped against her channel, pattering out a quick rhythm against her flesh. His command echoed in her head as the pressure built within her. She was losing control of it. *Oh, but his damned fingers.* As they slid into her he moved them about scissoring against her walls.

"Come for me, Kitten," his rumbling voice pierced into her soul. Her eyes fluttered open once more and locked onto his intense gaze.
She felt herself scream as her release broke free of the dam deep inside her. She shuddered and bucked against

his palm. "Gods, yes, thank you, thank you, Sir!"

"Of course, Kitten. Such a good girl. You did well holding out for me," he murmured to her, as he continued to wiggle his damnedable fingers inside her. The crash of her orgasm pummeled her, shattering her and swallowing her whole.

Finally, he slowed his assault and she felt the tsunami of her quell to a raging river. She gasped and sucked in breath after breath. "Oh, thank you, Sir," she whispered.

His rumbling chuckle rolled over her skin and she felt his amusement mix with his need and desire. His large hands played along her skin, pinching and rubbing. They closed round her elbows bringing them together behind her and were clutched easily behind her back with a single left hand. The right hand pulled her left leg up. She felt a pressure against her opening as he settled between her legs.

"The fun is about to begin, my precious, little Hell Cat," he growled. She felt the head of him split her wet lips. He drove deeper teasingly slow into her sex. With an inch of him inside, he stopped his progress and she squirmed beneath him. She felt her walls accommodate his width, shuddering beneath him with echoes of the previous orgasm bouncing about the corners of her body and soul.

He began to withdraw, the sensation ringing up her spine. Again he stopped at the head of him just inside her and he reversed and drove himself back into her. Slowly, he eased himself in and out of her. Each time he claimed more of her, deeper and deeper. Her walls strained to contain him as he pushed into her channel, her nectar spilling around him as she felt the waves of her pleasure cascade back higher and cresting to fall. She felt a gasped "yes" slip free with each thrust.

When he reached the end of her, he stopped. She felt full and glanced up into his face. He had a pondering look on his face. He raised an eyebrow.

Her delight quailed at the eyebrow. "What's the matter? Did I do something wrong?" she managed to squeak out as her body shivered its delight.

He kissed her forehead, "No, Fraulein. I was watching your beautiful face. And waiting for you to be ready. I think you may just be."

He reached under her waist and grabbed her wrists as one with his right hand. He withdrew half of his member slowly. He then pushed back in to the end of her just as slowly. She quaked under him, her fingers flexing and scratching at the blankets as he pistoned in and out of her.

His pace was ponderous and steady. Driving deep and slow. Oh, the sensation was driving her mad. He drove in at one angle rubbing his head along her sensitive places inside. The angle of his withdrawal brought the length of him along her swollen nub at the top of her petals. She moaned as he pushed in and sucked in sighs as he withdrew. Her legs clenched against her lover's side. Her ankles curled about his legs and pulled him in slowly.

"Come with me, Kitten. I am going to fill your sweet, velvet walls to overflowing. Your tight sex has taxed my reserves and I feared I would not last this long. You are too much for me." He kissed her gasping lips once and began to increase the rhythm of his assault.

Her roiling climax hit her hard then. He seemed to have summoned her release with these words. She felt his member twitch as she clenched around his swollen rod. He let out a soft moan as she relentlessly spasmed around him. She felt him go as he slammed repeatedly into her. She had thought she was coming before but now she was exploding with pleasure. His and hers twisted and grew as they flowed together.

Such joy she felt was echoed by him. Acceptance. Fulfillment. Moments and hours were indistinguishable as the sensation continued to grow. Sometime later their shared orgasm abated. Their bodies were covered in sweat and steam billowed up from them in the cold air as he slowly continued his movement in and out of her. They sighed as one.

"Thank you, Sir."

"You're welcome, my little Witch."

26: Decision

1923, New York, New York.

Giulia stared at the signed document laying on her desk. They had succeeded. And easily. The Russo family had snatched at the scraps, and her brother had performed better than he had in their practice session.

Yet, she still felt empty. Her thoughts turned to the thickly-bearded, brown-eyed devil. *Who was he truly? How in the hells had he seen through her ploy? He was powerful.* She could feel that in the roped off area of his restaurant and in the tension of the room downstairs. He had swatted her curse, and it had laid still under his paw. She could still see in her mind's eye the gleam of the things behind his eyes. See the others in the room awaiting his command for violence.

Something low in her ached as she shuddered. How close to death they had been. And for egos of men. She was glad Matteo had followed her lead. Those men she had brought to the meeting were good men, and they had families. She hated the drama of it all, but telling wives their husbands would not be coming home broke her every time.

She drummed her fingers along the oak as she pondered her next steps. She needed to be closer to him. His control of her curse was breathtaking. She made a fist and slammed it down. *She would have to do something, but what?* She let out her breath in a heaving sigh. She had no idea.

Her stomach rumbled with hunger. She sighed once more. Food, it seemed, was her next step.

She stared out the window of the car. Her driver tapped a rhythm on his steering wheel as he waited patiently. The wooden sign swung in the light breeze.

The large bald wolf stared back at her. Her curse growled back at him. The wolf of the man stared placidly back at her. It just watched her.

She felt her lips twist from snarl to a smile. Her stomach rumbled again. She popped the door open and slid out onto the broad sidewalk, the car between her goal and herself. She stepped to move about the car. Remembering her driver, she called over her shoulder, "I will call the hotel when I'm ready, Antonio."

"If you say so, Miss De Luca," he replied as he started the car. *Good man.*

She watched the big man as she glanced up and down the street. She had plenty of time to cross, but not if she moved at a normal pace. Her belly once more reminded her how long ago the sandwiches at lunch had been.

The wolf across the street stopped leaning on the doorframe. He glanced down the road at the cars and work trucks moving about their business. He moved to the corner and leaned out over the curb. The next series of cars moved past him and he stepped out into the road. A few trucks rumbled to a stop and one driver said something in Irish at him. The big man waved an apology as he stepped up to her side of the street. The curse stood within her, a vicious growl echoing up her throat.

The bald man stopped an arm length away, "Afternoon, Miss De Luca. Will you be dining with us today?"

"Yes, please. I'm afraid I didn't want to chance crossing in this dress."

"Understand that. I'll escort you across, if you'll allow me?"

"Thank you, yes... uh, mister?"

"Mr. Caan, Miss De Luca," came the reply with a nod of his bald head. He offered an arm. She took hold of his elbow, and they moved to cross. There was a break in the traffic, and they walked across the cobbled street.

As they neared the door she felt her curse sniff the air, and her heart began to race. She could smell him. Over the wolf beside her she could smell him. *Mother Mary, help her.*

Her curse whimpered and strained to pull free of her. Caan seemed to stiffen a bit next to her, his wolf watching her curse, "Are you well, Miss De Luca?"

She bit back the rude words that burned at her lips. "I... no, gentlesir. I am not." She clutched at his arm and took a deep breath. "I will be better when he helps me. If he helps me," she forced out as her stomach rumbled with hunger. Her curse scratched about inside her, pressing at the walls of her soul.

She felt him then. The one she had come to see. A trickle of power and she felt her curse flop onto its back in submission. Instant, without question. She let out a sigh. She tugged softly on the big wolf's arm. He complied and escorted her to the door, which he opened for her easily. She could see the thickness of the door. Solid oak and banded in hammered steel. Yet it moved as a page in a book.

The scents hit her then. Acrid sweat interlaced with perfume and cologne warred against the mix of freshly ground pepper and crushed garlic with rich vegetables and tangy olive oil from the kitchen.

The soft tinkle of ivory was the next to hit her. It soothed the murmur of voices and the scrape of cutlery on porcelain. The piano played a sweet lilting song. The woman of the swords sat on the bench, caressing the keys. She saw the muscles of a fighter flex across her slender back, the blue dress leaving an unusual amount of flesh for polite society.

She felt the squeeze of the wolf's hand on hers, "Enjoy your meal, Miss De Luca."

She came back to herself and turned her head to face him, "Thank you, Mr. Caan. I shall remember your kindness." She slid her arm free of his and turned to find the blond woman standing near. *Grace was her name? Yes, that was it.* "Ms. Grace, pleasure to see you again."

The sun and earth seemed to radiate from her slight frame as she raised her eyebrows and smiled back at her. "Is it, Ms. De Luca? Welcome back. Follow me, if you will." She turned and began to lead her back to the roped staircase.

Grace frowned as Duncan led the De Luca girl inside. *Why was she back? Had she not been direct enough when she had flirted with her Mister?* She sighed as she moved forward to be polite.

Allen felt the young wolf tearing at her cage. He rubbed his face and let his beast knock the young wolf onto her back. His wolf stared down at her, and she exposed her belly to him. He sighed. Grace and Helena were going to be annoyed by this development.

What to do then? He tapped his chin.

Grace crossed the ropes, nodding to Ted. She led the way deeper into the private area towards a darker corner. *She would have her answers.*

Giulia swallowed hard as she watched the petite woman walk towards the shadowed part of the room. She could smell the coiling power swirling about the woman now. She could taste no fear in the air besides her own. The terror threatened to break her as she forced herself to follow, her feet moved slowly as if she fought against a gale of wind.

Then just as suddenly, with the feel of silk across her eyes, she was free of the storm and the dainty blond woman stood before a black door. Anger had replaced the polite smile. Her blue eyes swirled with black and gold and red and blue and white and brown then black once more. She stared Giulia down as she reached her right hand backwards and pushed the door of darkness, opening a way into a void.

For a long moment, they stared at each other. The flickering colors in the small woman chilled her core.

Then Grace turned and stepped into the dark portal. Giulia struggled to swallow the terror threatening to strangle her slowly. With force of will alone, she pushed through the inky darkness.

She halted, surprised by the feel of wind and sun on her face. She found herself in a small glade. She smelled the rich scent of moss and underbrush mixed with pine and maple. She heard the rustle of leaves and a chirp of a bird. Looking up, she saw boughs move in the light breeze. She spied a red breasted robin as it chirped once more. Its small eyes watched her as her eyes gazed in wonder back at it.

She smelled chimney smoke and fresh baked bread. Following her nose, she pushed through the wild forest. *Where was she? Where was the woman she had followed to this place?*

Minutes seemed to pass in a haze. The clearing she came out of the trees into was breathtaking and odd. Purple flowers she didn't recognize mixed with daisies and lilies. A lone chimney stuck out of a large green mound in the center of the clearing. A swirl of smoke lazily drifted toward the clouds and sun from it. Walking about the mound, she found the ivy covered door. The soft wind caressed her cheeks and fluttered the ivy leaves.

She closed slowly on the door. The scent of bread wafted through the cracks about it. In the center of the door a small cat face knocker slept. She got closer to peer at the knocker and it yawned. She jumped back with a yelp of surprise as it blinked its brass eyes at her. "Not polite to stare, Puppy."

"I... what?" Giulia answered, baffled.

"You heard me, Puppy. It is not polite to stare. State your business or be gone. And be quick about it."

"I, uh, was following Ms. Grace and I, uh, had come to Mister's to eat and talk with Mr. Wells?" Giulia replied, unsure of ... everything.

"Bor-ring. Go away. No doggies are allowed," the cat closed its eyes.

"What?" Giulia asked. *What is happening? Why am I talking to a door knocker?*

The left brass eye opened a finger's width, "Go away. No doggies." The eye began to close again. "You are boring as well."

She growled and bared her fangs at the cat, who was nonplussed. *Wait... her...* she looked down and saw a fur covered body of a wolf. A long fluffy tail curled about the feet. The long hairs of it bristled but calmed as she stared down at them, her anger fading to shock.

The door swung open and Grace popped her head out the frame to peer at the brass knocker, "Ambros, stop that. You knew I was waiting for her." She turned her eyes on Giulia, "Ah, well, that makes more sense then. Hmmm." The calculation whirled with her power in her eyes. "A few years after the attack then. Not in control at all. Let's do something about that."

She lifted her hands out and drew an oval the size of a melon in the air. One of the vines from the door pulled free and twined itself neatly in the same shape. Plucking the growth deftly and snipping it with a pair of small silver scissors, Grace lifted the plant up and laid it over Giulia's shoulders. The vines shrank about Guilia as her form shifted back to that of a human once more, now wearing a silver necklace with a leaf shaped amulet around her neck.

"It will not stop the full moon, but now you won't get fur on my rug. Come in, and let's have some tea and bread. I'll tell Ambros to get you something else to eat as well," Grace looked pointedly at the brass cat. It yawned, curled in on itself, and disappeared.

Then she turned and slipped into the shadowed chambers beyond the doorway, leaving Giulia alone outside. Giulia's head was spinning with all of the craziness and with wonder.

She heard a kettle let out a whistle from inside. She peeked inside. Grace was lifting a kettle off a swing arm. "Do come in. We need to get back, sooner rather than later."

Giulia noticed a table to the side with a lace tablecloth and a fine china tea set atop it. She slipped in, fingering the amulet resting against her chest. Feeling awkward, she sat down and peered at the tablecloth. Strange symbols comprised the art of the lace rather than the usual brocade. *I wonder what these all mean.* Looking about the room, she saw jars full of different things, spices perhaps, and plants drying on lines that hung from the ceiling.

A small glass piece on a shelf caught her eye. It was a small statue of a wolf battling a large cat. *Perhaps a tiger?* It was difficult to determine at this angle. Behind this she saw another statue; this one was a porcelain angel. It had long black hair and blue and black painted wings. *Odd.* The angel seemed to be watching the glass piece's battle, a short sword clutched in one arm.

Grace stepped over and began filling the teapot with water from the kettle. Setting the kettle to the side, she plucked a glass jar from a nearby shelf. She tucked her dress under her knees and sat down across from Giulia. Her eyes still shone with the otherworldly lights.

"So, since time is of the essence, you will tell me why you are so interested in my Mister." She began scooping out a fine smelling tea into the teapot. The rich smell of the tea as it seeped was calming and heady. Giulia blinked and opened her mouth to speak, but Grace cut her off, "Truth, now."

Bristling with the implication and the insult, she bit her tongue and counted to three. *It would not do well to insult a witch in her home.* And there was no doubt in Giulia's mind that Grace was anything but that. And a powerful one, considering the displays she had shown her.

"I am a cursed being. I was turned into this monster when a monster tore my fiance apart. I have taken great care to keep my secret and, with my brother's help, my curse to myself.

"I seek your mister, whatever that means, because he can control it, and I would live a normal life if given the chance.

"That and he is gorgeous. And he saw through my careful script in the meeting with the Russos. Easily. He intrigues me on numerous levels.

"I would give him my maidenhead. I would be his kept woman, his whore, anything and everything he wanted from me. I would give him access to all the resources at my disposal. I would give him all of me.

"Truth enough?" Giulia finished, watching the twitches on the woman's face as she talked.

The witch sat staring at her for a long moment. The colors swirled in her eyes joined by fire and lightning. Giulia watched as anger warred with contemplation. Grace let out a sigh as she closed her eyes, sealing away the flames and lightning. She sipped her tea as she continued to battle with her emotions.

"You may present yourself to the Mister. You will do it tonight. And we shall see what we see. I do not want to share him with another. Helena will be furious I am sure, but that is your problem.

"You will let your brother know you are staying here this evening. I do not want the De Luca family stepping on the Mister's business.

"Ambros has arrived with our food. You will eat and leave. I will leave it to Sir to decide," Grace opened her eyes as she finished. The lightning and fire were gone, but the anger remained. The colors swirled around her pupils slowly.

Giulia nodded slowly.

A cat in a suit appeared with a platter balanced on one paw. It stepped forward and yawned. It waved a hand and two bowls of stew floated to the table. It smelled delicious. The cat in the suit turned and disappeared once more.

They ate in silence and sipped the tea. All were of excellent quality. Giulia savored each bite and sip.

Sooner than she wanted the meal was over. "Thank you for seeing me and for the gift. I... I am sorry that I am weak. I did not mean to step on your toes or Helena's for that matter. But the heart wants what the heart wants. Perhaps I can be content with the gift you have given, though you know that is not what I want. My primary concern was my curse. I will return at dusk to meet with Mr. Wells?"

The witch hesitated, "Yes, that will suffice. I will tell Duncan to expect you."

Nodding, Giulia rose and made to leave. The brass knocker winked at her as she passed. "Bye, Puppy!" It called as she scowled back at it. She pressed into the forest and made her way back to the spot that held the black portal.

27: Presents and Presence

Allen sat in his chair behind the desk, his right calf resting on the corner. He flipped the next page of his book, then flipped back when he realized he hadn't read the last page. Sighing, he set it down on the desk. *How long were they going to...*

He felt the young wolf leave Grace's pocket. A circle of Grace's power sat around Giulia's neck. *Interesting.*

The young wolf lingered at the hostess area for twenty minutes, then moved outside to wait. No doubt for a car.

He felt Duncan interact with her, through the pack threads. *He seemed at ease with her, yet differential. An alpha recognizing an alpha? Hmmm. He seemed much more at ease then when she first arrived.*

Just as her car arrived, he felt her beast sniff for him. The young wolf inside her whined as she sighed.

He felt Grace emerge. He felt her emotions pulse down their tether. Annoyance and anger at the young wolf. She must have felt him as her love for him pulsed hard with a determined resolve, with undercurrents of annoyance at him. He grinned and let his love for her flow with a touch of his power down the tether.

She was on her way to his office and him.

Grace shook with fear, anger and anxiety. *Who did that young she-wolf think she was? Had she overstepped? Would her Mister take her in? Would he do all the things De Luca wanted? What would she do if he did? What should she do?*

She felt him soothe her emotions through the
bond with waves of desire, love, and affection.
She let out a breath and knocked on the door.

He heard her let out a deep sigh and knock.
"Enter," he called. He watched as she pushed
the door open slowly, her eyes peeking
around it at him and dropping when they met
his gaze. She slid into the room, her slender
shoulders held back and proper, if slumped
slightly. *She expected some reprisal it seemed.*

He dropped a pillow onto the floor in front of
him. It was something he kept in his cabinet. It
was a feather filled one with a green silk case.
She looked up at him briefly and dropped to
her knees deftly onto the pillow. She knelt
there with her hands behind her back, staring
unblinking at his belt buckle.

He sighed, "You're not in trouble, unless you
want to be." He curled his hand in her hair and
pulled her down against his inner thigh.

She let out a strangled sob and looked up with wide eyes. Tears welled up and pooled around her shimmering blue globes. They climbed higher and higher. He stroked her cheek softly with a thumb and she broke. The dam that she had been holding came pouring out. It cascaded down her face, smearing her makeup, and out the bond between them.

He felt all her worry and despair roar out of her for him to take. And he did. He took it all, rubbing her cheek and humming softly to her. She cried wracking sobs in the fabric of his pants as she clutched to him. Her fingers dug deeper into him, pulling herself closer and closer as she gasped and bawled, chest heaving against him. He watched the relief come over her as he took charge of her and their future. Like he always had.

Minutes passed before she managed to slow to hiccupping snorts and a soft snore. She had fallen asleep, her face pressed against his crotch. He smiled and wiped at her tear-streaked face. He pulled free a handkerchief and dabbed away all the moisture, starting with her eyes then to her nose.

Minutes later, she woke as he continued to stroke her cheek. Her eyes slid open lazily before she stiffened slightly, a reaction from waking from comfortable sleep and the proximity of her face to his crotch. "Better, Fraulein Grace?"

She looked down and replied, "Yes, Sir. Thank you, Sir."

"Do you want to talk about it now?"

He felt her emotions as he watched her face. She seemed to be a swirling eddy of hurt, self doubt, a need for reassurance, concern, gratitude, jealousy, inadequacy, and protectiveness.

He smiled at her, "I understand your concerns. I need no one, save you and our delightful Angel. What can I do to reassure you? Ah. But I do have a surprise for you, when you are ready for it. Perhaps tonight or tomorrow?"

"Oh, you should expect the De Luca woman this evening, Sir," Grace replied, with an ounce of stress flooding the bond between them.

"Very well," Allen said, pondering that bit of information. He pulled on her nose. He stuck his thumb out between the fingers after releasing her nose and wiggled it at her.

She smirked at him. He reached out with the same hand, helping her to her feet. Then he promptly pulled her down into his lap. She let out a quick peep of delight and fright. He squeezed her waist softly.

She leaned against him. He kissed under her chin. Allen continued to consider the troubles that seemed to be blowing their way.

For one, another woman being about might cheer up the "pack." Unfortunately, that woman seemed to be fixated on him, if the emotions rolling off his favorite witch was any indication.

Furthermore, she was from the De Luca family and the Russos might take offense to him taking her in, quelling any sense of neutral stance. However, she would grant access to a powerful family from Italy, and that may or may not be helpful.

And it appeared she was not in control of her beast. However, the ward woven into the necklace and amulet Grace had given her would no doubt help her from losing control during high stress and emotional states.

He needed to decide on a plan or two before she arrived. Or, at least, some options.

Ted and Duncan sat across from their boss. *He had a vacant look on his face. He seemed to be lost in thought. He had sent for them and only waved them to their chairs when they had entered. He had been mulling his words before they arrived. It had been a few minutes since then. The boss was not a man without a plan most times.* This display was beginning to unsettle Duncan.

Just as he was going to ask, Allen sat upright in his chair, fixing them with his dark brown eyes. He could feel the power of his alpha roll over them, as his gaze flicked between them. "Tell me what you think of the De Luca twins."

Ted looked to Duncan, who nodded, "They seemed to be bright individuals. Much better than the local hooligans who frequent our establishment; though even those have some in their number that have honor."

Duncan piped up, "The beast in the girl is strong. She saw the danger we posed on the night of the meeting and acted accordingly.

Her brother has shown decorum and has made contacts throughout town with many of the other groups in the city. They seem to be making quite a few moves in a short time. Do you think there will be war?"

Allen sighed, "Possibly. And with the young wolf coming to see us, we may be pulled into it. I am debating on preemptive action. I would rather spill their blood before they would threaten our own."

Ted and Duncan nodded at this. They had had to do something similar when they had first arrived. The Irish had been disagreeable. But after a change of management it has quieted down considerably. There was still something of enmity between them, but none could prove the death linked back to them.

"Counsel?"

Both men shook their heads.

"Very well. You are excused."

They stood as one and left their boss to ponder more.

Grace stared at her hands. She wondered what to do with herself. Her section was taken care of by one of the other girls that worked here. She really must thank Sally later. Her regulars had come and gone for today.

Her thoughts kept bouncing between the anxiety of the situation and the giddy excitement of whatever the surprise her Mister had for her. *She could not wait to let it all go and just not think. His pleasure and direction was what she craved. The fact that he was so caring and mindful of praise for doing what he commanded was … perfect. And, gods, relaxing. Her favorite thing was when he would read from a book while she plied him with her mouth. It was so intimate and soothing. His voice and grunts filled her with joy, while her mind was blank other than her task at hand.* She smiled.

Well, she considered that wasn't her favorite but one of them. She sighed. *It would all work out, somehow. Mister wouldn't take chances. Not with their safety. He probably would come up with a back up plan. Or seven.*

She stood up from her stool in the Mister's hidden office, dusted off her skirt of the nonexistent dirt, and checked her face in the mirror. She touched up her makeup and went back down to see if any of the girls needed help. She doubted that they did, except perhaps a large order.

The night brought wind and rain from the north. The cold spattering of rain pelted pedestrians, cars and buildings alike. People bustled to their destinations and out of the fierce storm.

The evening crowd thinned quickly as it grew darker. With the downpour the stragglers, few in number, had hurried off to their cars or cabs swiftly.

Mister's closed down for the evening. The last few factory workers having drinks were shown out. Those that were too drunk to walk home had cabs called for by the staff. After all were gone the doors were barred and locked. The tables and chairs were put up and lights turned down.

Fifteen minutes before nine o'clock there was a knock at the door. Duncan opened the door to find Giulia, two men in suits he didn't recognize, and Matteo. He frowned at the unexpected men. "We are closed for the evening. How can I help you?" he said in a bored tone.

Matteo exchanged a glance with his sister. "We are here as was required of my sister. I would like to speak with Mr. Wells. Out of the rain, if possible."

Duncan looked over the drenched individuals. The rain was coming down at an angle and was cold as it splashed off of the four huddled awkwardly in the doorway. "You are welcome to come in, but your men will need to wait with me while you speak to him." He swung the door wide and those waiting hurried inside. Rain dripped from hats, coats and noses to puddle on the foyer floor.

Janet, one of the waitresses who was also a wolf, hurried over with towels and a mop bucket. The newcomers thanked her and began to dry themselves as she smiled at them and set to mopping up the mess behind them at the door. Duncan considered her.

She was a short, cheerful, young lady with curly brown hair and an athletic form. She had been a recent pack entry. She took instruction well and had been his submissive a time or two before settling into a power exchange relationship with Jim.

Duncan rued the loss for the hundredth time. He determined he needed to find someone to fill that part of his life. It was a need that he had put off sating, and he had caught himself gritting his teeth on numerous occasions.

He shrugged that thought away as he turned his attention back to the De Lucas and their escort. The two men in suits under rain slicks were formidable sizes, if only human. He could see the telltale bulges of large firearms. He could smell the gunpowder and gun oil. He did not, however, smell the tang of silver that would mean lasting damage. As such he dismissed their weapons. *Let them have their security blankets.* He angled his head to a nearby table as the two men shrugged out of their raincoats. They looked over at it then turned their heads to Matteo. The De Luca man nodded his curly black haired head and they moved to it. They pulled down two chairs and slumped gratefully into them.

Janet finished cleaning up the rain water. As she was passing, Duncan said, "Bring some coffee for our guests. And ask one of the others to escort Mr. and Ms. De Luca." She nodded and walked away quickly. He walked over to the seated men, who tensed, and pulled a chair down for himself. He sat into it and returned their blank stares.

A few minutes later, Jim walked out with his hands clasped behind his back. The bear was a medium sized man and clean shaven. His eyes were piercing steel blue and locked on Matteo. His red wavy hair was cut short and combed to the left with some sort of hair product. Duncan didn't know much about hair things, since he had started shaving his head. *Whatever.*

He knew Jim was strong, especially when channeling his beast, having sparred with him on multiple occasions. Jim and Duncan shared a quick glance and nod. Jim motioned to the two De Luca twins. They followed him as he walked back the way he had come from the kitchen.

A moment later, Janet reappeared with coffee. Duncan leaned back in his chair to wait.

Allen sat in his hidden office, his feet up on the desk. His right hand traced through Grace's hair as she leaned against his thigh. He had been brooding for some time now. She wondered if she should say something, when Ted poked his head in, "The De Lucas are here. The boy would like to speak with you, Sir."

She felt his leg twitch beneath her head and his fingers halted mid-combing, "Certainly. I have nothing better to do with my time than suffer the whims of all the gangsters in town." He let out a heavy sigh, "Send them in, I suppose. We might as well see this farce through." He patted her head gently, and she sat back on her stool, pouting. His eyes met hers, and he quirked his left eyebrow at her, "Do you not want your surprise, Kitten?"

She pulled her bottom lip in quickly and gave him her most innocent smile, "Yes, Sir!"

"After all the pomp has been taken care of we shall see what we shall see, then we will have some fun. I will give you your treat tomorrow if you are well-behaved tonight," he grinned his evil, dark smile at her.

It made her inside curl with fear and her heart hammer with excitement. She could feel his desire spike and knew he could smell and feel hers. She gulped and nodded sharply.

"Good girl," he said as he turned to the door. She heard footsteps on the stairwell. A moment later, Jim opened the door with the De Lucas following close behind.

Giulia felt a thrill as she locked eyes with the creature that called himself Allen Wells. Her curse panted and flopped on its back in submission. It was all she could do to not emulate it.

She shuddered with giddy pleasure at his attention. Her brother gave her a sideways glance. She pointedly glared back at him. He dutifully looked away, cringing.

They approached the desk Allen sat behind. He rose politely as they entered the room. He had on a dark, grey suit with red pinstriping. He had on a black silk shirt and a red silk tie with black brocade. His clothes were well fitted to his muscular body. Heaven help her, yum.

As they approached, she caught sight of Grace seated on a stool to his right side. She was wearing a long lush green velvet dress stitched with embroidery and emeralds. She had a matching pair of gloves folded in her lap. The blond woman had a friendly smile on her face. Giulia noticed it did not reach her eyes. In fact, the demure woman seemed to be glaring while smiling. That was quite the feat. And utterly terrifying.

Allen watched as Jim slid to the side to allow the De Lucas to enter behind him. Jim held the door out of the way, met his eyes, nodded to him, then stepped outside the door, closing it behind him without a word. Allen knew with his keen senses he would be able to hear the conversation inside.

Good man. Allen raised his left eyebrow, "Do sit, Mr. De Luca. What can I help you with?"

Matteo sat down in the well made leather chair and seemed to stiffen a bit, "It would seem you know exactly why I am here, Mr. Wells. You have entertained my sister a couple times this week. And you told her to come back here tonight. I want to know why."

Allen sat himself after Giulia slid into her own chair. He looked at her, "You said that he knows your affliction?" The question was pointed and came out rougher than he would have preferred.

But being talked down to just because this man was a noble of this era made him bothered. Self-worth paid for by a line of rich ancestors and happenstance did not a noble make.

Duncan and Ted had said he did fair dealings and treated his people well, according to their spies. But this display of peacocking was trite and unwelcome.

"Yes, Mr. Wells."

"Mr. De Luca, she has sought me and mine out. Not the other way about. She has come to me for aid in controlling what she has referred to as a curse. She had said you have aided her in the past. So, hence, I assume you have knowledge of what all that entails?"

"Yes, Mr. Wells," the much younger man said, through clenched teeth.

"Good. Now. Do you know why she turned to us in particular? Possibly, would you like to know?"

"Yes, Mr. Wells," Matteo repeated.

"That is because I am also 'cursed.'" Matteo's eyes went wide with this news. He began to speak, but Allen held up a hand and continued, "I will trust you with this information because you have guarded your sister's secret. But I will be forced to take action should you prove less than the honorable man that my sources have made you out to be." With this he stood, "I shall call in the morning to invite you for breakfast. Or you can just invite yourself as you did this evening. The morning meal begins at seven sharp, Mr. De Luca. Is there anything else you need answers for?"

Matteo stood shakily, "No, Mr. Wells. Ah, well. Yes, I do have one. You will protect her, on your honor?"

Allen smiled. *He had not heard this phrase in some time.* "On my honor, no harm shall come to Ms. De Luca by outside forces."

Matteo squinted his eyes, "That isn't what I asked. But I suspect it is the best I'm gonna get." He reached down to Giulia and they squeezed hands. He whispered, "See ya in the morning, sis. Be careful. I hope you know what you're doing."

She squeezed his hands back as she replied in an equally whispering manner, "Me too, brother, me too. Thank you."

With a sigh and a quick glance at the two behind the desk, Matteo De Luca left.

Giulia swallowed as she watched her brother step out into the stairwell and the door close behind him. She turned back to Allen and Grace. He was studying her with his dark pools for eyes. An expression of contemplation pulled his mouth in a straight line through his well groomed beard.

Giulia had dressed well for the evening. A form-fitting black evening gown with matching gloves and hat. A string of jewels hung around her neck and dipped into her ample cleavage. Shimmering black opals and onyx stones were nestled in white gold and caught the light well, drawing one's attention. Her long legs were crossed at the knees and were sheathed in black stockings. Her shoes were no doubt something Italian and of good taste.

The she-wolf stared up at him where he stood. She had the look and smell of prey. He felt his beasts watch her as she sat there. The big cat was not impressed. But the wolf was drinking in her scent. *Complications. We will see how she does.*

He broke off the stare and turned to Grace. He leaned back against the desk. "Ready, my dear?"

Grace smiled coyly up at him, "Yes, Sir." She raised a hand to him. He grinned at her, catching her implication. He reached down and snagged her hand. He easily pulled her up to him and slid his right arm around her slender waist. He pinched where his hand came to rest which tickled her for a moment. This had the desired effect of her squeaking and slamming herself sideways into him.

"Sir..." she turned her eyes up at him. She had a hint of a pout on her lips and her eyes were sliding into a squint.

"Come along, Fraulein. People are waiting," he smirked down at her. He slid his arm back from around her waist and caught her hand in his. He pulled her along, leaving Giulia to catch up with

them as they walked through the door that had
opened at their approach.

Jim pushed it wide and stepped to the side. He
nodded to the bear and helped Grace down
the stairs, Giulia and Jim close behind.

Allen and Grace entered the Court Below. It
was one of the largest rooms buried deep
under Mister's. It was also where he held
court on the days of ceremonies or events.
Much like today. He kept his face neutral as he
passed the crowd of wolves, a couple of bears,
and a few tigers.

The large chamber's walls were huge cut
blocks of black stone. In each corner, round
pillars held the ceiling. Intricate carvings
wrapped around each pillar, showing
creatures of all kinds in an elaborate dance.

The far end of the room held a dais. An ebon
wood throne sat upon it. Cushions lay about

the room providing seating or lounging for those in attendance.

Helena knelt on the left beside the ornately carved chair on one of several cushions near it. Grace stepped from his arm to take her place on the right of the seat, kneeling easily and smiling up at him.

Allen smiled back at her then at Helena, who was beaming at him. He turned about, facing a slightly frightened Giulia. She was holding a mask of nonchalance over her pretty features, but he could smell her fear. Judging by the sensation coming from the pack, they could smell it too.

Now we will see what she is truly made of. Allen sat down on the throne. The rest of the assembly knelt on their cushions and held still as statues. The room had gone silent, all trace murmurs having died as he had sat. Now the only one that was standing was Giulia. He could feel her unease build.

"So, young wolf. You have come looking for a place of refuge. A place of belonging. You have found it." He watched the unease seem to drain from her and her lips began to curl towards a smile. He continued, "However, this is more than just a place of work for most. Those too young to control themselves on the night of the moon are trained by those older and more experienced. You should know that the one who trains you is based on your performance tonight." Her expression grew confused and she opened her mouth. He cut her off.

"You will fight in order to establish your place. Would you like to begin now?" he watched her as numerous emotions flickered across her face. "No lasting damage and not to the death," he clarified. "We aren't savages. Just savage." A chuckle swept about the room from half amused members.

"I... yes, Mr. Wells. I would like to make my place here. I would request to be given the right to fight you to see if I am ready."

"Lofty goals, young wolf. But, no, you have felt me keep you from the change under duress. There are few in the world with this ability. Where the change causes most of our kind great pain, I feel none. Where the beast is who they are, it is only part of me. I am not looking to bruise your ego, but you may fight ... Jeffrey. If you beat him, you may present yourself to one of the alphas for training. If not, then Jeffrey shall train you."

She did not look pleased by this. Spoiled rich child. Used to getting her way. But this is not the human world. This is the darkness. He waved a hand at the wolf named Jeffrey.

The young wolf had shown promise and had gained control and confidence in the last months. He was almost ready to be one of the alphas, but he was still half in the human world. His family still lived, and he doted heavily on his mother and two younger sisters.

Jeffrey kept to his feet and began disrobing. Giulia noticed this with shock and looked up at Allen. "What?"

"Unless you want your clothes ruined by the change, I suggest you do likewise," Allen smirked.

She stared back at him for a handful of moments, took in the expectant faces about her, and began disrobing as well. Allen watched her careful nimble fingers as she removed garments. He could feel her beast lashing at the bonds of her amulet. She did not seem to notice.

He looked down at Grace, meeting her gaze. The lovely woman nodded. *She had noticed also. Giulia was an inferno missing a spark. Jeffrey may not be enough of a challenge. This was an odd development. Had she been bitten by an elder? He would need to address this question sooner rather than later.*

Giulia stood naked facing an equally naked Jeffrey now. She took a stance in an Israeli fighting style. Jeffrey dropped into a wrestling crouch. He could feel their beasts chomping at the bits.

Allen leaned forward. "Begin." As he said this he pushed his power into both of them and they began to shift. Both of them shook as their forms shifted to a wolfman hybrid. They both screamed as bones shifted and slid to rearrange themselves to fit in their proper placement.

This was a crucial moment. The first to regain their senses would have an instant or two over their opponent. Giulia won. She completed her change first. But she lost it in the moments after flexing her fingers, now claws, and shaking her head as she adjusted. Had she never been in hybrid form? Or had she never had control before?

Jeffrey came out of the agony a moment later. He swung a paw immediately at Giulia's head, but she just managed to spring back out of the way.

Minutes passed as the two fought furiously, neither able to land a lasting blow or get a good hold on the other's person. She was conserving her strength however. No reckless attack or overreaching risk. Smart. She was dangerous when in control of her beast. Jeffrey appeared to be tiring and was lashing out with more aggressive and obvious attacks.

Finally, she struck him hard, rocking his jaw and sending him reeling from the impact. He struggled to regain his balance but a knee to the chin, and he fell backwards. She pounced even as he was falling. Her teeth bared and her claws extended towards him as she jumped for him.

Allen had seen enough. He stood up and shifted to his wolfman. The room fell into a hush as Giulia and Jeffrey abruptly shifted to humans. They fell in a tumble of limbs. She leapt back to her feet. She swayed a moment then turned her eyes to him. *She was moondrunk.* He pointed at a nearby cushion and she plopped down onto it.

Grace slipped forward and checked over a groaning Jeffrey. After making sure to touch some of her ointment into the larger cuts, she nodded to Allen. He looked back to Giulia, who still had some moon in her eyes.

"Well enough. You shall train with Mr. Garrison. He will teach you how to keep this kind of control over the next few years."

She frowned but managed a nod.

"With that done, we can move onto Court business. Bring out the feast."

Several men hurried to a side door and came in with several trays overstuffed with multiple roasted animals of all kinds. They set them down and the pack descended on the food with gusto.

28: Iron

Grace had been excited all day for this evening. *Not that she disliked working at the diner or even the speakeasy, just that the day had seemed to drag on for eternity. Her Mister had promised a new surprise for her and his surprises were always delicious and just what she needed, even if she hadn't known she needed them.*

She almost bounced down the stairs toward the lower rooms, her fingers running over the hewn stone. It was cold to her touch, but without blemish. She hummed the tune that Helena had been playing. *Such a lovely piece*, she thought to herself, *haunted and happy at the same time.*

She leaped the last couple of stairs as she came to the bottom, hurling herself towards the hallway and the rooms beyond.

Allen sat in a chair, watching her placidly. An elbow rested on the armrest and his chin was on his fist.

His eyes twinkled with mischief as she grew closer. His lips turned up into an evil grin, making her lurch in her chest. She knew she was wet, just with that look. *Gods help me, this man*, she groused to herself, silently.

She felt her throat constrict as she came even closer, stopping a few feet from him. "Good evening, Sir!" she chirped happily.

His eyes slid over her, drinking her in with unguarded desire. They seemed to flash with yellow then green as he took in each article of clothing and curve they hid. From her pinstriped red and black half jacket and matching corset, to the bright red silk shirt, to the loose black tie between her breasts, to where the skirt clung to her waist, down her legs clad in their black hose, to rest on her black slippers.

Then they flashed once more to her eyes. They were shining green. She could see the rolling red begin to rise around him.

She felt his beasts coil inside him as his evident hunger for her flicked over her. Her corset and skirt suddenly felt too tight, her breaths coming in gasping pants.

"Good evening, my delightful little Hellcat. You look like you are excited for tonight," he said slowly.

She blushed lightly, gave him a coy smile, and said, "Yes, Sir."

His power bit into her middle, making her back arch, "Mmm, show me your excitement."

She whispered, "Yes, Sir," as she spun around, quickly unzipped her skirt and bent over pushing it to the ground. She could feel the cold of the hallway play over her soaking underthings. She stepped free of the skirt, folded it, set it to the side, and grasped her ankles.

She felt him roll his knuckles over the wetness of her. She heard him hum softly to himself as he touched her through the fabric, bouncing lightly from the button at the front to the valley of her lips.

He pressed through the silk into her sex. His soft hum moved in pitch to a growl. She could feel his need and desire through the tether of his power as it rolled over her, his fingers pushing deeper into her.

The pressure eased from her sex slowly. She felt a quick yank at her hips, and the coldness of the chamber was against her bare flesh. She glanced over to him around her hips and she could see her torn undergarment clenched in his left hand.

She felt two fingers press into her tunnel as his low rumbling hum continued. She let out a soft moan as she felt them flit about inside her. "Good girl," he intoned his lit eyes catching hers as she stared back at him. He pushed forward into her sex rubbing deep inside her. She felt herself clench with the attention to that location. Waves of pleasure crashed over her, shattering and splintering to drift through all that she was.

"Good. Right at the precipice. I can feel you squeezing and clenching your velvet walls around me. It wouldn't take much more to have you cascade into your orgasm. So. That is where we will stop that for now." With that, he slid his fingers slowly free of her.

She pushed out her bottom lip at him in her prettiest pout. She felt his beasts churn under his skin and pressed against her aura in response.

She shuddered at the touch and pulled back her pout. He let out a chuckle as she did. He stood up and slapped her bottom softly with his right hand, "Come, come, Hellcat. There is much fun yet to be." He turned and opened the door behind him, pushing it to swing on its well-oiled hinges.

She stood and followed him into the room.

A large bed sat in one corner. The mattress was covered in a black silk sheet. The posts extended up to the ceiling with large steel rings attached at one-foot intervals. There were no pillows or blankets on it, though there were shelves with both on either side of it.

Along the wall were many of the tools he used to give her and Helena such delight. Paddles, crops, switches, canes, and floggers of all shapes and sizes hung down from their posts or hooks.

Across from them were the many different sized and varied purposed restraints. Leather, cloth, silk, steel, iron. Buckles, clasps, ties. Numerous locks.

Hooks and rings also hung along this wall next to various lengths of ropes of various colors, material, and braids.

But what drew her eye was the new piece of torturous delight in the middle of the room.

An iron lattice the shape of a man rested on casting wheels. Many shackles and locks were nearby on a wooden table. Her eyes roved over it, at a loss for where one would even begin.

"Stand here, Kitten." He was pointing at the ground in front of the piece. She quickly obeyed. "Undress and turn about."

She again quickly obeyed folding each article and setting it on the table next to herself and spinning about to face the door.

She heard him pull a shackle off the table. He leaned forward and latched it to her left wrist. Another scrape and he repeated the process with her right wrist. Minutes later, she had a shackle around each limb, knee, elbow, waist, and neck.

Allen's beard brushed across her shoulder, and he nipped at her right earlobe, "Are you ready, Kitten?"

She nodded her head anxiously and quickly squeaked out, "Yes, Sir."

She felt him kiss her neck and move back from her. Her ears strained to hear what he was doing, shuddering with excitement. She heard the rasp of metal on stone and felt him move closer with the sound.

He took her arm in one hand and locked the manacle to an iron rod. He moved about attaching more and more rods to her restraints.

He stepped about to the front of her. He had a devilishly evil grin twisting his lips.

"Nothing pinching, Kitten? Nothing too tight?" he leaned forward inspecting her and her restraints. He reached out with a finger and ran it along her belly just above the restraint on her waist.

She tried to look down at his finger and track its movements, but her neck was held fast and the collar prevented her from leaning her head down.

She flexed her fingers, strained each limb, and leaned against each of her restraints. *She was immobile. There was no give in each of the restraints, yet none were tight enough to hurt.* "N-n-no, it is perfect, Sir. And very secure."

He grinned broadly at that, "Just the beginning, my dearest Kitten." He stepped around her to the apparatus she was strapped to and she heard the click and clank of gears moving. Slowly, she lifted off the ground. Her feet began to lift as her head stayed in the same location. The rods took her weight and she let out a shriek of shock. Slowly and steadily, she tipped back until she was looking up at the ceiling. It looked a bit closer than she was used to seeing it.

Then the clicking and clinks stopped. She heard his footsteps once more. His lips pressed into her ear. "Now, the same question. No discomfort?"

She nervously stuttered out, "N-n-no, Sir." She could feel her arousal dripping from her.

He chuckled and bit into her shoulder, "Delicious. And now we begin."

He stepped away from her, back to the device. A click was heard from over where he stood and she felt her left leg spread by the restraints on it. Another click.

More soft taps of his feet tapped along the floor, followed by another click, and her right leg was moved away from the left. Another click.

She heard him move again. *From the direction of the sounds of his footfalls, he was walking to the side with the impact play tools.*

She heard his return and felt him run a slender implement over her bare skin. He ran it over her feet, inner and outer calves and thighs, and over her bottom.

She knew the feel of that device. It was one of the bamboo canes he had shipped over from Asia. Goose flesh spread out over her skin and her nipples stretched out toward the ceiling.

A finger teased along the outside of her petals, spreading her juices along the inside of her thighs. "Such a messy Kitten."

He tapped the cane back and forth along her legs, from her calves to inches from where his fingers continued to tease at her sex.

He slid his finger up and down her slit, as the tap-tap of the cane continued.

The taps slowly increased in pace, until it was a light flurry along the inside of her legs. Then all at once, he slid his finger away from her and the tap-tap of the cane disappeared.

She jerked with the sudden lack of stimuli. *What?* Her thoughts began to flood back into her.

Then he slid a finger into her to the base and began to tap at the outside of her left leg.

It was too much. Oh, gods, she was going to explode. His finger was curling and exploring and stroking her inner walls. Deep, deep within her.

Then he disappeared once more.

His chuckle was dark and evil. So cruel. She could feel it roll over her skin.

Two fingers slammed into her. They writhed inside her as her right leg received light taps along its outside.

His thumb ran along the swollen clit as he pushed up on the inside of her belly. He slid the fingers in and out of her, writhing as he went.

He spread her inner lips and a hot tongue flicked over her distended clit. Her body jerked against the restraints and her fingers scrambled to latch onto something, anything.

"Oh, goddesses," the words escaped her as the touch of his tongue and her inability to move and the insistent tapping began to overwhelm her.

Then his mouth sucked her into him and his teeth bit into her softest place. His teeth nibbled at her clit and the tip of his tongue flicked against her clit's tip. Her hips ground against him as he continued to lash at her.

As she got closer and closer and closer to the cascade she so desired, he vanished once more.

She jerked again, her hips still grinding frantically at her hidden tormentor. She clenched her fists and let out a frustrated, "No, no, no... please, please, please, please..."

His dark chuckle echoed through the room. "Yes, yes, yes, little Kitty. It will be a long night. Do you like my new toy? It is one of a kind." The growl was back in his voice. It rolled over her skin and goose flesh sprouted behind it.

Her hips slammed forward at the sound of his desire and she quaked with a touch of his power as it bit her here and there.

A lump curled in her throat as she strained again at her bonds. His words "long night" echoed through her mind. She nervously squeaked out, "Yes, Sir."

His cane reappeared, flicking against her bare bottom, once along each cheek.

Her hips drove forward as she gasped. She let out a soft cry as he dipped two fingers into her, withdrew them, and flicked each cheek once more.

The lashes against her backside continued, followed by a teasing probe of his callous fingers deep inside her. She felt her mind slip and free itself to the rhythm of his touch.

The lashes suddenly stopped and his fingers pushed deep into her curling against her walls, writhing around and touching every inch of her.

She felt her walls tighten around him. His fingers pushed back all the harder. Her hips rocked forward, meeting the base of his fingers driving them deeper into her. "Please, please, please, please..." she whimpered.

"Not yet, Kitten."

The reply belied what his fingers administered to her. Pleasure coursed up her body from her core. "Oh, no, no... pleeeeeease...?"

A smack of the cane and the thumb pressed down on her clit, twirling it in a lazy circle. His fingers tortured her with circles of their own inside her, pushing up to the limit.

She twitched, writhed, and whimpered in such joyous torture.

He eased off the pressure of each finger and thumb as she neared her climax. "No, no, no, no... pleeeease?"

"Not yet. Patience, Kitten."

Then he was gone from inside her. *The lack of him was almost as startling as the flurry of quick sturdy strikes with the cane over her rigid form.*

Where there had been waves of torturous pleasure, now there lived only delicious pain. Calves. Thighs. Bottom. Soles of her feet. Sides. Inches from her sex.

It all roared to life with the sweet nectar of swift stinging pain.

Moments flew by in long wrenching hours. Her hips thrust forward repeatedly, jerking against her tethers.

Then it was all gone.

Silent absence.

She drifted about in the singing joy of the stinging pain as it swirled with the aftermath of the crashing against the struggle of not being allowed to come. She sucked in breaths and gasped them out.

A moment or two of swirling sensation. That was all it was.

He bit her left shoulder. She hadn't even heard his approach. She jerked against the device once more. He released her shoulder, kissed it.

Another long second of nothing. A shiver of excitement. Then he bit into her right side. She spasmed. *The part of her that he had bitten into was the same area that he teased with tickles until she frowned at him. Now, however, it was delightful agony.*

He released her again. *Another eternity of a second.*

He bit her left thigh just below her bottom. She cried out, "Oh!"

He released her again.

A tongue played over her right calf. He bit into her Achilles heel. Her hips beat against the waist belt.

He let go.

That hot tongue flicked along the sole of her left foot. He bit lightly into her foot at the arch and sucked her big toe into his mouth, holding it with his teeth.

"Come for me now, Kitten." The cane flicked up against her backside. He released her toe then was sucking on her clit and thrusting his fingers in and out of her sex. The fingers working all around and touching all of her.

She had been thrashing against each of her restraints. Each bite made her edge ever closer to the brink. *Now. Now, she had permission.*

She felt the dam explode and the warmth of his desire mingled with the vibrations of her keen need to make him happy. Her body lit on fire and swirled like water. Every inch of her thrummed with it. The spots he had bitten most of all. It wrapped her in booming, crashing waves. Her body was alight with fire.

It blasted out from her core and echoed from the bites, lashes, that thing his teeth and tongue were doing, and the eels he had for fingers. Goddesses! She whimpered over and over her thanks.

Finally, he let her slowly come back down from the maelstrom. She drifted for she knew not how long. His palm stroked and patted her bottom. The other hand's fingers slowly rubbed inside her.

29: Up is Down

Grace sighed in a happy bliss. Her body still spasmed and she subconsciously pulled on the restraints holding her firmly in place.

"Such a good girl. Now. On to the next part." His tone was still very much full of need. Need for her. The feel of it rolled over her skin and touched her all over. Gooseflesh sprouted and a shiver jolted down her spine.

She felt herself react once more to him as his growling voice rumbled, "I hope you did not think that was all I had planned."

"Huh? Oh, um, no, Sir. I didn't think... anything," she said, "It was lovely."

She heard a click from the machine and the rods that suspended her in the air seemed to loosen from their rigid state.

Then she fell.

Her feet swung up as her head swung downward, performing a sudden cartwheel. She screamed out in terror as her head rushed toward the unforgiving stone floor.

And just as suddenly, she stopped. The manacles bit into her skin holding her fast as she jerked in them. She continued to scream a moment or two longer.

She was upside down now, her legs still splayed wide. She could see his booted feet out of the corner of her eye.

"Delicious. I love to hear such honest emotions. But, I have you, little Witch. Now. The fun can begin anew," that same desire filled rumble caressed her ears.

She watched him step around and stop in front of her. His fingers teased her opening with a finger, then with something else. *What is that?*

She felt the soft yet firm object push down into her sex. It moved in and out of her an inch or two, drawing a low moan from her lips.

A low sound of flint and steel snicked overhead. She felt a small splash as something dropped onto her. *Oh and it burned.* She cried out in surprise, "Ah! What is that?"

"You tell me, Kitten. You are the one holding it." She could hear the slight laughter in his voice.

She felt the heated liquid quickly cool on her skin as it ran up her stomach. She shuddered and felt more droplets fall and splatter on her bottom, thighs, and again on her stomach.

Exquisite pain racked her body as each droplet made her shake and spill more onto herself. "Ah, ah, ah!" she cried out as more and more of the shockingly hot but not too hot liquid rolled down her skin and began cooling.

Seconds stretched as she tried in vain to still her movements. A drop fell and cooled along her breast, trailing its path toward her nipple.

She watched his boots turn to the side and she saw a new step of his plan swing into view. *On purpose, she was sure. A long crop. The long leather strap at the end he had used to tease her body with many times. The thin maple rod was overlaid with many thin leather braids.*

As the implement swung past her vision, reality and horror struck her.

Just before the crop did.

Snap! The leather thong snapped against her nipple. She jerked again.

Another trickle of hot liquid cascaded over her body. She shrieked out in a mix of delight and pain. Another jerk of her body at the sudden heat spilt even more.

The splash hit her inner thighs and splashed over her bottom and back. A few droplets fell onto her stomach and both breasts.

She was screaming now. *What delicious, evil pain.* She tried to still her body, but each infitessible movement of her body dribbled more hot wax onto her.

She watched the crop swing by. Another snap of the crop, aimed at her other nipple. And she was jerking and moving once more, pouring more from the candle to cool onto her.

Again her tormentor swung the switch past her vision. Only to have it snap against her backside, making her jerk once more in her bindings.

Splash.
Snap.

The seconds began to blend into a rhythm she could see. Seconds turned to minutes.

She was gasping for breath now. She had stopped screaming a few minutes ago. Her head was getting a bit fuzzy. She must have made an odd noise. She saw his eyes level with hers. Then he stood once more.

She felt the machine move again and the blood seemed to slowly make its way back to her extremities.

She felt his arms wrap around her and carry her over to the bed. She nuzzled up against his chest. His low rumble in his chest thrummed through her as his hands moved about her. She let out a light, heady giggle as she felt wax break off and fall free. She welcomed the darkness as it swallowed her as completely as his arms.

30: Payment

1097, Nicaea, Anatolia.

Allen wiped the sweat and blood from his face, looking about for the next threat. The heat was oppressive. His skin was dry and ravaged by the sand. The march from Italy after a long travel from Wessex by ship was almost as unwelcome as the screaming berserker Turks.

Allen spat out a chunk of bone and brain to the ground. The red glob splattered on the soil next to the Turkish fighter Allen had cleaved with his greatsword. The blade had been dulled by days of fighting, making the blow more of a crushing force than one of cutting. This had been the reason for an untimely taste in his mouth.

He worked a bone shard out of his cheek as he leapt forward to block another screamer's curved blade. He kicked the man in the left knee. The man crumpled in pain as his leg gave way. Allen pulled a dagger from his belt and drove it down into the man's eye. The man jerked as the blade bit into his brain, the hilt slamming against the eye socket.

Allen straightened and swept a slash at another foe that had encroached as he had finished the last man. They clashed metal for a few blows. The man staggered as the heavier greatsword drove into his saber. The man unslung a mace from his belt.

The man came forward, swinging both of his weapons in a reckless flurry of attacks. Allen stepped back, deflecting with the long blade of his weapon. Allen watched for an opening as the man continued his assault.

There. Allen pulled a throwing knife from his belt and whipped it forward toward the man, slapping the Turk's weapons to the side. The blade dug into his throat and the man fell to the side. Blood bubbles gurgled out of his mouth as he choked and drowned.

Dismissing him, Allen glanced about. The fighting was falling away from him. Pocket resistance was all that was left. Allen went about retrieving his weapons, wiping them off on the fallen soldiers' shirts or pants.

Allen sat in the shade of a porch watching the rest of the men pull women and children from their homes. The city gates had fallen after a siege.

Frightened faces looked about frantically as more and more of the innocents were pushed into the otherwise empty city square.

Monstrous. Allen kept his thoughts to himself but made no move to aid in pillaging the hovels or dragging the "heathens" from their homes.

He had tried to tell himself the gold was worth all of this but the thought twisted in his gut as he watched. A "crusader" kicked a woman in the back that was not moving fast enough with an armored boot.

Allen gritted his teeth as the woman fell, her son pulling her towards the mass of people huddled a short distance away. A knight on horseback watched from nearby. Most likely a nobleman.

The knight barked out a command from his seat. The crusaders drew their weapons, closing the circle about the frightened people. The killing that followed was by no means holy.

Minutes later, Allen was found in an alley by a patrol. He had retched up his lunch on the cobblestones. The patrol leader wanted to know where Allen had been. The heretics were not going to kill themselves.

Allen had flung himself at the man and been promptly beaten down and dragged off to be put in chains.

That night they had flogged him twenty-five times. He had lost count after the first dozen. He only knew the count because the Prince of Taranto had said loudly in front of everyone how many he had earned by denying God's will.

Allen woke in a pile of blood and mud. He was chained to the center pole of the tent. He could hardly see through his swollen eye and the blood running down from his brow.

What had woken him? He looked about the tent and saw very little. *Wait. Was that a pair of cat eyes?*

Green slitted eyes stared back at him steadily. He watched them. They were much too high up to be anything but that of a large predator.

A thickly accented voice rolled out softly from the darkness, "You did not find the butchery to your taste like so many of your people?" It was a woman's voice.

He tried to respond but his throat was parched and his lip was cut and swollen from the beating he had received.

"I have seen you, infidel. You are a terror with a blade. Many have been sent to see their god. Yet, you do not kill all you see. Why are you here? Does not your god desire our death?"

"I am not here for a holy war," Allen managed to croak out. "I have come to fight for money. Their crusade was an opportunity to feed our village." His throat ached and seized. He coughed and spat out a mouthful of blood.

"I see," the voice from the darkness, no, the large cat said. "You are a fighter then. You fight so that you may fight."

Long moments passed and Allen felt himself weaken as his blood pooled about him. His vision began to darken as a tall naked woman stepped out of the shadows of the tent. Her brown skin was tight around her, showing ripples of muscle beneath it. Long black hair cascaded down bare breasts, which swayed with her rounded hips as she strode towards him.

"Then you will be mine, infidel. Your payment for killing my husband and standing by as your people killed mine." Her mouth opened wide as she stepped over his prone form. She pushed away his feeble attempts to ward her off. She smiled a toothy grin at him.

He noticed they were all sharp as the evil smile got closer and closer. Then, mercifully, he lost consciousness.

Allen woke up once more. He felt much warmer than before and something was pulling at his member. He looked down to see the woman astride him. Her hips slammed down once more, sheathing him in her deep.

"Your gifts with weapons seem to be of great value. And it seems to extend to your manhood," she smiled her wicked grin at him once more. "Now, fill me with seed and we shall leave. We need to be going soon. Your wounds should be closed by now."

Allen realized he did not feel the pains from his back and he could see. He pulled his hands toward his face but found his chains were tighter now than they had been since he last fell asleep. But nothing was left of his aches and swelling. *And, gods, she was so tight about him.*

The swaying breasts and hammering of her down on his hips was bringing him closer and closer to the edge.

She smiled at his reaction. "Good. You like this body. Because you will be serving it for sometime. Now, give me your seed." She extended a claw to flick at his nipple. *Wait, claw?* He confirmed a long black claw extended from where her index finger should have been and it tapped at his nipple. She slid it down toward his navel, bringing his attention to where she slid him in and out of the pinkness half hidden by the hair there.

Her folds sucked at him as she pistoned up and down on his shaft. He felt her clench around him and she slammed down. She shuddered atop him, gyrating her hips as she drenched his loins with her juices. Her body squeezed and pulled at him and he quickly lost himself to the feel of it, spraying deep into her. She shuddered once more as he pumped more and more into her.

"Good. We shall leave now," she stood up swiftly. Their mingled juices dribbled down her long legs. She reached down and broke the shackles holding each of his limbs in place.

Much too strong. He sat up and watched her stride to the entrance. She glanced back at him and beckoned him to follow her. He stood up slower.

She dashed from the tent and he heard a startled cry go out. Then there were shouts echoing throughout the camp.

He followed. She had ripped off one man's arm and disemboweled another. The third man had been the one to let out the cry of alarm. But he was dead now, his throat had been slashed a moment too late.

She frowned as they watched the torches closing in, "We go, infidel." And they ran.

Naked and alone though the desert.

Allen stared at the cave wall. He could smell the arid air flowing down its length and hear the scattering of the scorpion in the corner. He could also smell the sleeping woman. She smelled of ... rich incense, dogwood, and lotus blossoms.

He felt strange. He had been on the edge of death and left to succumb to his wounds. Now, he felt he could swim the English Channel. He flexed his arm and watched the muscles ripple along it. *Odd.* He was unsure of what he should or could do next.

Going back to the village was not an option. He would be counted a traitor or coward, having left the army. Resting his elbows on his knees, he looked at the stranger.

She was lean and athletic. She had long, dark hair that seemed to shimmer in the shadows of the sunlight that bounced around the corner from the opening.

She was facing away from him as she slept. Her deep brown skin shifted as she breathed in slowly. He had no idea how she could sleep on the clammy rock floor. It was by no means smooth, yet she slept like the dead.

Her naked flesh glistened with a light sheen from the heat. *Who was this woman? And what did she want with him?*

He sighed as he wrestled with his mixed emotions. *He was a simple man. The blade was his life, since he had trained as a child. Now he had not even a scrap of clothes to cover himself, much less a sword.*

But the cold green eyes. He shuddered and went back to studying the wall.

\- - -

He must have dozed. The night had come and with it brought the chill of the desert. He could see his breath as the whistling breeze played along his bare skin.

He heard a padding of feet as someone neared him. He sat up and reached for his absent weapon, habit taking over.

She stood there, watching him. Her cold eyes bore into his soul, face placid. "Did you sleep well, infidel?" Her voice was playful and teasing.

He smirked back at her, "Well enough, I suppose."

"Mistress."

"What?"

"You will call me, Mistress. Your life is no longer your own. You will say 'yes, Mistress' or 'no, Mistress.' There is no other answer that is permitted," her dark eyes flashed green as she glared down at him.

"I think not. I will not be spoken to in this..." the rest of what he may have said was lost as she lunged forward and slapped him across the face.

"The words are yes or no, followed by Mistress. If you speak out of turn again I shall punish you once more," her smile was sinister. Allen could feel the danger lurking behind those eyes.

Yet he could not stop himself, "I shall do as I please." He caught the slap before it connected. Surprise registered on her face as he pulled her roughly forward and closed his hand around her throat. He pulled himself up and glared back down into her furious eyes. He also spat his next words, "You will not touch me in this manner again." He could feel something claw at the inside of his skin as his voice became a low growl, "I am the master of me and no other.

I am grateful for the aid you have lent
me. But you will not lay your hands
upon me. I shall not whimper and
cow to you." He bared his fangs as
his claw tightened.

Wait. He glanced down at his arms
and saw the fur there. He probed his
mouth and felt the teeth sharpened
to an array of stilettos.

She twisted in his grasp and stepped
away from him, breaking his hold
around her neck and wrist. She
studied him as she slowly circled
him.

He turned to keep her in front of him,
wary of more violence from the dark
skinned stranger.

"You are one with your beast already?
How is this possible?" The woman's
voice was suspicious and incredulous.
Her arms were held out to each side,

fingers splayed out and curled into claws. She stepped carefully. Her legs never crossed and her steps padded lightly on the balls of her feet.

"You know more than I do about this. How am I to answer questions I do not understand?"

Her eyes seemed to darken as she peered back at him in curiosity, "The beast within that I have given you. It takes most until the rebirth of the moon to draw upon its strength. Yet, you, a new cat, have had this gift for no longer than a day, if that, and draw it to you effortlessly and seemingly without thought or will to do so." Her brows furrowed as she studied his new form, "And you are not a black jaguar as am I, which bades the question asked, who are you that the beast is changed?"

He stared blankly at her as he turned her words over in his mind. Visions of nightmares of story playing over in his mind. Men that turned into foul beasts with the changing of the moon. Foul beasts that ripped and tore apart friends and family and strangers alike with reckless abandon. He rubbed his face and tried desperately to make sense of it all. *This woman had turned him into such a beast? He did not want death for being a "traitor to the will of God," but neither had he wanted such a fate as this.* He let out a ragged sigh as he dropped his hands and stared down at the stranger. Then glanced at his flesh noting that he had resumed his human form, again without realizing it.

"Who are you, infidel?" The woman asked in a soft whisper.

The next few months passed in a blur of faces and training. He learned the were-leopard woman who had rescued him was named Aylin. From what he could get out of her, she had lost her husband in the war of the Crusades and had gone into the wilderness to die only to see what had happened to Allen. She had thought about breaking him to her will after changing him.

She taught him some of the region's culture and what it meant to be a were. However, Aylin seemed to be cold and uneasy in his presence. Her discomfort was not enough that she would not talk to him or ply him for fornication, but he sensed there was some part of the first week that had unnerved her to the core.

He learned quickly all that she had to teach and was able to make her sweat when they had sparred. Then one day as he awoke to her cooking a rabbit, he found that she was watching him warily out of the corner of her eye. A spear with a barbed head that he had never seen before sat within easy reach of her hand as she flipped the cooking meat on the hot stone upon which it cooked.

"You must find your own path this day, Infidel Allen. You have learned all you can from me, mastered it, and have now surpassed my strength," she paused as she said this pointedly watching his face before she continued. "It is unheard of that one should surpass their Patron, much less in the span of such a short time. You are destined for something. This much I see." With that said, she lifted half the rabbit in one hand and scooped the spear up with the other. "Farewell, you that travels. May you find what you seek one day." Then she turned and left.

31: Demand

1923, New York, New York.

Darlene was done crying. She had mourned long enough for someone who really hadn't given a rat's ass about her. She pulled open her wardrobe and began to rifle through the numerous outfits. She pulled them out one by one and held them up to her. An hour passed as she finally decided on the blue dress. She set to dolling herself up. She was on the prowl.

The town car she had ordered for her came to a stop in front of Mister's with a clunk of the brakes. The large, tasty man Duncan Caan opened her door and lent her a hand out. She squeezed it and let herself be pulled out to the sidewalk. His big hands steadied her as her shoes clacked on the sidewalk, one still holding hers and the other resting on her waist. She looked up at the big man to thank him and was surprised to see outright lust billow in his eyes before he slid his professional mask into place. *Hmmmm,* she mused.

"Here to see the big cheese, Mrs. Johnson?" he asked in his rich deep voice. *She could listen to him read the daily rumble til the sun fell outta the sky.*

"Is he available, Mr. D? Seems my hubby was a sap, a pooper, and a red-hot grifter that got on the bad side of a rub-out, savvy?" Darlene whispered as she slipped her arm into Duncan's and waved off her driver. The car rolled away into traffic, horns blasting their annoyance at the driver.

"I had not heard all that. I don't believe I had heard of your husband's demise. Are you sure you are feeling copacetic?" he pulled the door open and they turned down the hall towards Mr. Wells office.

Her heart started hammering against her ribs as they neared it. "I am sure I'll be the cat's pajamas by the morning. Don't you fret over me, you big lounge lizard."

He squeezed her arm a little and rumbled, "As you say, Mrs. Johnson." He leaned forward to tap his big hand on the door.

"Enter," came the command from behind the large door.

Duncan spun the knob and poked his head in, "Mrs. Johnson to see you, Mr. Wells."

"Oh. I see. Get Mr. Blackburn to stand at your post and return. Come in, Mrs. Johnson, and I will put an order for some tea in."

Duncan opened the door wide for her and closed it softly after her. Mr. Wells loomed behind his desk, a pen poised in one hand as he pulled a tasseled rope to one side of his desk.

She felt herself twitch low and deep inside as his fingers curled and his forearm flexed with the motion. *Golly, she was such a chippy bim,* she thought to herself, trying not to drool. She noted her mouth had fallen open as she gaped at him and snapped it closed. She slid into the chair across from him as he stood.

He moved around the desk easily and sat back on the end. She felt her eyes drawn down towards his belt line and caught herself.

His smile was easy on his lips as her eyes met his. As if something occurred to him, the corner dropped on the left and he let out in soft consoling tones, "I heard your husband died. How are you holding up?" His dark eyes pierced deep into her soul as he waited for her response.

"As I mentioned earlier to Mr. D, I will be a sight better now. He was no good to anybody, least of all me. He was a scoundrel, cad, and crooked, if all the fuss is half true." The words came out biting and harsh, but he didn't seem to mind too awfully much.

"Be that as it may, Mrs. Johnson, you have my condolences, and support should you need it. We think very highly of you here. Please, do not hesitate to ask if a need arises."

"Thank you, Mr. Wells. That means quite a fair amount. I would be appalled if I had to move to a flophouse or run a gooseberry lay to make it through," she paused here, not sure how to proceed. *But her soul was wrung out; she needed to slip into that mindless euphoria he could offer.* "I actually have a request. If... if it isn't improper, I'd like to have a session tonight and melt off some of the hell this past week has been. That sounds awful. I only recently became widowed, but here I am throwing myself atcha like a moll that had a mickey finn..." she trailed off her eyes watery as she stared up into his dark eyes.

A flash of sorrow raced across his face, followed by possibly determination or resolve. "Mrs. Johnson, I would propose a counter offer. As much as I enjoy training and pleasuring you, I think you are ready for a full time Mister. Or possibly a full time Master. That would be between you and the dominant. And by that, I am going to refuse you. Not that I did not revel in the carnal pleasures with you, but that I think you have outgrown the fling that we have been having. And, as such, I would recommend finding another of the Misters here to quench your needs."

She felt crushed and dejected. She fought back the tears and thought about what he had said, pushing her libido and selfishness to the side. She dug into her feelings and thoughts on what he had said.

"Not to say you're wrong, Mr. Wells, but why? It seems sudden. And I haven't had any lovers other than yourself and my late husband. I feel a bit out of my depth here," she whispered.

"Well, there are a number of delicate issues that have sprung up that I cannot go into with you that require my careful attention. On top of all that, I have found myself with little to no time for more fun with those that I would like to. This is not fair to you and the other ladies who have been enjoying the dungeon. So, the other Misters are picking up the slack for me going forward. You have come a long way and little training by your new dominant for their taste and it will be a joy, I assure you. Which is why..." he broke off as Duncan slipped his large frame into the room.

Allen watched Duncan come to a poised position to his left. *The man was rigid and trembled slightly at his core. He knew something was happening but not what,* Allen could see. *Better ease his tension. Let things see themselves through. Mayhaps a good time for a gesture of goodwill for both of them.*

"As I was telling Mrs. Johnson, I will not be her dominant any longer. I would like for you two to see if you think your auras will mesh and as such I..." he broke off again as the tea service arrived, carted in by Jane, a tiger that worked the kitchen under Ms. Ricci. Her short hair was pinned back in a small bun and her uniform was immaculate, no creases or flour to be seen. He nodded to the left end table and she began unloading the tray. "As I was saying, I would like the two of you to have dinner in the VIP area. Mister's will pick up the bill. Ms. Janet, see to it that Ms. Grace is aware. Thank you." The brunette tiger bowed to him and left the room taking her tea trolley with her, now empty of the service. "You are welcome to use this room to talk about it. Enjoy the tea. I have a meeting with Mr. Russo," he bent over her hand as he pressed it lightly to his lips. "Again, Mrs. Johnson, you are welcome here any time. Do call on us again." With this, he strode from the room, waving to the two of them as they stared back at him dumbstruck.

Darlene's head swam with a whirlwind of emotion. Surprise, dejection, humiliation, intrigue, and desire. The final mix to the heady cocktail was added when she glanced over at Duncan to see a myriad of emotions warring across his usually stoic face.

She took a moment to catalog the flurry of twitches and barely contained emotions as he stared back at her. Lust was evident but she only caught glimpses of the others as he fought them. *Hmmm. Such a mystery. Maybe he needs this as much as I do. What to do?* She watched him a moment longer before she made a snap decision. *Allen had always called her a brat, but he had smiled when he said it. Maybe Mistah D would like a brat as well.* She hopped up onto her feet and moved over to the end table. She leaned over and gave him a fair look at her rump as she set to making two cups of tea.

"Mistah D? Wouldya like a bit of sugar? In your tea that is," she called out in a sing-song manner as she peered over her arched back at him. The corset she was wearing under her dress digging into her sides.

He stared at her for a moment, his eyes flitting from her backside to her face half hidden by her shoulder and hair. He clenched and unclenched his hands. Then she saw the control drop over him, "No sugar, Mrs. Darlene. I think you will be sweet enough for my tastes." He sat down in one of the chairs and awaited her.

She giggled to herself. *This was going to be fun.*

Duncan watched as she sashayed back to where he sat, a cup on a saucer in each hand. *He was going to enjoy making that face turn from a smile to a slack-jaw, whimpering mess.*

Grace walked towards Allen's public office. She heard the feminine giggles and a soft rumble of chuckles. She smirked. *Seems they are getting along.* She knocked once before opening the door slightly. Duncan was leaning towards Darlene. She was red faced and out of breath. *Oh my. Maybe she interrupted something.* She cleared her throat and said clearly, "Mr. Caan, your table is ready for you. Ms. Janet will take you to it when you are ready."

"Thank you, Ms. Grace. We will be right out," he replied with a knowing smile. She returned it and gave a half bow. She closed the door behind her. Immediately, there was a gasp and more giggles.

32: Acceptance

1913, Suszyca Mountain near Bolesławów, Poland.

Shadows and blood. That is all he could remember for the last several years. He had spent more time in fur than as a man. The other wolves fled him if they caught his scent, but if he managed to come across them they would snarl as they backed slowly away.

He was jealous of their simple nature.

He brooded as he watched the villagers move about their daily lives, greeting each other with waves and smiles. He bristled at the sight of what had been stolen from him without his permission. Just the thought of Jacobi's toothy grin made him furrow the ground with his nails. He had been wronged and robbed of a life he had wanted since he was a small boy. Not that he had been small for long. He had always stood head and shoulders over his classmates in primary school.

Now... Now, he had no control of his life. If only he could go back and say no. But if wishes were fishes, he would never be hungry.

Thinking about fish made his stomach rumble to remind him it had been several hours since he fed himself.

Grunting, he pushed himself up to all fours. He was a large wolf, four meters long, nose to rump. He shook the leaves and dirt free of his coat it had collected during his stay and trotted off in search of a królik. *The chase usually was good and would break his mood.* He hoped.

He had caught five when he was done with the chase. His mood had brightened to a degree, but he felt unseen eyes on him. He cracked the leg bone of the last prey with his large teeth and sucked the marrow free.

A twig broke to his left and his hackles shot up as he rolled his eyes to peer that way. A bearded man stood a half pace away. He drew in a deep breath and smelt no fear in the air. *Odd.*

The man glanced over his shoulder and said something to someone behind him. Not a villager, the words the man spoke were not of a language he knew.

The idea that a man was so close, without his scent reaching his snout, troubled him. His hackles rose and he snapped the bone in his maw viciously. The man slowly turned his head back to lock eyes with him.

But, still fear was not in his manner or demeanor. There was something else...

Duncan jumped up onto his paws, bared his teeth, and let out a fierce challenge. The man showed him his palms. Gloved fingers spread wide and extended outwards as the man spread his arms in a placating gesture. A woman's voice, unintelligible, came from behind the man. The man answered in the same clipped language.

Duncan snorted and spread his lips wider to allow his teeth to gleam in the sun he had been enjoying until these interlopers had arrived.

The man smiled an unfriendly smile and Duncan felt a pressure press against his beast. Pain wracked through him as he shifted back to a man. Darkness swam over his eyes to claim him.

Duncan woke to the crackle of a fire. He remained motionless as he took stock of his surroundings. A blanket was draped over him where he laid on another. A pillow of sorts was propped under his head.

There was a sweet smell of a woman drifting to him from his covering and pillow. Intrigued, he pulled in deeper on the scent but his beast slept on inside him.

The man's voice called, "I can tell you are awake. Care to join us, young man?" There was no malice in the voice; however, it brokered no choice either. It had the taste of a command.

Duncan swept his eyes about him as he sat up. To his left was a tall brown-haired woman with her hair tied back in a braid. A sword of all things rested against the log she sat on. A metal plate sat in her lap, balanced easily. She was dressed in hunter's garb and had a blue bandana holding the braid in place. A curl bounced with the breeze over her bright blue hazel eyes. She had a placid yet ready look to her face and the set of her body.

To her left was a shorter blond haired woman in a green bandana. Though hers hid more of the short, golden locks and kept them neatly tucked out of her face. She also was dressed for the wilds, but with more green cloth than the brunette's brown leather. She had one hand up holding a green globe that shimmered and danced as she stared down into it as it hovered over a quartz, an amethyst, and an emerald on her palm. Her eyes flicked up to his and she let out a quick smile before dropping them back to the ball.

To her left and his right sat the man from before. He wore a green linen shirt with a green dyed leather vest and long brown woolen pants. He was armed with two long hunting knives sheathed at either hip. His forearms leaned against his knees as he waited for Duncan to complete his assessment.

A small fire crackled in a pit that had been well dug and lined with rocks to prevent the fire from escaping. A spit held a skewered królik that sizzled and dribbled grease with the licking flames.

His stomach rumbled again. He grimaced. The man pulled a knife free, lopped a leg from the roasting animal, and tossed it to him. Duncan caught it easily.

He mumbled his thanks and bit into it. Spices and juices flooded his mouth as he tore at it with his teeth. His eyes momentarily closed as he swallowed. He slammed them open as he realized his lack of caution. He saw none had moved save the man who was wiping the grease off of the knife with a cloth.

Duncan waited a bit more, then he set to devouring the leg.

The brunette seemed to take his appetite as lack of aggression as she dismissed him and continued her own meal.

The blond asked the man something in that unknown language he had spoken before. The man nodded and she seemed to relax. The green orb disappeared and she put the crystal and gems into a pouch on her belt.

The strangers ate in companionable silence as did he. The man seemed to be watching him without looking in his direction however. That unnerved Duncan. His beast remained subdued and did not stir when he touched it. It was for the first time since he was turned by Jacobi's trick that he was free.

Finally, his hunger abated, he looked up from his meal of meat and roasted potatoes. The rest of the group had long since finished. Their stomachs had not been black holes of hunger.

"Thank you for the meal. Now, who are you and what do you want from me?" Duncan questioned them.

He could see a blank look on the man's face. He looked over to the blond woman, saying something in the unknown language. She dipped her into her pouch, pulled free the shards of stones, and mumbled something. The green orb bloomed over her palm, her fingers splayed in a nova.

The man nodded and turned his bearded face back to him, "My apologies, friend. We do not speak your tongue and are using the power of Gaia to bridge that barrier. My name is Allen. My two friends are Grace and Helena. I took from your expression you wanted to know who we are and what we want. You look like a man long since removed from society and friendship. No doubt due to your beast trapped inside your soul. We offer a place to call home. A place to belong. You do not have to take our word for it. You feel my beast holding yours at bay. Reach inside and touch it."

Duncan felt his wolf stretch and yawn with a lolling of the tongue and flex of muscle. He felt its eyes meet his and the humor in them made him chuckle aloud.

Then he saw the paw that held the large black wolf in place. It shifted between a large cat and a wolf. Then the flickering paw came away and he felt the control flood back into his body.

"That is the gift I offer. Control of both selves," the man named Allen stated calmly.

Duncan flexed, feeling the roll of the power rolling through his body and limbs. "Very well. At what cost?" he looked at the man.

Allen waved the question away, "There is no cost. I give this freely to those in need. I have found there are many of us Moontouched across this small world of ours. And I would hope to help all I can, that would take the gift. Would you join me in this?"

Duncan rolled that over as he watched him. He pulled the scents of the group in through his nose.

The man was one of the moon, though he smelled of more. The two women were not, however. His eyes roved over them. The brunette's steely eyes bored into him. The blond wasn't watching him, instead peered into her green, flickering sphere.

"Very well," he conceded, "Where do we start?"

"First, we will need to speak a common tongue. Then, we will find like-minded people."

Reserved hopefulness bloomed in his chest. It throbbed against his ribs, threatening to crush his heart. His wolf whined softly as the hope wrapped its tendrils into him. He gritted his teeth, pushing against the longing. "And then?" he let out with a soft growl.

"Help them. Teach them to control themselves, if needed. Give them whatever aid they need that is within our power."

Duncan let that settle in his mind and soul, "Let us begin. Your task seems noble, if not somewhat ludicrous."

33: Coy Conversation

1923, New York, New York.

Sitting in the darkened alcove of the VIP, Duncan watched as Darlene savored the meal. *Miss Ricci had outdone herself.* They had both had to wipe their mouths at the smells when Jack had brought their meal, which had been a tray covered in oysters cooked every which way.

Oysters Rockefeller, spinach and onion baked to perfection with just enough lime spritz to make the dish sing.

Another dish held the oysters boiled in a rich garlic sauce topped with fresh ground romano cheese.

Another was an oyster stew, creamy with various herbs and seven different cheeses mixed with salty potatoes.

Another was blackened oysters with a tangy pepper and lemon marinara sauce to dip them in.

Another was deep fried oysters wrapped in bacon and breaded with another side of garlic butter.

There were more, however he hadn't had room for them, having stuffed himself comfortably full.

He watched as Darlene reached over for an oyster on the half shell and raised it to her mouth. She had a teasing smile on her face as she flicked her tongue out to jostle the muscle in its resting place. He felt himself flex against his slacks, rigid and aching.

He coughed unnecessarily into his hand and leaned forward, "You keep that up you might find yourself only able to get that much meat later."

She blushed prettily and licked her lips. She broke the shellfish from the shell and slurped it down, covering her mouth with a napkin as she chewed. *She was exuding pheromones and desire from every pore.*

He swallowed his need down and steepled his dark fingers, resting his elbows on the armrests. He asked slowly, "You know the Rules as you've played before, Mrs. Darlene. Do you have any hard limits I should know about before we go downstairs and begin?"

Darlene seemed to ponder that as she swallowed, her dainty neck jumping as the meat slid down her neck. *This woman was making him lose his mind.* She dabbed at her lips before she replied, "Nothing with blood or bathroom play. Don't mind the threat of blood, Mistah D. But actual blood, no thank you. Other than that, I don't think there is. And if I get uncomfortable, I will just call Red and we can discuss it. I don't care for degrading names either. Sorta reminds me of that lowlife I was married to. So, I'd like that to be a softish hard limit, at least, until you and I are peachy keen." With this last part, she winked coyly at him.

"All of that is within reason and amenable. Would you like dessert before we retire for the evening?" he managed not to say without growling or cracking. He smoothed out a wrinkle as he held her eyes.

She blushed prettily as she replied, "No, thank you, Sir. This has been a treat, but I'd rather have something else between my lips."

He did let out a soft growl at this. *Gods, he was going to really have to do something about her brattish nature. He didn't know how Allen had dealt with her. But, now she was his and her training could truly begin.*

34: Ache

Giulia was tired of the ache of her muscles. Not that it was a bad ache, she just felt hollow. Training had been vigorous and thorough. And Mr. Garrison was relentless, barely letting her catch her breath before launching another barrage of attacks at her until she was slammed on her back on the ring again. Over and over again, just as she thought she was getting faster, he would do something she hadn't expected and the leather mat would crash into her backside or head.

After each session he would take her through each of the moves or attacks at human speed and show her how to counter them. Then, once he was sure she understood, they reset and go again. And she would kiss leather. Over and over, the cycle repeated.

Then, after the day turned to dusk, there was a nap-sized helping of food, which they both devoured. She would take a cab back to her apartment in the Roosevelt hotel and sleep until dawn.

But the empty hole in her soul gnawed at her. She had caught glimpses of him, as he met with the other Misters. She kept having to wipe at her mouth to keep from drooling.

The casual power, his dark knowing eyes, his lean muscle wrapped in silk and cottons, and the intellectual mind that she had witnessed in that meeting made her ache for him. He seemed to not even notice her, while talking to her teacher.

She felt foolish for it, but she wished he would take her into the ring, slam her onto her back and press her down into the leather as he had his way with her.

She thrummed with need as the thought of him driving his length into her wet slit, pounding his hips against hers until she was screaming as he filled her with his seed. She panted as she rode the feather pillow. She gasped as she climaxed and fell over into her blankets, sucking in breaths. *Why did the most desirable man since Binidittu have to be taken? What had she done in her past life to deserve this?* She thought about an encounter from earlier today. She had been leaving to take a shower when she turned to see his two women stroke his arm and back as she passed. The blond had given her a dark look as she curled her body around his arm.

She sighed up at the ceiling and closed her eyes. At least, it was Sunday and she could work with Matteo tomorrow morning on numbers and planning for the family. Not that he needed the help, but they had been good at spotting something each other had missed.

"Benny, I miss you," she whispered. A moment passed and she drifted off to sleep.

35: Dismissed Doubt

Darlene felt her heart racing as she undressed. Duncan had deep blue eyes that bored into her soul as her dress fell to the ground. She glanced down at his crotch to see a straining seam at the front of his slacks. *Mmmmm,* she smiled to herself, pleased with the reaction.

She had always been a tad self conscious about her body. She was plumper than the social beauty standards, but not unhealthy so. Occasionally, at the Policeman's Ball, she would catch snippets from the other wives. *It was never flattering.*

But she had been a good wife, until the day that Georgie had come home breaking of sweat, sex, and booze. And when she had asked him about it, he had hit her. Repeatedly. The shiner had been a bother to hide. She had been lucky to have turned her head just enough that it hadn't done more damage.

She couldn't remember how she had found out about this place. But it had become her refuge and safe haven. *Odd*, she thought, *the place I come to get my backside tanned is my safest place.* She rolled that over in her heart as she slid the straps of her red lace bra down her arms. Mistah D followed her hands with his eyes.

She shivered with anticipation. His gaze was drinking in every inch of her. She dropped it to the side then traced her hands down her corset to her waist, her pale fingers slid down the red leather corset under her red lace panties. She eased each side down alternately, tugging and pulling them slowly down her hips. She turned around and peered at him over her right shoulder as she pushed them down over her rump. The chilled air kissed her backside as it popped free of the mostly sheer fabric. She leaned over dramatically as she pushed them down her black hose covered legs, exposing her most private places to him.

He let out a grunt as she arched herself back to standing, pushing her chest out letting the swell of her breasts bounce against the top of the leather around her torso. She tugged at the garter belt, fitting it better around her, then she let it snap back against her flesh.

Duncan was going to burst. This woman had him straining at his slacks and he hadn't even touched her yet.

He had watched her slip off her clothes with the allure of a spider dancing along a web. He needed to show her how much he had enjoyed it. "Come over here," he let out with a hint of his beast in the tone of his voice, a low rumble of a growl. She did as he bade her. "Kneel," he commanded. He slid a pillow under her as she dropped to her knees.

"Service me," came the next command. She smiled as she unbuckled his belt and pulled it free of his pants, tossing atop her own clothes.

She unbuttoned his slacks and the bulge of himself pushed his undergarments out of his pants. She let out a whimper as she squirmed on her knees, pulled down the linens, and wrapped a dainty hand around his girth. She licked her lips as she leaned forward and flicked her tongue against his purple head.

Her mouth sucked him in and down into her throat. Her eyes met his as he felt her tongue swirled around him, slickening the length of his member. Her eyes were alight with desire and he could smell her sex thicken the air with her scent. She was wet with her need.

She slid her mouth up and down his length forcing as much of him into her as would fit, gorging him down. She cupped his balls and pressed them under his shaft towards her. She stuck out her tongue and licked them as she moved her head back and forth. She held them there as she bobbed back up and down, fitting a half inch more into her throat. Her tongue lapped at his shaft and balls, her eyes half closed in pleasure.

"Gods," he murmured as he felt his first twitch, then he emptied himself down her throat in heavy spurts. He grabbed onto the chair as her eyes widened and she quickened her pace. More and more of him shot down her throat and she swallowed hurriedly.

He finally finished and she slowed, sucking and lapping at his rod. The slow pace she worked his manhood had him hard and ready for more in mere moments.

"Good girl, Mrs. Darlene. Turn around and show me how wet that made you," he demanded.

She blushed and eased him slowly out of her bright red lipstick covered mouth. He could see that she was leaving streaks of it on his hardness. She spun on her knees and leaned forward, placing palms to elbows on the stone floor. She placed her endowed breasts and forehead a moment later, and arched her back.

"Good girl. Now, spread your legs so I can look at you."

She let out a soft, "Yes, sir, Mistah D." And she slid her knees apart. Her petals glistened and dripped with her desire. A strand of clear wetness dripped slowly to the floor as he watched.

"I am going to have my way with you now. You may come when you want, but I am not going to stop until I come, or if for some reason you need to call Red. Understand?"

"Oh, God, yes, sir, Mistah D," she moaned.

He stood up and dropped the slacks and linen underwear to the ground. He stepped one leg over her, grabbed his shaft, and pushed the head of himself into her wet slit. She let out a sex drunk moan as he advanced deeper into her channel. Her body tightened around him as he invaded her inch by inch. She shuddered as he got halfway and her moans became cries of orgasm. He withdrew half of the hardness and drove it in and out of her. She bucked against him as she screamed out her pleasure.

He kept his stride, three inches in and out. He felt her clamp around him halting his momentum. She shook from head to toe, back arching up and down, as she came repeatedly.

He gave her a moment to calm down then forced the entire length of his member into her slickness until he was pressing his hips against her bottom. She gyrated as he split her, shaking with the effort of keeping still as another wave of climaxes buffeted her.

"Now, Mrs. Darlene, I am going to get started. What is your safe word?" he asked.

"My - my safe word is Red, Mistah D!" she cried, as she squirmed.

"Good girl." He withdrew and began to pummel her, taking pleasure in the moans, gasps and whimpers from her mouth as he felt her pulsate around him. He pulled free an inch and drove it into her, leaning on the beast that watched within him to give him more speed. The slap of his flesh on hers was delicious.

He grabbed a handful of her hair and her hips. He lengthened his withdrawal and continued slamming it into her.

Oh, my God, he was so deep! And his pace was ripping her breath away. She barely had time to gasp in pleasure from the fullness of her sex before he withdrew and slammed his juicy meat back into her. She screamed again and again as she vibrated with the repeated waves of building and roiling pleasure. She thought her heart might just explode as her next orgasm began before the last one stopped.

"Yeeeeeeeeeeeeeeeeeessssssssssssss!" she screamed at the top of her lungs into the dark room. The word shaking and drawn out by the force of her climax. She savored the feel of him stretching against her inner walls, the pull of him against her lower lips, the veins along the length rubbing deep inside her, the feel of his tip drawing lines along her, the feel of his hand pulling on her hair, the other holding her in place firmly, and the slap of his balls against her clitoris. Divine! "Oh, my God, Mistah D! Oh, my God!"

Then she felt him twitch and fill her with a warmth she couldn't describe. Her entire body exploded and sang with repeated shakes of climax. She felt the drool dribble down from her mouth over her chin and to her cleavage. Her eyes rolled back in her head and she fainted.

Panicked, Duncan checked her for a pulse. Quickly, finding one he scooped up his sub and carried her over to the couch. He cradled her to him as he watched her drool in her sleep. He let out a contented sigh and let himself relax for the first time in a very long time.

36: Assessment

Jim had never been big on pack politics. Being that he was third meant he had to play his part as enforcer or deal out some humility to a Moontouched that wanted to challenge for Duncan's place of second.

This had been the main outlet for his destructive nature. He thoroughly enjoyed hitting people. The need to hear whimpers and grind of bone under his knuckles called to his beast.

He was different from the other bears he had met. William, the only other one in the pack, was the most carefree individual he had known and extremely slow to anger.

But Jim's Kodiak sent him into a tizzy if he hadn't pasted a palooka with his mitts longer than a week. Which, until recently, had forced him to seek out trouble.

Now, he was training the wop woman. And while she was a quick learner and sharp as a tack, he was really getting enjoyment out of slamming her into the mat and making her cry out.

The fact that the dish carried a torch for the Big Shot was obvious. She went jingle-headed anytime he was nearby. If they were in the middle of a match when this happened he would ramp up his speed and give her a reason to not be so dangled.

She wasn't a chippy. He could tell she was smart, ruthless, and keen, if he was honest. But she was gunning to sit at his table.

Jim found himself at Allen's office door. He hesitated before rapping his knuckles.

"Enter."

Jim pushed the door in and slumped into one of the chairs. Allen seemed to only briefly acknowledge him before continuing to work on paperwork.

"Problem, James?" Allen asked.

"No, sir. Just complications I wanted to talk to you about," Jim replied, his gravelly voice grinding the words.

"I see. What is on your mind?" Allen said as he set a sheet of paper to the side and switched his attention fully to Jim.

"You know the De Luca woman is infatuated with you, right?"

"Her attention has been noted, yes."

"Then either you need to address that or stay away during training. Her attention to you will find her in trouble if she has to defend you in a battle. It has earned her extra lumps already on her pretty head."

"Very well. I suppose I will send a runner next time you are needed. As to her intentions towards me, I have enough and more women on my plate. Ah, that reminds me. I have a need to divert my clients to you and the rest of the Misters, as many as you can stand," Allen steepled his fingers as he leaned forward and looked Jim deep in the eyes, "There is going to be a conflict and I want to make sure we survive it. I will need the hours that would have been spent on such delicious frivolities." Allen thumbed through a stack of paper and pulled a small folder free, "Look through these. Theodore has prepared them in quite a fair amount of detail. Talk with the others and see which ones will fit into your lives."

"Yes, sir. I would like to reiterate that I think you are putting off the inevitable. She has the mindset of a feral wolf. She is locked on you, stalking you when you appear to not notice," Jim chuckled. "Then Ms. Grace sees her and gives her a proper glare."

The two men chuckled over that. Allen shrugged back at him.

"You are probably correct in your assessment, but it will be when my two Lovelies are ready. Another reason for the divergence of my submissives."

Jim tucked the folder under his arm as he stood and waved at Allen. "Best of luck then, boss."

With that he left to sort through the file. *Maybe, he could get Ted to go over it with him. Speaking of, he couldn't remember seeing the man today.*

37: Winter and Wings

1923, A Place Somewhere.

Mac Sgiath Òir stacked the last ten coins next
to the others. *His horde had gotten quite large
over the last few millennia. Helping that elf
and his wife beat his yellow cousin really had
been the best decision.*

A chime echoed in his demiplane. He turned
his scaled head at the shimmering looking
glass in the corner. A white hue coalesced
along the ornate metallic frame. He stalked
over to see what the Winter Witch wanted,
dropping into the frail human guise.

He touched a hand to the runes and her pale
form came into view. "Beannachdan dhut,
Seann Òr," she said in her beautiful sing-song
melody of a voice.

"Good morrow, Winter's Mistress. What a
sight you are," he responded carefully. *The fae
were great manipulators of the spoken words.
You had to be sure never to show gratitude or*

hint that they had done you a kindness to keep yourself from owing them a debt. He had danced this game before with her, but to call upon him now seemed unfortunate timing.

The white haired fae frowned slightly. "My apologies if this is a poor time. The Winter Court is arriving on the New World for a visit and I wanted to give the Wanderer and his people fair warning. Five favors is more than enough to owe the man. Though I am coming with a small retinue, I would like my Servant back while we are in his territory."

"I shall talk to Him for you. I am sure we will be happy to entertain should you desire."

"No, that will not be necessary, though I would like to introduce him to my niece. It would be delightful to see what his women do. Mayhaps, Dae will let me steal her away from his Castle in the Green. I am rambling. We should arrive by the end of the fortnight."

"That is two days," Òir managed to contain his annoyance at the Queen. *She was playing a joke. He was certain Mr. Wells would not be amused.*

"Ah, so it is. Until then, Golden Wing," she winked as the spelled mirror shifted to show his thin form with blazing golden eyes.

"Thrice-damned me," Ted groused at his reflection.

38: Surprise

1923, New York, New York.

Grace slowly pushed herself to wakefulness. She remembered Allen had said something about a surprise for her, but they had just climbed into bed after he had allowed her orgasm.

She began to stretch and found she couldn't move. Blinking her eyes she found she couldn't see either.

She took stock of herself. A hood was over her head but her mouth was not covered. However, it was full with a device holding her mouth open and something else held her tongue.

Her arms were behind her and her elbows were bound together, as well as her wrists. She felt ropes against her waist and shoulders.

She believed herself to be suspended from the tug at the ropes and slight sway in herself.

She pulled on her legs and found no give in the restraints about her ankles, calves, and thighs. Her legs were open wide and she was certain she was fairly exposed. A blush crept over her face at the thought of that.

As she pulled at her various bindings a tug on her nipples let her know there was a reasonable amount of weight hanging from the piercings that Allen had insisted on her getting through them a month ago.

She felt callous fingers tap the inside of her thighs.

"Good morning, little Kitten. Do you like the surprise?" His deep rumble of a voice came from the right side of her head.

She tried to respond but with her mouth held open and tongue held in place, she was unable. All she could do was grunt and huff.

"No? Such a shame. I guess I will have to get my thanks from Helena while you listen."

She flexed and let out a garbled response but the sounds of slurping came to her from where he was. *Damnit!* she thought as she bucked against the restraints. The other woman moaned out loud, her mouth sounding quite full.

"Very good, Angel. But I think she is ready for me to use her now." She heard the pop of him pulling free of Helena's mouth, then her tongue was free. Without warning her mouth was suddenly full of him. A hand wrapped around her hooded hair and forced him deep into her mouth.

A tongue lashed against her taut nipples as he drove his member deep into her mouth and out again, swinging her on her bonds. Drool dribbled free from her mouth as he used it. The head of him ran along the roof of her mouth to crash against her throat. She lashed out at it with her tongue and tried desperately to touch all of him with it.

"Good girl. I think I will come down your throat first," he continued to thrust into her mouth. Then she felt the first twitch of his member and he filled her mouth with his thick seed. More and more of it shot into her mouth and down her throat as he held her down over it.

"Clean it up. I will have Helena check your work."
She hurriedly swallowed him down and licked at him
the best she could.

He pulled himself free and she swung in the
restraints. She gasped for air, as drool and remnants
of him ran out over her lips. She heard him click his
tongue, "Such a messy girl. Clean her up, Helena. I
will get something to punish the girl who can't
swallow all her food."

The lashing at her nipples stopped and the other
woman kissed her way up her body to her face.
Helena began licking at her and murmuring delight,
"You taste so good, Kitten. And it's twice as good
with the Master's seed on you as icing."

A hand came down on her bottom hard. "If she isn't
clean enough by now, I will have two naughty girls to
punish. Let's have a look now, shall we?" A hand
curled into her hair and roughly dragged her higher.
Helena dropped away as she rose. She gasped at the
suddenness of her head being yanked upward
around the device holding her teeth apart.

"Hmmm. You missed some on her neck, Helena. Bend over. We will finish your punishment then I can concentrate on the messy girl." Her head eased down as he relieved the pressure on her hair and let go of it. She heard the slap of leather on flesh, a dutiful count from Helena followed by the four repetitions of the same. She felt the quiver of excitement run down her spine and sudden slickness of her drip from her channel.

"Good girl." She heard him walk alongside her down to her bare bottom. A finger trailed up through her folds, "The thought of the strap has you excited, doesn't it, messy girl?"

Knowing her mouth could make no sound, she bobbed her head and squirmed in her bindings. She let out an "aahaa" just to be safe.

"Maybe I should tickle you instead. If the strap is going to be a pleasure, it wouldn't be that much of a punishment, now would it?"

She let out a squawk of displeasure and disagreement. She thrashed and felt herself swing slowly in a rotating half circle.

"No?" he let out a half chuckle and teased a finger down her waist. "Very well. Firm spankings it is then." The blow came suddenly.

"One, Sir!" she tried to say. The second blow came as quickly and surprisingly.

Punishment in a hood deprived her of seeing his backswing and the fall of his arm.

"Two, Sir!" she tried again.

The next blow crashed into her.

"Three, Sir!" she screamed around the device in her mouth.

The next blow came down as she finished her last call.

"Four, Sir!" she gasped.

The last blow came down and it was all she could do to call out, "Five, Sir!"

"Mmm, good girl. I have such delightfully good girls." She heard him move again. A warm pressure pressed against her opening then he was inside her and rigid as stone.

She felt him pull on her arms as he pumped his firmness deep into her and filled her.

Repeatedly he pummeled her as she sucked in air. A wet tongue lapped at her clit as he drove himself in and out of her, head to hilt. His hips slapped against hers, Helena sucking and licking at her.

"Come for me, Kitten. I'm going to fill your womb and you are going to milk me with your wet slit."

"Aahaa," she tried and the dam broke, pouring free of her as he emptied spurt after spurt into her.

"Mm. Good girl," she heard him say as he stroked her bottom. She felt their fluids dribble free only to be lapped up by Helena's eager tongue.

39: Lesson

1654, wilds of Virginia.

Allen watched the stag graze on the grass. He had been stalking it for the better part of the day. Slowly, he placed a paw forward as he inched towards his prey, keeping his body low.

He inched towards it. Closer and closer. He began to bunch up his muscles as the stag raised its head. Its eyes were wide open with fear as it looked away from him up the hill. Upwind. The smell of a dog hit him a moment later. *No, not a dog, a wolf.*

The reality of it hit him as the stag shot away from him. He let out a snarl of rage as the pack burst free of the neighboring underbrush and began to give chase to the spooked deer.

Allen hunched down as his stomach rumbled. He agreed with the growl. This was the third time this week the pack had ruined his hunt. He had been forced to eat an entire family of squirrels due to their sloppy habits.

That tears it, he thought to himself. He stood up and stalked forward. His claws extended and raked at the lush grass as he neared where the five wolves dined on what should have been his kill.

The largest of the wolves noticed him and turned, pulling its lips back in a menacing manner, canines red with the stag's blood. The rest of the pack noticed him, and leaped up to stand with their leader.

He dropped his mouth open and drew their scent over the glands in his mouth. Pops. The eldest and largest was perhaps five years old. He huffed his aggravation. *Where was the leader of their pack? Surely, these youngsters were not the entirety of it. Unless this was a new pack rising.*

The leader, seeing him not make aggressive movements, appeared to grow bolder, letting out a series of growls and barks.

Allen, unperturbed, raised a paw and flexed his claws. The one inch razors popped free and he slashed the wolf's nose. The wolf let out a yelp then snapped his jaws closed a moment after Allen pulled his striped paw back out of range. Allen snarled at the alpha pup, retracted his claws, and popped him once more on the nose. Blood dribbled down into grass as the pup's head rocked back with the blow to his snout.

The rest of the pack charged up to the flank, and Allen caught the rest of their scents clearly. Two males and three females, one with a litter on the way, teats distended with the belly. He leaped backwards as they crashed into each other.

There was something else in their scent. *What was that?* He batted another lunge into the turf as he slipped easily to the side. *Human under wolf scent?* Slowly, it all seemed to fit.

He slid a quarter of the way back to his human form as the beta male made a leap for his left side. He punched the beast in the temple and it fell unconscious on the grass bed. In short order he had knocked the alpha down beside him as well. He eased back as the three females protected their fallen, who were now slipping back to their human forms, with noisy pops and grunts of pain.

A pack of young weres, not wolves. Probably a group of settlers that had gotten ambushed by an elder were. The young men that lay snoring in the heather seemed to be young but man grown.

Allen sat back and licked his claws clean. The wolves watched him teeth bared. He chuffed a dismissal then turned to go.

The alpha female charged at him as he turned his back to them. He slipped to half form and caught her mid leap and tossed her back to her pack.

They considered the standing cat, peering down at them, flexing his claws. He growled a challenge but none of them replied. His stomach echoed his anger.

He stepped wide about them to the bleeding carcass and ripped a leg free. He dared them to stop him with his dark eyes. They watched him from their defensive stances over the males.

He slid to full human and walked away into the woods. He waved a hand over his shoulder as he pushed through the brush.

40: Annoyance

1923, New York, New York.

Allen watched Grace fume as she sipped slowly from the black tea. Helena twirled through sword forms with her two blacksteel shortswords twenty paces away.

"Sir, why is she coming here; did she say?" Grace asked her voice cool belying the anger he saw reflected by the landscape around them. He knew how close this haven tied into her being. The wind would dance through the leaves when she was amused. The rain would pour if she was upset. Sunbeams would dance through the clouds if her joy was complete. The brisk breeze nipping at his skin, tempting him to change, was evident of her cold rage. "First, the De Luca wolf, now this. What is next, Sir? Your Matron is going to come and try to steal you, too?"

"We both know that I am not a thing that can be 'stolen,' but I catch the meaning. I am going nowhere. Why she would tempt our patience is beyond me."

Grace knit her eyebrows together, rolling the conversations around trying to find the angle that seemed to be evading her. She let out a heavy breath. "I suppose we should just be on our guard and do our best to not give any ground. I will follow your lead, Sir."

"As will I, Master," came from Helena, as she ended a complicated swirl of her weapons, her dark hair cascading in a fan along her taunt back.

He nodded, "Very well. See to it the staff is aware of our incoming guests. None are to speak to any of Her entourage. I don't want any of our people 'borrowed' by any of Her creatures." With that he stood and held out his hands. Grace took one in hers and Helena, rushing over in a sprint, took the other. He reveled in the difference of their texture and raised them both to his lips. He kissed each. His eyes and soul promised much more, as his eyes met their eyes. They both shuddered and watched his back as he left for the portal.

41: Torture

Pain. She had felt pain throughout her entire being in what seemed to be a never ending cycle.

Blood and sweat oozed off of her naked flesh onto the floor to mix in the cesspool at her feet. Thick iron manacles bit into her arms at numerous points. It burned her soft skin. Her pointed ears twitched as she heard him enter the room once more.

His thoughts slammed against her mental defenses as he neared her. His cruel voice echoed against her mind walls. *You will tell me the place she keeps it. None shall find you in this place. I have gone to great lengths to keep her from being able to find you.* His cruelty bled through the intrusion his mind tried to force upon her. And she felt his power dig again into her walls.

More pain. As she struggled against the sickly blue tendrils in her head, he pulled out his curved iron knife. A swish of his deformed fingers and one more cut opened on her slowly regenerating body. The iron proved to be just as much an anathema to her healing as before. What should take but moments to close took minutes. Her core was dry as her lips. Her brown curly hair was matted to her forehead by blood and sweat.

Her usually melodic voice was just a croaking gasp as she let out her defiance, "Never."

The ever-twitching tentacles that hung from his face spasmed with what she had come to learn was mirth. *We shall see. You shall soon run out of energy and your defenses shall fall. Until then, we shall continue.*

Three more cuts and she let out another hoarse scream. *How many days had it been? And how much longer would she have to endure?*

42: Suplication

1923, New York, New York.

The following day was a flurry of preparation. Grace refreshed the wards on Allen's upstairs office, adding numerous conditions that allowed only those from his circle of power access to their powers. Helena and Duncan saw to the more martial of preparations. Checking their firearms again and the sharpness of their blades, they were meticulous in their inspections.

Allen closed the restaurant for the night of the expected arrival. The staff, dressed in their finest, stood in rows awaiting the entourage.

Only Duncan stood at the door outside, a nervous Darlene clutching his hand. A nearby town car waited for her as he assured her that he would see her soon.

A clattering of horseshoes on cobblestones rang down the street. White mares pulled a midnight carriage through the fog rolling from the bay.

Duncan pulled Darlene's chin up to crush her lips with his own. "See you on the morrow lover," with this he opened her door and hurried her into it. They shared a long look as the towncar pulled away. It turned a corner and she disappeared from his sight.

A staccato of hooves clattered and the carriage with its darkened windows pulled alongside the door. Opening the door, he held up a hand of support for those inside.

A slender porcelain hand, dwarfed by his own, took the proffered hand and the first of the fey stepped from the darkness. As his eyes were dazzled by her unnatural beauty, it was in this instant he realized he couldn't see into the cab. A magical illusion of some nature kept him from looking in past the door.

The ivory hand in his was the hand of a silver haired elf. Her shapely form was hugged by a silver dress, swirling in her wake and with patterns of runic stitching and a multitude of diamonds in a rainbow of hues and plethora of sizes. A black diamond on a silver chain nestled between her breasts caught his eye for a moment as it was jostled by her hopping down from the lowest step. His eyes flicked up to her face, finding a smirk on her lips and a twinkle in her gaze. She had done that on purpose.

"Greetings, Duncan. I hope you are well?" A coy smile graced her lips as she continued, "Seeing off a lady friend?"

"As a matter of fact, I was. She is not of our worlds but highly spirited. She doesn't understand the importance but could sense some of the tension of your arrival." He kept his voice neutral and conversational.

The Winter Queen frowned, "Yes, ah, I had not arrived to tease you about your love life. Rather to introduce the Wanderer to my niece and talk with him about a matter of urgency."

As she finished speaking a slim hand snaked out and took one of Duncan's proffered hands. A slender pink faced maiden slipped free of the carriage and stepped lightly down the stairs. She had a firm grip, yet soft hands.

He felt calluses on her index, middle and thumb. Shelving that away for later consideration, he helped her the rest of the way to the ground. Her shimmering lilac gown swirled around her as she moved. Lamplight glimmered in amethysts and opals set into the lace that spread along the garment. Her hair bobbed around her neck and was as myriad of colors as a rainbow. Her eyes caught his and stuttered his brain. The left eye was a vibrant green and the scent of fresh meadows bloomed in his mind. The right eye was an iridescent red that pooled and swam with golden flecks. They were set above a button nose and full lips. The pouty lips curled in a frown as he realized he had been staring.

"Welcome to *Mister's*," he hurriedly opened the door and held it stoically as the Queen tittered and the pair slipped past him.

He let out a breath and released the door. Leaning against the frame, he silently wished Allen luck.

Grace took in the pair of magical women walking in as Duncan held the door. She noted the faceted gems and designs of the lace. Magical women was not quite a true statement, but they were definitely flush with a ready supply.

She wondered if the garments were being worn for the fey's personal needs, or if they were wearing them to bring them into Mister's in order to influence the people there.

She felt like she had her work cut out for her if the meeting lasted longer than expected. She teased her lower lip as she began to worry about the protection spells she'd put in place holding up to that kind of raw magic. Not because her magic wasn't good enough, but just because she was worried about her people staying safe.

She felt Allen's aura crashing over her and her fears were pushed to him. She felt Helena's bond through him and knew that if it came to a fight, they would be ready.

Allen felt Grace's tension and sent her reassurance. He felt Helena echo him with her vibrant belief in him. He let an easy smile play across his lips.

The ageless beauty, Nevvie, floated soundlessly across the floor to him. Her companion stepped up to her right, a respectful distance behind. She was a pretty thing, but he noticed as her sharp eyes took in everyone and the room at large.

As Nevvie stopped in front of him, Allen and she nodded slightly to each other.

"Well met, Wanderer. May I present my niece, the pride and princess of Summer, Violet Verci." She indicated the young lady to her right, who curtsied low at the mention of her name. Her eyes dropped to the floor in front of her as she held the position.

"Welcome, Winter. Greetings, daughter of Summer. May your stay in my circle of power be well and to your liking. You shall be afforded all guest rights. Shall we adjourn to my study?" Allen watched as Violet looked to Nevvie for the decision.

"Please, that would be most agreeable. Perhaps some refreshments and a bite to eat." Nevvie purred the last, the tones sultry and low.

Allen smirked, "Cucumber sandwiches and tea will be ready in a moment, if that is to your liking?"

Nevvie's eyes twinkled like onyx stones. "As you say, Friend."

They had moved to the office where sandwiches and fresh tea were brought in by Tom. He had then bowed to his patron. As he had stood to leave, she had pulled him back to her and whispered something low into her ear. Allen had forcefully not listened, humming a light tune as he chewed his bite of sandwich. Tom nodded and left the room.

Now, there were just the five of them in the room. Nevvie and Violet each sat on overstuffed leather bound chairs. Allen sat in the center of an equally overstuffed satin couch, Grace seated to the right and Helena to his left.

"So, now that pleasantries have been observed, we can get to the heart of the matter. I have come for aid once more." The Queen of Winter looked pensive and the Summer Princess appeared equally dour.

Allen sighed internally. "I have plenty to keep myself busy. I am afraid I do not have the time to fetch more trinkets to add to your collection."

"No. I have not come for a fetch quest or a menial task. My cousin of Autumn has been taken by a being of darkness and madness. I am unable to find her. I beg you to find her and bring her home safe. I know that this is a task of great difficulty as I am unable to do so. But I ask, nay, plead for you to do so. I will swear any oath that you require should it not put my people or family at risk. I only ask you to do this for me."

Her words and trembling lips assured Allen she spoke the truth. He could taste no lies in her words or demeanor. He watched as tears began to pool in the corners of her eyes as the seconds ticked by. He turned to first Grace, who looked thoughtful, then Helena, who had a look of mad glee behind her eyes. *His Thinker and his Warrior. How happy and lucky he was to have them.*

He turned his gaze back to the fey. "Very well. I see no reason to deny you. Grace, find out what you can from our esteemed guests about what they have tried. Helena, see they have suitable living quarters for their station and satisfaction." He stood, nodding to the two royals and stepped from the room, Helena following behind him.

43: Glean

1923, Witch Glade.

Grace tapped her chin as she studied the crystal ball. She had worked tirelessly at the device since her Mister had gotten it for her months back. She referred to the two open books to her left on their pedestals. The dialects were obscure and she was muddling her way through as she took notes in the ledger held in her left. She put her pencil in her mouth and turned the ball slightly clockwise.

An image of a brunette with curly brown hair and long pointed ears came into focus from the brown smudge she had been a moment before. She seemed to be alive, but only just. Long cuts covered every centimeter of her body and slowly closed as her body drew upon her magic. Grace felt a tear roll down her cheek as she stared at the horrific image within.

She spat her pencil out and called out in a clear voice, which rang out in her cottage, "Ambros. Prepare for guests."

"Yes, Mistress," the cat's melodic voice chimed.

With that done she placed her notes to the side and dashed back to her portal. She had not thought it would have only taken her a week to find the lost elven Queen, but now time seemed to be even more of a hindrance than a virtue. Her sandaled feet pounded on the soft forest floor as she dodged trees and their roots.

—

1923, New York, New York.

Allen finished his appointment with the Hoffmans. He shook the two brothers' hands as the meeting completed. Uri, the older of the two, dabbed at his mouth with the napkin. "Please, give our compliments to the chef."

Noam agreed, "As always, it was fantastic."

"I will. Thank you for coming to meet me. I will be sure to bring the documents that we discussed later this week. Ms. Verci will be grateful when I share the news with her." Allen tilted his head forward. "She is finding permanent lodging or she would have been here."

The two men nodded as they headed for the velvet rope around the VIP area. Ted unclipped the rope as they neared him. He nodded to them respectfully as they passed.

A shimmer came from the corner that held the door to Grace's pocket forest. The ebony door slid open and his breathless witch popped free of the pool of darkness beyond.

Allen raised an eyebrow as she panted and waved to him. "Ms. Grace, are you well?"

"I... I...," she gasped out, "I found her."

Allen's other eyebrow joined the first. "Well, I believe your news is better than mine. I secured financing for the Summer estate. The Hoffmans agreed to our proposal." He beckoned to the table as Janet cleared the plates. Grace nodded as she gulped down air and began catching her breath.

Janet pulled a tray off of her tea station. A kettle of black tea and a pot of black coffee with a small velvet cake sat atop it. She began pouring them drinks to their preferences as Allen pushed in Grace's chair. He slid down into his, steepled his fingers, and looked over them at her.

"Well, I have a general idea of where the Autumn Queen is, but I cannot say for certain. The ball doesn't give me clear enough surroundings. But I think with the two elves helping we should have the necessary power to widen the image with a spell."

"That is astounding. Ms. Janet, leave the plates and call the Vercis for me."

The young wolf dipped her head and hurried off.

"Grace, my dear, well done." He raised his cup to clink against hers, "Hopefully, we can get this business over sooner rather than later and have a moment to breathe."

"Wouldn't that be nice, Sir." Her eyes twinkled at him over the rim of her cup as she sipped her tea.

44: Face of Terror

The fey barrelled into Mister's through the speakeasy. Duncan had met them at the street and showed them up to the VIP area. Ted had met them at the ropes and indicated to the table that Allen and Grace stood up from. Grace led the group into her realm and a quartet of deer had appeared to be their mounts.

The strange deer had bowed to Grace. A quick pat on their noses and the group raced through the forest surroundings. Violet drank in the dense foliage and returned the gaze of numerous small animals. "It is quite pretty here. Reminds me of Father's lands in the summer."

Grace gave her a knowing glance as she sat uncaringly sidesaddle on her mount, "I should hope so. This land is based on magic that he had the decency to trade with me. There is a touch here and there that I changed, but only so to suit my needs."

"You know my father?" The fey princess leaned forward on her mount. She had a bewildered look on her face. "What did you trade to acquire the ability to create a Veil? This is powerful magic and you speak off-handedly about welding it."

The clearing that held Grace's cottage came into view and the muddled feelings Violet held in her heart came out in a rush. This place was quaint but called to her. It buzzed with power. The echoes of the crystals to the south, the forest at their back and the lake to the west made her swoon in her "saddle." She began to topple as it overcame her practiced defenses. Then muscled arms snaked around her, cradling her neck and knees. The smell of the creature that held her was intoxicating as was the aura she felt mingle with hers before retracting as Allen set her carefully on her feet.

"Are you alright?" His voice tickled at a place deep in her she had been ignoring for some time now. Rich as chocolate and vicious in intensity. *You could listen to that voice for...*

She got her mind back to the task at hand. "Yes, quite. Thank you. It was just a bit overwhelming. I am well now." She brushed nonexistent dirt from her dress as she wrestled her sudden need and schooled her thoughts. Her head clear, she turned to a frowning Grace. "My apologies. You know Father?"

"Yes. Allen, Helena, and I made a trip to Ireland years back and helped him set up some rune work for him. Amplifier for him while monitoring the underworld traffic. He wanted to know what kind of dangers were slinking into his lands so he could properly defend. Your aunts no doubt benefitted as well." Her frown lessened as she spoke but she seemed to be studying her.

Violet swallowed and nodded. She turned to study the clearing, as a cat sprang into the clearing. It wore a bow tie and had a towel draped over one forepaw. "Tea is ready, Mistress."

"Very good. If you will follow me, esteemed guests." Violet felt the bite of the last word. *She had noticed her taste of Allen. Of course, she had.* Violet groaned inwardly. *It hadn't been intentional, yet the faux pas had been rude.*

She pondered apologizing but dismissed it as it was secondary to their goals. Aunt Briar first, reparations after.

They moved into the cottage and the thrum of power exponentially crackled and snapped at her defenses.

"Grace. Not now." The soothing voice of Allen slid over her skin. A dark promise lay in those words. She wished it was meant for her.

"Yes, Sir." The reply from their host had a sullen timbre to them. Violet looked at her to find the woman's ice blue eyes promising a reckoning.

They sat at the table and the feline began to pour out tea. The green slitted eyes in its head never left Violet's. Violet sipped and savored the rich flavor.

"Now, the spell I managed shows me the Autumn Queen. She is alive but not well. The defense of her captors has not allowed me to look at her surroundings. However, if you two lend your power, we should be able to push through that and expand my vision. It may even be done to not alert our foes. But that is also a possibility, if we are not careful."

"I understand," Aunt Nevvie stated. "You will have as much of our help as you need. What do you need from us?"

"Hold this and channel your magic into it and I will mold the spell to draw from it." Grace handed them each an uncut gem. Aunt Nevvie received a bird sized opal. Violet received a grapefruit sized emerald. Allen was given a ruby the size of his head, that drank in his aura as a fine wine. Violet started at the ease of seeing his control.

Then she set to her own task. The vibrant colors in the gem echoed her soul and it easily accepted her. The stone soon sang the Song in her heart. She was lost in the many voices that echoed her father's. She remembered fondly her mother and the stone began to vibrate and pulse with her lent power.

The witch began to hum, a regal purple amethyst nestled in her lap. Violet watched as the four stones they held released a thread that twined into a fine rope. She felt the others along the tether. Allen was the primal rage and feral power. Aunt Nevvie was the destruction and rebirth of Winter. Grace was lightning, water, earth, fire, and wind.

Violet felt the threads of Grace and Allen melt to one and vibrate the other two strands. A choked gasp slipped free of Violet's lips, but she fought to maintain her task. The bond between their hosts brought forth envious thoughts.

Why not that for me? A voice she had pressed down for ages murmured in the back of her soul. She crushed it back down and redoubled her efforts. The Song deepened and mingled with the Winter Cold.

The two threads wrapped around a clear crystal ball set into the middle of the table. A myriad of colors lit their faces as runes of salt and black sand activated.

Aunt Briar came into view and she felt and heard the sob choke off in her throat. The shredded skin of her aunt slowly healed. Then a flick of steel undid the tension of the woman's flesh.

As they fed more power into the spell, more of the room came into focus, swimming outward from her aunt. A monstrosity with the passing semblance of a human held a knife up. A tendril pulled a strand of blood from the knife to its circular mouth. The teeth of a lamprey quivered in its head as it moved to cut once more. Its movement was sure as it sliced once more into Briar's skin.

The tendrils on its face quivered and the bulbous head pulsed like a heart. Purple and black skin rippled with the effect. It waved a seven fingered hand and paced about the room. Black sigils that hurt Violet's eyes bloomed and squirmed into her aunt, who shook and screamed with the violation.

"I can take us there. I can see where they are." Grace's voice shattered the horror with a chance of hope. "We will need to hurry. I could feel her resolve failing her."

"Yes." The cold hate-filled word slipping free of Winter. "Let us go soon."

Allen closed his eyes and after a moment opened them. "Our Angel is ready. She can meet us at the entrance."

Grace nodded and twirled her hand. The stones lifted from their laps and disappeared. "I am ready, Sir."

45: Trust and Trial

Helena was laying her tools out on her bed. Fifteen knives weighted for throwing. Two dirks with keen edges. Two silvered shortswords. A quartet of silver alloy needles the length of her hand. A pair of revolvers, modified for eight rounds instead of the normal six, with five quick loads. She tapped her lips as she looked over the arrangement.

Her bedroom door slammed open with a clatter. She whirled, her short sword in one hand swinging up as she lifted a knife in the other to throw. Her eyes fell on the De Luca she-wolf.

Helena let the tension of her coiled muscles fall away. "You should be more careful, child. Your haste almost made me do something regrettable."

"I want to join the rescue team!" The words spilled from the young wolf in a rush.

Helena rolled her eyes. *Children. Always in a hurry to die.*

"I am ready. Trainer says that I am aptly skilled. I only need Mister Wells' permission." Guilia bit her lip then continued, "But I can't seem to find him. Do you know where he is, Ms. Helena?"

"He is in Grace's pocket with the fey guests. I am certain he has a mind for who he will take on this journey." With a dismissing wave, she began to ready for battle, strapping each tool into their place.

"No, I must be able to go. All I have been doing is training and working on controlling my beast. I need to stretch her and find my limits. There are more than enough people that will be guarding the Mister's home. I will not be useful here. I need to find my place and to prove my worth."

Helena sighed, exhausted mentally from the woman's tirade. "Fine, fine. He will be out soon enough. I'm certain if you blather at his ears as you have mine he will at least consider your words. Now, get the Hel out of my room before I test my sword on that pretty neck of yours."

Allen found Helena waiting as he came out of the portal. She stood in man's clothes colored in black. Her arsenal hung from her neatly, hilts and handles within easy reach.

"Mr. James has let the staff know we are closing early. Wait staff has begun closing tickets and Mr. Duncan has turned away more clientele as they've arrived." The pale hazel eyes of the angelic woman flicked to her right. "The young she-wolf is waiting for you in your office, along with your gear."

The two of them began striding to the back stairwell that led to his office. "Do I want to ask?" he asked, feeling a tension knot in the spot between his shoulder blades.

"Best she poses it, I think. Not that I envy you having to make the decision." the tall beauty shrugged.

"Very well. Grace and our guests are working on our entrance and magical needs. They said they would be ready within the hour, our time. Grace sped up time there so they could work out details." Allen waved his left hand in a dismissive wave.

He strode into his office briskly with hardly a pause to open the door, with Helena hot on his heels. Guilia sat on one of the chairs across from his desk. Her lithe and elegant form wrapped in clothes not dissimilar to that of Helena. She had a long Remington rifle resting against her upper thigh. As he strode to the desk where his equipment lay neatly arranged, she stood, her unflinching green eyes meeting his own.

"Yes, Ms. De Luca? You needed to speak with me?" He finished his trip to the desk and began changing into the loose black linens folded on his chair.

"Ah, yes." He could smell her arousal blasting from her as he draped his clothes over the back of the chair. "I, uh, would like, no, I mean, I need to join the rescue team. I need to prove my worth and find my place. There," her words trailed off as he stepped out of his pants. She whispered "Oh, my."

He felt the heat from Helena as he slipped into his linen pants. He glanced over to see both women drinking him in. He pushed his feet into the boots. He cleared his throat as he pulled his shirt over his head.

"Right, sorry, uh. There are plenty of people staying behind. Teacher says I am ready, with your permission." Guilia stammered out the last.

He eyed her while he draped his baldric and greatsword over his shoulder. He checked the draw, finding it suited him. Looking at Helena, he asked, "Angel?"

"As long as I don't have to be guarding the knýtirakki, I have nothing to add, Master."

"I do not have time to argue, so do not make me regret this, Ms. De Luca."

"Yes, Alpha." She nodded, a grin worming its way across her face.

46: Lost to Lust

Guilia drank in the Alpha's flesh. Corded muscles rippled under taunt skin. Veins stood out across his hair-covered torso. A swathe of the hair carpeted his bulging pecs and slithered down his flat stomach to the line of his briefs. She swallowed as she tried to jolt her brain back into motion. Unfortunately, all her brain could do was imagine running her fingers through that hair and caressing the hardness beneath it. Tracing her fingers down to the line and grasping him firmly and pulling the heat from his body with her mouth.

Her brain shuddered as she imagined his form changing to his wolf and forcing her own change. The scene continued in her mind, him filling her slickness with his manhood while his teeth pulled at the back of her neck. A moan almost escaped her as his beast filled the room and sniffed her skin. She met its eyes and her beast whined.

He stepped into his pants and shirt. Her mind caught up and she continued with her reason for wanting to go. He frowned slightly as he strapped on a large sword. He seemed uneasy with her joining, so she pleaded with her eyes. He asked the Nordic beauty and she seemed unperturbed. He came to a decision and told her not to make him regret it. She vowed to him and herself to not. Soon he would see her worth and perhaps let her in.

Guilia stood in the witch hollow, body tense and thrumming. Her wolf danced about as the greenery buffeted her senses. Small creatures scurried unworried in the underbrush. The rich scents of the trees, herbs, and flowers tickled at her nose, acutely aware of each different species. A gentle breeze carrying the hint of a billowing storm crackling at the horizon caressed her cheeks.

However, with all the beauty of the place, her eyes were affixed to the diminutive blond

German woman. She had walked through the portal to this realm and had felt the frost in the air as their eyes had met. Now, she was working in tandem with two other startlingly beautiful women to open a magic gate. The slender white haired woman had not even bothered to acknowledge her existence. But the one with hair that shimmered and changed along the colors of the rainbow seemed to even now be considering her. Pale eyes flickering under raised eyebrows watched her even as she held the massive diamond pulsing with blue and green lights.

Tom, Helena, and Allen stood nearby. A variety of auras to be certain. Tom tasted the same as the white skinned fey, a touch of humanity underneath. Helena tasted like steel and key lime pie. *Odd.*

The Mister, however, tasted of power, sex, brutality, and whiskey. Yet his stern face was also welcoming and dragged her off balance internally. The gears in Guilia's head spun as she tried to figure out what that all meant.

Grace drew another sigil into the air as the two others sang softly. It floated up around the ball of white, blue and green, joining the other dozen sigils shimmering there. "All done, Sir."

"We are ready then, unless you three need a moment to replenish your expended energy?" Allen's voice made her beast quiver and shake herself from snout to tail.

The three magi exchanged quick glances then shook their heads. "Splitting the cost has allowed us to draw on my plane and it is ready, as are we."

"Very well. Good work, ladies." Allen slid his huge sword from his back, "Let us begin."

Grace waved a hand in a swirl of fingers and the ball of energy bloomed, opening a green circle that passed to blue then white then shimmered to a view into a room of darkness.

Allen stepped up to and through the black, quickly disappearing from sight.

The rescue of Autumn had begun.

~ Fin ~